PUNK ROCK
GHOST STORY

David Agranoff

deadite
press

deadite press

DEADITE PRESS
P.O. BOX 10065
PORTLAND, OR 97296
www.DEADITEPRESS.com

AN ERASERHEAD PRESS COMPANY
www.ERASERHEADPRESS.com

ISBN: 978-1-62105-230-2

Printed in the USA.

*Dedicated to my lost brother Peter Spielman
and Tom Rager, who is keeping his spirit alive*

"Your '87 is our '82.
It makes no difference what we've been through..."
—Face Value

"Kids think the old school was some magical era. They don't realize how frightening it was to live in a world where people were violently opposed to you. I was in one of the biggest cities in America, L.A., where you'd think there'd be some tolerance, but people wanted to kill us for the way we looked. Today that doesn't seem possible."
—Greg Graffin, of Bad Religion

"Too much horror business, driving late at night..."
—The Misfits

PROLGUE

Some things can't die. No matter how hard someone tries to kill them. In the dark, dank basement, the screams still echo decades later. If you sit on the unfinished dirt floor long enough you can still hear the echoes of that rage. They weren't huge crowds that gathered there, but the sweat and energy shared in that small space was like a nova bursting inside the concrete walls. Power chords drove the insanity. The group madness of youth.

The scene changed. The world changed. It was a past too powerful to die. A moment in history that could not be forgotten...

***

The Chevy van coughed and spit like a cat trying to cough out a hairball. After thousands of miles in the short two years of the van's life, it was already pushed beyond reasonable expectations. Frank was white-knuckling the steering wheel, trying to will the engine not to die. Smoke rose from the hood. His bandmates were waking, putting down magazines and realizing the danger they were suddenly in.

Dickie reached up and turned down the Zero Boys on the mixtape blasting from the stereo, so all the cursing and pleading could be heard. He'd just been nervously playing with the safety pin he put through his nose after he lost his nose ring. Oscar rolled around in the loft that housed the bed over their equipment, looked out the window and squinted at the desert sun. His mohawk looked saggy and flattened by sleep.

"What happened to the freeway?" Oscar asked as he slid down onto the seat next to Gary. There wasn't anything to see but two lanes of sand-swept highway.

"I don't even know. Where the hell are we?" Gary asked as he rolled up the comic book he'd been reading. Dickie pushed eject and the tape popped out. They could now hear the wheezing death of the engine. The van pulled off to the side of the road snap, crackle and popping the gravel.

Things had been tense most of the tour, but since the Houston show the tension had become open warfare. It should have been one of the best of the tour. They had been looking forward to playing with the local act D.R.I., since they booked the show months ago.

Oscar had put the last of his speedballs in his arm that afternoon. That made him grumpy and sickly. Only a handful of people showed up and even though D.R.I. offered them their cut of the show, it still wasn't enough to pay for gas. They emptied their pockets to get to the show in Austin and pulled into town just in time to find out that show was canceled.

The promoter was evicted from his house and the basement was his venue. Oscar was insufferable when his stash dried up and he began detoxing. They spent the night in Austin digging in dumpsters for stale muffins and cakes. They didn't go hungry, but if they didn't gas-and-dash a few times they would never have left Texas.

"New Mexico," said Frank. He squeezed the steering wheel so tight the pleather ached.

"Mexico? Oh shit," Oscar said in disbelief.

Dickie turned in the seat and hit his jonesing guitar player with a rolled-up copy of *Maximum Rock and Roll*. "New Mexico, dumbass!" Dickie understood it wasn't just the lack of heroin giving Oscar the shakes. This tour had gone from adventure to insanity and they were all scared.

It had been three weeks since they left Indianapolis, and it was impossible for any of them to remember what life had been like before. Days and nights ran together and time passed in all kinds of fucked-up ways. The Fuckers only had one 7-inch record that they sold through a classified in *Maximum Rock and Roll*. This tour had no business working, but after two years of trading letters with the members of Black Flag, they offered Frank a show.

It was to be a straight trade, a basement show in Indianapolis for Black Flag, and a spot opening for their heroes in L.A. Frank got a list of phone numbers from Flag's roadie and started making calls. Pretty soon they had shows in basements, backyards, and even a sewer drain.

Dickie bought the repo'ed 1980 Chevy van from his Uncle's repair shop. An ugly white van, but in amazing shape considering the price. Gary and Frank worked for six months at Dairy Queen to make their payments.

The manager was pissed when they quit for tour. They built a loft that looked like a short bunk bed so they could sleep over their gear and plastered the back in stickers. All their favorite bands were represented: The Clash, Dead Kennedys, Sado-Nation, and Black Flag.

They tested it with a show in Louisville opening for Squirrel Bait. All the equipment fit, and it was perfect for tour. What could go wrong?

Frank turned off the engine and jumped out, waving his once white, now brown Circle Jerks shirt around trying get rid of the smoke. The rest of the band sat in the van staring. A part of all of them felt better with Frank out of the van.

Dickie, Gary, and Oscar watched Frank in silence. They'd all grown afraid of him since the tour began. The vocalist opened the hood, and for a moment they were out of his line of sight.

Dickie looked back at his bandmates. "I told you we should've gone home."

"We're gonna die out here," Gary whispered.

"It's him or us." Oscar said softly.

"It's just overheated," Frank yelled. "Needs some water."

They were tired, strung-out, and hungry. Frank was the only member of the band to never suggest quitting with their tails tucked and going back to Indianapolis. They had planned to spend the entire month of July in the summer of 1982 on their mission.

The Fuckers and their shows meant everything to Frank.

9

No matter what happened, he seemed to love every second. He was born for this. 200% grade A Punk Rocker.

Oscar was higher than a weather balloon during most of the tour so he never noticed a thing. No one complained because it never affected his guitar playing. Dickie enjoyed the shows, but worried constantly about the van, that he was still paying off working as a mechanic after school for his uncle.

Everyone chipped in, but the title was in his name. Gary had basically run away from home, stealing his older brother's bass guitar and spent the first leg of the drive scraping off the embarrassing KISS sticker.

Frank was the only one old enough to be done with high school, but he quit or got kicked out depending on who was telling the story. All three of them replayed the many warnings they got from everyone when they started the band with him. No one from his older brother to lifelong friends thought doing a band with Frank would be easy, but the reality was he was good at it. His lyrics were sharp, his vocals angry and on point.

"We'll make the Phoenix show," Frank promised as he grabbed a gallon jug of water out of the back. When he opened the back the burning desert air hit them. They were already shirtless, uncomfortable, and sweating.

"Hotter than Satan's asshole out here," Frank said as he disappeared in front of the hood.

Gary shook his head in disbelief. He didn't know anything about cars. His brother and father once restored a '65 Mustang together, while he was up in his room learning Ramones and Black Flag records on his brother's barely-used bass guitar.

His father hated Punk Rock and gave him the *'Why can't you be like your brother'* stare/speech a lot. More than once, Dad threatened to send him to military school or shave his hair off. He'd been afraid to go home to face the fam, but at this point staying on the road with Frank was far more frightening.

"What if it doesn't start?" Gary asked.

They all knew the chances of four spiked-and-dyed Punk Rockers getting rides hitchhiking in New Mexico: Less Than 0%. A sign just up the road read '*Holbrook 60, Flagstaff 100*.' No one wanted to think about walking across the desert.

"Even if it starts, we have to go home," said Oscar.

Dickie nodded. Born Richard Abrams, he was called Dickie by his whole family. The Punk world knew him by the name Infected Dick. Frank had thought they needed funny names on the insert for their record. He was Frank Fucker on vocals, Hairy Gary on bass, and Oscar the Crotch on guitar. Oscar was pissed when he saw the record, even if Dickie had the most reason to be upset about the name Frank gave him.

Dickie was the second oldest in the band, after Frank. He would still graduate in the class of '83, like Frank was supposed to. They met each other in first grade, discovered Punk Rock together when KISS started to sound old and boring, and had skated more miles of Indianapolis together than the van had traveled.

If anyone could reach Frank, it was Dickie. He looked at Gary and Oscar and they were silently begging him. Dickie closed his eyes for a second.

"You don't know him like I do. Look, he won't fucking quit."

"He is fucking crazy," Oscar raised his voice slightly. "You don't say anything, I will."

"Maybe we should just do the Flag show," said Gary. Oscar and Dickie shared a look. They were both starting to wonder if Frank hadn't invented the Flag show to convince them to go on tour.

The next summer wouldn't work. Gary and Dickie were supposed to be starting college that fall; Dickie at IU an hour south, and Gary at Ball State an hour northeast. The band's shelf life didn't look good. Oscar was already growing tired of Frank's act.

Frank drained the water into the radiator when Dickie walked around the front of the van. Dickie looked down the road. It had that wavy heat look for miles in the distance. His skin felt like it was baking under the sun. He had a hard time

11

believing that van would start any time soon.

"Hey Frank, can we, uh, talk?"

Frank poured the last of the water into the radiator and threw the jug in the sand, causing a small lizard to scurry away. Frank leaned against the front of the van and pulled his cigarette pack out of his pocket. He opened it and sighed seeing he only had three left. He put it in his mouth and fumbled in his pocket for his lighter. Dickie lit the cigarette with his before he got a chance.

"You have any smokes left?"

Dickie shook his head. "No money, dude."

Frank blew out his first drag and offered one to Dickie. He lightly puffed before handing it back to Frank.

"We get the van started, Frank, we have to go home."

Frank laughed. "Quit? You want to quit. Two fucking shows from Flag in L.A., and you want to quit?"

"We all do, Frank. This tour has been a fucking nightmare. Rednecks, jocks, cops, and we haven't made a fucking dime, man. Oscar ain't the only one losing weight."

Frank was a naturally big guy, recruited for the football team each year, but he never played. The team was filled with the jocks that picked on him before his growth spurt. Classic rock listening macho assholes, who stuffed his friends in lockers, were afraid of one Punk. He was the only one that didn't get called a faggot or weirdo in the hallways. Other Punks had to worry about rednecks jumping out of trucks and attacking them.

That was all before three weeks of eating only what he could dumpster and steal. Now Frank had bags under his eyes and his frame was showing. He looked scary for a different reason. Now it was behind his eyes.

A semi-truck came down the highway going well past the posted fifty-five. Oscar and Gary got out to wave it down. It flew past so fast, Dickie almost fell over. The dust swirled around them giving the moment a surreal, hellish feel. Gary and Oscar were cursing the now-distant truck.

"We're finishing the tour," Frank said.

Oscar stepped forward. "Don't give us the speech man.

I'm calling a fucking band meeting. Right here in the asshole of nowhere."

"We are not having a meeting," Frank laughed.

Oscar shook his head in disbelief "You're outnumbered. We all want to go home. Sleep in real beds. Eat real food."

"You're all a bunch of pussies," Frank flicked his spent cigarette towards Oscar. "You forgot to score real junk, Oscar. That's the real issue. Isn't it?"

Dickie tugged his Mohawk back out of nervousness. "I don't care what you call us, Frank. We are in deep shit thanks to you. I am not talking the tour and the van. We just wanted to play music man, we didn't want trouble. We didn't plan on no fucking war."

Frank nodded. "We didn't start it, but we have to finish it."

"See." Oscar pointed at Frank with an unlit cigarette. "Crazy man. Can't reason with him."

Frank walked back to the back of the van, he returned with a wooden baseball bat. It had "Peacemaker" carved in it and was stolen from a bartender in Philadelphia. "Get back in the fucking van and shut the hell up."

Dickie knew in that moment that Frank was crazy enough to beat them with that bat if they didn't get back in the van. All his sanity had been gone for days, weeks even. Something wild and untamed had taken over Frank.

He couldn't shut off the feeling of being on stage. His addiction and drive was as powerful as anything Oscar put in his arm. Nothing would stop him from this tour, this mission. It consumed him like a burning flame.

They had only one choice to survive this. They had to put out the flame. He couldn't believe it had come to this, but he knew, Frank stashed the pistol under the driver's seat. He just hoped he could get there first.

13

CHAPTER 1

May, 2006

Nate always closed his eyes when this song started. Scott held the distorted note, bending his lowest string just slightly. Denny tapped the cymbals to create a buildup before Ericka slid her fretting finger across the bass.

The low slide was their cue to break into one of the faster songs in their set list. They all banged their heads as the guitars rolled and the drums galloped. It was the first and best People's Uprising song. Nate wrote it on an acoustic guitar and played it for Ericka in his dorm room when the band was just an idea.

The song was called "Third World Rebellion." It was a little metallic compared to their other songs, but no one complained about the powerful reaction the breakdown got every time they played it. Each one of them couldn't help but dance in place, despite the cramped space in the garage.

Between the random storage and the old mattresses uselessly trying to hold the blare inside, it was like practicing on a packed bus. This song was magical and they all felt it. More than any other one in their fifteen songs, this song was a conduit for all of them to connect.

The garage had no ventilation. The sweat poured off them, pooling on the concrete floor. Even in the late spring, the air felt oven-like at this point in practice. Yet they all got a second wind when it came to this song.

They never talked about it, but it just sorta became their closer. They couldn't play anything else after the climax of this song. Nate screamed the vocals. He always had a strong voice, taken after his father who could be heard across the stadium screaming, "You moron!" at football games after a bad play.

But towards the end of this song his voice always cracked, giving way like a slightly loose tooth or ladder rung about to snap. He just squeezed the microphone harder and went with it. Ericka told him it gave the last part an added sound of desperation. It fit the moment just right.

The drums galloped to the end. The guitar crunched with an open E-chord. Nate screamed through a cracking and dying throat as it ended, "And we will fight! We will fight!"

As the song ended, Denny leaned back against the mattress lining the wall. Spent, he enjoyed the shaking pleasure knowing they'd just blasted through band practice in record time. No fuck-ups, a perfectly tuned machine.

"Fuck yeah," Scott said as he did every time they practiced "Third World Rebellion." Ericka put her bass down and shook her head. Nate smiled so big and goofy that Denny laughed at him from behind his drum set.

"We're so ready for tour," Ericka said as she propped her bass in its hiding spot. Nate looked slightly nervous for a moment. He wasn't ready to talk about tour yet. They still had a month left before they were supposed to leave, but they were missing one important thing and their summer depended on it. He was still red-faced from practice, and didn't know how to tell them his plan. He didn't think they'd like it.

"Wait a minute." Scott gently placed his guitar in his case. "I don't remember hearing shit about a van."

Nate cringed. There it was. The subject he'd avoided all week with them. Despite having most of the money and a promise of help from his mother, he hadn't found a van that worked for them. They needed a cargo van, but all he found were mini-vans.

Denny and Scott loved playing in the band, but hated dealing with all the nitty-gritty of doing it. Ericka was busier with school, having a more serious major of Biology with an eye towards teaching, so it fell mostly on Nate to make the band happen.

"Nate?" Denny asked.

"I'm going to Indy on Friday after class to look at one," Nate said. He didn't want to explain how he found it. Denny

15

dramatically dropped his sticks on his snare.

"Dude, we have a month." Scott was the most unhappy about it. He was always looking for an excuse to get out of tour. He had a new girlfriend, Mel, and he barely made it through practice without calling her. He was with her every minute she agreed to see him.

As if on cue, his cellphone rang in his pocket. They all knew it was Mel. "Band meeting!" Denny declared.

Nate nodded as he backed into the door leading into the main part of the house. In typical Fort Flop fashion, a hitchhiking crusty was asleep on the couch. He rolled over, and through sleepy eyes looked at Nate (who ignored him.)

During his freshman year while still living in the dorm, Nate had dreamed of living at Fort Flop. Many bands used the basement for practice over the years, and the living room was a home to shows when they pushed the couches out on to the back porch.

Someone was always there hitchhiking through from Oregon, Florida, or even many punks from Europe. They always had a disappointed look when they saw it was just another house. The legend had grown when Against Me! played a song that was recorded and bootlegged entirely out of one of the bedrooms. Even after the band sold out, the Fort Flop recording was considered their best in part because the sing-alongs were louder than the band.

It put Bloomington, Indiana's small political punk scene on the map. In a college town that was almost 65% Indiana University, this little punk house became a legend. It had a cemetery on one side, and musicians of various genres living on the same block. The lease passed on like a venereal disease, but somehow despite new punks coming in and out, Fort Flop was in its sixth year of hosting shows.

Nate looked at the crusty on his couch and wished he had anywhere to sit. The other couch never made it back inside after Saturday's show. The guy had taken fewer showers in his life than he had band patches sewed onto his pants. He never asked if he could stay, just showed up and never left. Nate wasn't even sure he remembered the fucker's name.

At the end of Nate's sophomore year at IU, the dream of Fort Flop living had come to this. Standing in his living room wishing someone wasn't always sleeping on his couch. Ericka and the rest of the band came in. Scott and Denny were townies, they grew up in Bloomington and didn't go to the university. They seemed to hang around the campus most of the time now that they were the same age as most of the kids that went to school there. Scott was dating Mel, who was in her freshman year, and that drew them into the university scene.

Scott looked sad as he put his phone in his pocket, forced to endure another half hour without his girlfriend. Denny walked up to the couch and kicked the base. "Hey, Tick, move your ass."

Tick sat up enough to give Denny a seat. The drummer sat and stared at Nate. Ericka pulled up a chair from the kitchen. Scott sat cross-legged on the floor and Nate found a spot next to him.

"Tick, you mind if we have a band meeting?"

Tick looked around for his once-green, now-browned frame pack. "Yeah, I'm needing to get some breakfast."

Tick got up and stretched off the sleep. He didn't seem bothered by the late afternoon sun coming in the window. He looked through his bag and didn't find food. He looked around at the members of People's Uprising. "You guys know any good dumpsters close by?"

They did, but no one felt like explaining the competitive dumpstering scene of a small college town with a large population of migratory crusties. Nate was considering his answer when his housemate Zeke walked into the kitchen behind them.

"It's complicated, man. I'll make you dinner," Zeke said as he looked in the fridge. Tick walked toward the kitchen. Denny shrugged, Nate normally was the gung-ho one in all band meetings. Scott looked at his watch. Clearly, he didn't want to waste time.

"We need one of those sweet family cruisers like Wasteland toured in. It had a DVD player in it. They watched

17

movies and shit," Scott said, laughing.

"They had to pull a trailer. I would rather build a loft and pack our gear." Nate repeated this every band meeting.

"Nate likes things old-school, buddy." Denny smiled. "We'll be lucky if we get a tape deck."

Nate knew Denny was onto him. He was born twenty years too late. He had a certain picture of what a punk rock touring van looked like, and it was all about the 80's. He loved retro-punk.

Everything about that era was magical to him. He considered himself a historian. The only thing as big as his record collection was his collection of zines. Some went back before he was born. He read and knew everything about the scene back then. He didn't like to admit it but Denny had him pegged.

"Old vans break down. I don't think it is a good..." Scott whined

"Breaking down in the middle of nowhere is a Punk tradition," Ericka laughed. "I'm handling it."

***

Ericka plugged in her laptop and sat on Nate's bed. He was at his desk waiting for his own computer to come on. He had half a plate of tofu and potatoes that Zeke and Tick made. Everyone wished it tasted better, but ate them. Scott ran out the door the minute the band meeting was over, and Denny wasn't far behind him.

Ericka always stayed for a bit with Nate to update the band's Myspace page and in the last few weeks they would work together to book the tour. Ericka was always looking for an excuse to stay. Nate didn't mind.

As a band, People's Uprising hatched in Nate's brain. He and Ericka had lived in the same dorm, Collins Hall, and saw each other in the dining hall long before they ever talked to each other. She had classical good looks that Nate felt were enhanced by the shirts she wore of underground bands.

The first time he saw her she was wearing a Born

Against shirt, his favorite band from the nineties. Even in the alternative dorm, that was a pretty obscure band. He knew right away that they should be friends.

He wanted to talk to her, and she even smiled at him that day. The next time she said, "Hey there, Old School," because of his Zero Boys shirt. There were over a dozen punks in Collins dorm, and slowly they all ended up eating together most meals. Ericka always sat near Nate.

She had grown up a bit, and changed her style to be a little less mall, but after few days Nate remembered that she was from Muncie and played bass in a band called Crash Causal. He had liked the band and remembered that she played well. Nate played guitar well enough, even in a few bands growing up in Indianapolis but he always wanted to front a band.

So one day, after a grade z plate of dorm spaghetti, he popped the question. "You wanna start a band?" A year later, they were best friends and their band had an EP released on Happy Couples Never Last records and a tour to plan.

***

Presently, Ericka looked up from her laptop. "We need a Pensacola show, but it's a Wednesday." Nate leaned back in his chair. "It'll be a small show anyways. Half the scene in that town is traveling in the summer."

"Small show is better than no show."

Nate took a bite of his food. "I don't know about that." He put up a finger, asking her to wait, as he felt his cellphone ringing in his pocket. He looked at the number and knew it was Jake from FlyTrap Records. Nate rolled his eyes. "Jake."

Ericka sighed. "Don't let him cancel the Philly show!"

Nate shrugged. Jake was an ambitious show promoter and guitar player in a band called Far Left. They had hosted Far Left on a spring break tour in trade for help with a Philly show. His band was based out of Atlanta, but Jake grew up in Philadelphia and promised to have contacts.

Nate just threw the phone on the bed unanswered. "I don't wanna hear it." They both laughed.

19

***

Nate responded to over twenty e-mails before standing up to go to the bathroom. All the lights were off in the rest of the house. Zeke and Brooke, the other two housemates, both had class in the morning. He looked at the clock that hung in the kitchen on his way to pee. It was after ten and Ericka had moved on to her studies. Still on his bed, they had both been focused and hadn't spoken in an hour, both with headphones on and listening to their own music.

Nate found the bathroom door closed. He opened it slowly. The bathroom was always an adventure. He only had two housemates on the lease, but it was Fort Flop. Half the Punk Rock underground had called these walls home for at least a night. He hesitated at the light switch. Sometimes sanity was better protected through pissing by the faint orange street light that came in the frosty window.

Brooke had her own bathroom, but Zeke was a slob. It was a safe bet Tick wasn't clean. Nate flipped the switch and the bright light was a mistake. The seat was up and looked splashed with something brown, and it was decorated with enough pubes to justify the nickname name Denny gave the toilet—Fidel. Denny always said he needed to water Fidel when he had to pee. Worst of all, the bathtub was filled with what looked like Tick's greasy former hair. Nate opened the closet and found his clippers jammed back in their case.

Nate unzipped his pants and thought about one thing - The Tour. He wanted away from this house, this town, this state. Fuck reality, he wanted the adventure of the tour. It couldn't happen soon enough.

Nate washed his hands and walked back to his room. The only light was from Ericka's laptop screen. It wasn't the first time she had fallen asleep here at the house, or in his room. This made him nervous. He had a crush on her, like every guy in the scene. Once the band started he did everything he could to think of her as just one of the guys, despite the inherit sexism of that, which went against his normally politically correct nature.

"Ericka?"

She didn't stir. This was all too dangerous. A relationship could doom their band. Nate went to the closet and got out his sleeping bag. Last time this happened he slept on the couch. Last time Tick wasn't sleeping on the couch with a freshly-shaven head. Nate spread the sleeping bag on the floor. He started to take his pants off, because he couldn't sleep in anything more than boxers. After the shirt came off, he noticed Ericka had one eye somewhat open.

"I'm sorry, I dozed off. You want me to head home?"

Her walk home took her across downtown Bloomington and the edge of campus. It seemed cruel to make her walk when she was tired and he would never let her make the walk alone.

"Nah, it's OK. We can talk about the tour on the way to class in the morning."

Nate sat on his floor and unzipped the sleeping bag. Her laptop closed and the room was suddenly as dark as it was quiet. He heard a gentle pat on the bed. He didn't look at her, just pretended not to hear it. He slipped in the sleeping bag. Honestly he loved her more than all his ex-girlfriends combined.

It was gut-wrenching to ignore. Nate fell heavy on to the sleeping bag and stared into the darkness. He laid there trying to think about the tour. *What still had to be done? Where they would go?* But in all that thinking, Ericka was always there. Three times he thought about climbing up into the bed but just turned on his side and thought about the road.

CHAPTER 2

Nate walked out the Fort Flop front door and spent more than a minute unlocking and untangling his bike from the dozen that were piled on the porch. The sun was barely up, but he needed a good start if he was going to make it to Indianapolis in time to check out other vans. He sat on his bike, took a deep breath of chilled spring air and looked down an empty Saturday morning Second Street. Bloomington was quiet on weekend mornings and this neighborhood filled with students up late the night before.

Nate never cared much what people thought of him. A political hardcore kid, he went through brief phases during his punk coming of age. His gateway to punk rock was Green Day when he was thirteen years old, but he quickly grew out of that phase. Short mosh-metal and straight edge phases followed, but in college he had settled in a slightly anarchist political leaning and a desire to play meaningful music. He didn't need to wear patchwork punk patch suits or dread his hair. Looking pretty normal, he was punk rock inside.

Nate adjusted his helmet. His mother, who hated that he rode his bike, offered to come get him, or pay for bus tickets. He only accepted the offers deep into winter. Driving in a car from Fort Flop to his parents' house took just over an hour if traffic on State Road 37 was light.

On his bike, his record was six hours of nearly empty backwater two lane highways. The first time he wore headphones and listened to music, but a Kroger truck came up so close and fast that it almost blew him off the road, so he decided that wasn't a great idea.

These long bike rides were about silence. The only sound was his breath, bike chain, and the wind in the corn fields. One stop at the Bloomingfoods Co-op to get a tofu Ruben and Clif bar for his lunch and he was off.

Ericka had offered to drive him. She didn't like it any more than his mother. He hadn't spoken to her since they walked to class. He knew she would hound him until he agreed to the ride. The reality was, it was one of these rides over a year ago when he first saw it. He had to go this way.

The front door to the house opened. Tick wasn't close to fully awake as he stood in the doorway. Nate saluted across his bike helmet

"Where you headin'?"

"Indianapolis." Nate grinned.

"The city?" Tick pointed to the west thinking it was north. Nate nodded as he pushed off and headed down the street.

***

Ericka stopped to pick up bagels and muffins, knowing they would need something to eat on the drive up. She had set her alarm for 6:15 am. She would have to get up early and be at the Fort to catch Nate. She pulled her Honda up to a barely-legal parking spot at the end of the block and got out with her bagel bag in hand, taking only a second to look at herself in the driver's side mirror.

She never worried about her appearance, not since she was fifteen years old. She had never in her life given a shit about boys. Nate was always different, and how ironic that the band had pulled them together like magnets, but also kept them apart. She kept waiting for him to just be a normal guy, throw caution to the wind and put her before the band, but he didn't, always the band first.

Ericka walked down the sidewalk and cringed when she saw the bike rack. Nate's street bike was gone. Tick sat on the front steps, shirtless, only wearing jeans that were almost completely covered in hand-screened patches of bands sewn together.

Ericka offered him a bagel. "Nate up?"

Tick took a bite first. "Yeah, but he took off. Said he was

riding to Indianapolis."

Ericka sighed.

"He like knew you had a car an' shit, right?"

Ericka nodded and handed the bag of food to Tick. "Oh, he knows."

"Thanks." Tick opened the bag and his eyes got wide. "Score!" Ericka was a few steps away. "He's crazy. That's a long bike ride."

She looked back not breaking her stride. "He's stubborn, and thinks he can do anything."

Ericka got back in her car and stared at the keys in her hand. She didn't want to go back to the dorm. She could wander the roads looking for Nate. She didn't want to look that desperate.

It wasn't like her, and nothing would turn Nate off more. She thought about what she could say. She could tell him it was about the band, finding the van for tour, but he would see right through it. Ericka pushed the keys in and got mad at herself for caring so much.

***

Nate rode for four hours before he started thinking about the sandwich. He had been writing songs in his head. It started with a political subject and then lyrics like a protest repeating in his head. He would hum the rhythm and the chord that would make up the riff would float there.

He'd just finished reading a book called *Sorrows of Empire* by Chalmers Johnson, and wanted to write a song about how fragile America's superpower status was. Half of People's Uprising's songs were conceived on long bike rides. Riffs and lyrics swirled around him like a mini-twister.

The miles rolled under and the minutes burned away. When the farms gave way to strip malls it was a sure sign that he was nearing the south side of the big city. Still passing farms, the land seemed to get impossibly flat as Indy got closer.

"It could end tomorrow, it could end tomorrow," Nate

whispered the rhythm between humming the riff.

He was in the home stretch and thought about riding straight through, but it was past noon. He looked for a patch of grass where he could sit and have his sandwich. He needed a farm house that looked the least Ed-Gein-like to stop at. The faded white houses all looked similar. Each had anywhere from two to half a dozen cars and trucks, many of which would have looked at home in a monster truck rally if they had wheels.

A few of the houses looked like they were built in the Fifties, all built further down long driveways. Half of the farmland was sold to build houses in the Seventies. Those were closer to the road and easier to see.

Nate had taken his bike down this road a dozen times, and always slowed down to look at the houses. They blended together until he saw the Grand Am. It was his marker. It told him to slow down. He was finally here.

It was funny-looking enough to catch his eye. A twenty year old Pontiac Grand Am with zero tires resting on blocks at the edge of the gravel lot, its body painted with faded purple and orange flames. Nate slowed down to a stop. It had four Black Flag blocks painted on the trunk.

He would expect something in this neighborhood to be painted with some kind of country music crap or Motley Crue at best. Nate looked around. The small two-lane highway was dead. It was close to five minutes since a car passed. He could see a truck coming from the north, but it was quiet enough to hear the wind blowing the cornfields around.

He could faintly hear music. Nate took off his helmet and held his breath enough to hear just that much better. It was so soft he would have missed it if he was still pedaling, but there it was, "Spanish Bombs" by the Clash.

"What the fuck?" Nate whispered. The truck was getting closer, tall on giant wheels. If Nate hadn't been so fascinated by the Punk house out in the country he would have noticed the truck slow down and the older man in a once yellow John Deere hat stare at him. The man shook his head at Nate like he was an alien invader and drove on. Anyone riding a bike here looked out of place.

Nate looked closer at the house. It didn't look different from the other farmhouses. The yard wasn't exactly overgrown, but not as freshly mowed as the others along the road. A new-looking Honda sat in the driveway closest to the house. The windows were left rolled down.

There it was, as it always was, behind the blocked-up Grand Am. It was a white Chevy cargo van. A tarp was tied across the front windshield and the van looked as if it hadn't moved since *Return of the Jedi* was first in theaters.

Nate stared at it a moment, from a distance it looked like the van he thought it was. A part of him just knew it. He had a feeling. He had never been this close before. He needed to see the back of the van to know for sure.

Nate got off his bike and pushed it slowly down the long gravel driveway. He came up the drive and walked around the Grand Am. Through the back window of the van Nate saw a loft exactly like the one he wanted to build. *Who else but touring bands would ever have a reason to build one of those?*

Now he needed to get a closer look. He set his bike down and stepped around the back of the van. Nate gasped. He couldn't believe his eyes. The van was covered in faded barely visible stickers for the Zero Boys, Black Flag, and the Dead Kennedys. The pattern of the stickers was familiar, but that wasn't what shocked him. It was the hand written message written with Magic Marker, so faded he barely saw it.

Ronald Regan can lick my Asshole.

He'd seen the back of this van before; hundreds, maybe thousands of times. The stickers weren't faded, and the marker ink was fresh and bold. Not like it was now. Four Punks stood in front of this van while someone took a picture. That picture surviving a generation or two of photocopies was the band photo for the one and only release of Indiana's most notorious Punk legends, The Fuckers. He had the insert for the record in his bag so he could confirm it, but he didn't need to. He knew it was the same van.

"Hey, asshole?"

Nate turned and saw an overweight man with long, graying black hair standing barefoot in the yard. He was a hundred and fifty pounds plumper, and twenty-five years of hard living older, but Nate knew who he was after a few moments of connecting the dots.

Nate stood there stupidly pointing his finger back and forth from the van to the man.

"Infected Dick?"

The man just shook his head in disbelief. Nate knew it now, after a few moments of staring at the old man's face. He knew that face. Dickie Abrams played briefly in every Indiana Punk band of the 80's from the Zero Boys to Toxic Reasons, normally filling in for tours. The important part of his history was his first band while still in high school. It was the band where he got stuck with the nickname he couldn't escape—Infected Dick.

The Fuckers.

"What the fuck are you doing at my house?"

"You live here?" Nate pointed.

"How old are you kid?" Dickie asked, ignoring the question.

"Uh, twenty?" Nate realized that Abrams was doing the math and figuring out that he wasn't even a gleam in his parent's eyes when The Fuckers were a band.

"Don't you have your own bands these days?" Dickie laughed and walked back towards the house. "Why you gotta harass me?"

"Wait, I mean, hey. I love The Fuckers record. The Fuckers were the best band of the first wave in the Midwest. Best thing to come out of Indiana."

Dickie stopped and turned around. "Better than Zero Boys?"

"You guys were first."

Dickie nodded. "That's right, but no one remembers us."

"I do." Nate grinned. "If you guys kept touring…uh. Us Versus Them, Carter Sucks…I mean they are classics."

Dickie looked like the color drained out of his face. Nate cleared his throat and walked over to the van. "This was your

27

van right, the same one you toured in?"

"Hey, stay away from that piece of shit." Dickie moved quicker than Nate would have guessed and blocked his path and view of the van. Nate put up his hands, and looked up at the man.

His teeth were yellow, his belly big enough to swallow a bowling ball. Nate was more scared of the man's breath than anything, but stepped back towards his bike. He picked it up and put his helmet on.

"I'm sorry, man. No offense, it's just..."

Dickie waved him off and walked back towards the house.

"What happened on that tour?" Nate asked, but Dickie opened his door to the blaring of the Clash and disappeared inside.

***

Dickie kicked the Heineken bottles from the front of his couch and looked at the silent images of the muted Montel Williams show on the TV. He turned off the stereo and fell hard on the couch. He looked at his shaking hands. He hadn't felt this exposed in a long time.

This farmhouse had been a weekend getaway for his family growing up. His lawyer father had threatened often to retire for farming but died first leaving the house to his son. He hadn't left the house much in the last ten years, even offering to play or jam in bands. None of those bands worked out.

Most successful punk rockers his age had either moved out of town to pursue their careers or were nervous about working with him. The wood shell of his drum set was molding apart in the basement and covered in a film of dust. He'd grown to accept that he would die alone and forgotten in this shit pit of a house.

He wished he never saw the kid out there in the yard. He was so young it blew Dickie's mind to realize that he could have been that little shit's dad. At least he was old enough.

That gave Dickie momentary pause, and he thought about what this could all mean. Why else would that little shit go through the effort to find him? He asked about the tour. After all these years, he thought it was forgotten. That they had outran it. Dickie closed his eyes and tried not to think about Frank and that day in the desert back in 82. He still heard Frank's voice faintly. *"Finish the tour."*

A knock on the door made Dickie jump up in his seat. He looked over at the door. The young Punk hadn't fucked off. He stood there with his stupid bike helmet under his arm waving at him. Dickie struggled to stand up and breathed deeply, making the short walk to the front door with the grace one expected from an ancient washed-up musician.

"Fuck off, I told you already."

"Hey, man, I'm sorry to bother you, but I want to see your van."

Dickie stood there dumbfounded for a moment. He couldn't get rid of the van. From the moment they got back to Indianapolis in 1982 he had tried. He tried to sell, trade off parts, and on a very dark and lonely night to drive it off a bridge. Nothing worked, he could never go through with it. Frank's voice always nagged him in the back corners of his mind like a record skipping. *Finish the tour.*

Dickie waited to hear that nagging voice rattling around his skull, but it didn't come. His jaw dropped slowly, he looked at the van out the window over the young kid's shoulder. That feeling of guilt and horror he felt whenever he looked at the van, all the memories of '82 stayed away for the first time.

"It hasn't moved in fifteen years at least." Dickie pushed the door shut. The young kid blocked it with his foot.

"So what's the problem, then? Sell it."

Dickie stood there, confused, sweat forming on his back. He wanted it gone more than anything but was waiting for Frank's voice in head, threatening him.

The young punk shrugged. "One hundred bucks then."

It's OK Dickie. It's time to sell it.

29

Dickie let out a long, deep breath. The kid stepped back a bit. Dickie knew he looked like a mess, but didn't care.

"Are you sure?"

"Yeah, I want it," the kid responded, Dickie wasn't asking him.

It's time Dickie. He is the one.

Dickie knew he sounded scared. He was. "You have cash?"

"I can get it."

CHAPTER 3

Ericka dropped her pick in the middle of their third song. There wasn't enough room in their garage practice space to even bend down and pick it up. She tried to pick her bass with her fingers, but she learned guitar first and didn't like playing without a pick.

Denny watched her struggle from behind the drum set, but kept playing. Scott kept his back to them when they practiced and he was thrown off turning around as the song fell apart. He flipped off his pick-ups as the guitar created ear-slicing feedback.

"What just happened?" Scott asked, but they all knew the answer.

Nate never missed practice, and they were all a little surprised when they woke up Tick at two on a Sunday afternoon to let them into the Fort. Ericka had stopped calling Nate's phone yesterday after the third time. Calling made her feel stupid. She'd knocked on his bedroom door before opening and realizing that he hadn't been back since he left for Indy. She could tell.

They waited till almost three before a nervous and annoyed Scott, desperate to get back to his new girlfriend, started setting up his guitar. He was ready to play the songs without their vocalist.

They'd all missed practice before, but never Nate. He played guitar and bass, and even if he wasn't the best drummer, he still filled in for Denny a time or two. He was the primary songwriter of the band and ran practice like Coach.

Denny dropped his sticks on the snare and shook his head. "This is a waste of time." They hadn't played this off in months. They didn't make it through three songs. "Where the hell is he?" Scott asked as he used his foot to flip the switch and turn off his amp.

Ericka was worried he was in some ditch between here and his parents' house. She avoided sharing that concern with the rest of the band. Instead, she pulled out her phone to see if his parents' number was still saved in her phone.

She had one missed call from Nate's cellphone. She smiled. It was during the last song. She was about to tell everyone when they heard a honk from outside the garage in the gravel alley beside the house.

Ericka put down her bass and pulled the garage door open. A tow truck was pulling up in the alley. Nate was in the passenger seat waving at them. The tow truck pulled a faded white Chevy van with rusted edges and chipped paint in spots. Scott and Denny stood with their instruments, staring in shock. The truck stopped and Nate jumped out with a big smile on his face.

"Oh, shit." Scott looked on in disbelief. Denny came around the drum-set and couldn't believe his eyes.

"You did it." Ericka smiled. "You fucking got us a van."

The tow-truck driver stepped out. Ericka assumed this was Nate's cousin, who owned his own garage. Nate tapped him on the shoulder and walked over to stand in front of the van like a *Price Is Right* model showing off a brand new car in the Showcase Showdown.

"Hey, everybody, meet the van. The Van, meet everybody." He tapped the van, and for a split second Ericka was worried the damn thing would fall apart. It was old. Not quite a rustbucket, but not far off from that status. She wasn't sure a single member of the band was born when this van was brand new. The tires looked brand new, with *'like new'* hubcaps, but the van was a disaster. Ericka's initial reaction went from joy to worry so she didn't even realize she spoke out loud.

"You're kidding right, Nate?"

"What a hunk of junk," Scott laughed.

Nate laughed. "You're just quoting Star Wars, but forget the age of the van for a minute." His cousin Kevin laughed and smiled. "How can they?"

Nate clapped his hands and rubbed them together in excitement. "I got it for a hundred bucks. This is more than just a van. It is like a rolling Indiana Punk Rock artifact."

"Yeah, but Nate," Denny sighed. "Rolling, sure, is your cousin going to drag it on tour?"

"Fuck, no," Kevin said as he dug out a Marlboro. "We built a practically brand new engine. Nate's useless in the garage, so you are all going to help me put the last pieces together. Few more parts come in and it will drive like new."

Ericka understood Nate's love of punk rock history and guessed it was probably the touring van for a band that Nate grew up listening to. "So, wait, this was some old band's van already?"

"Yeah, best part." Nate pointed at the van. "Who is the most important band in Indiana punk rock history? Total legends, tell me the first band that comes to mind?"

The three members of his band looked at each other and shrugged as a group. Ericka looked at the back of the van. She stared at it for a long moment, reading the faded stickers. She knew most of the band names, but nothing gave a clue. The license plate rusted in place from the eighties simply read 'Wonder Indiana.' It took her moment, but she turned and smiled.

"OK, I'm not sure I agree, but you think it's The Fuckers."

Nate put his hands up as if busted.

"No way," Ericka's jaw lowered slowly as she pointed at it. "This was The Fuckers' van. This Van right here."

Nate nodded. Scott finally sat his guitar down. "I give up. Who the fucking fuck are The Fuckers?"

"Right, I'm not surprised. You should know who they were, I mean that is part of the crime of it all. They were probably the first ever Indianapolis punk band. Sounded like a cross between the Meatmen and, I don't know, something smarter like MDC. They did one 7-inch, it had eight songs, and all short fast and brutal. Way ahead of their time. They had enough songs for an LP when, uh..."

"When what?" Denny asked Nate.

33

"The singer disappeared during their only tour. They never made it to the West Coast. He disappeared somewhere between Houston and L.A. They broke up."

"Why didn't they get a new singer?" Scott asked.

Ericka smiled and put up her hand to stop Nate from doing all the talking. "Frank Fucker was one of kind. He was the personality of the band. Could you imagine Minor Threat without Ian Mackaye? Dead Kennedys without Jello?"

"Yeah, they fuckin' tour with some other bozo," Scott chimed in.

"Right, and The Fuckers without Frank Fucker was just a bad idea," said Nate, just as Scott's phone rang in his pocket. They all knew it was Mel asking when he would be done with practice. Scott flipped open his phone and pointed at the van before answering. "I don't care if the Ramones toured in that piece of shit. It will never make it a month on the road." Scott walked away. "Hey, sweetheart."

"That engine is solid." Kevin dropped his spent cigarette. Ericka walked up and looked in the window. She saw the loft and raised her eyebrow.

"We need a CD player, and speakers if we are going to drive that much."

"Already in the works," Nate said, as he gave her a big hug. Nate walked beside the van and carefully stroked its outer shell. "It'll finish tour, we'll finish the tour. You'll see."

CHAPTER 4

The van sat in the backyard for two weeks. Nate was beginning to doubt his plan and knew that Denny and Scott had given up on the old thing. Scott suggested calling off tour altogether, but everyone knew his motivation wasn't an old van, but a new girlfriend. Kevin assured him that they would get the van going.

They had spent the entire Saturday morning tightening parts he could never name with a gun to his head. Nate didn't want to break his cousin's concentration, and frankly he didn't care what parts were called in the engine. Nate spent hours just staring at the van in disbelief. It was hard for him not to think about the history.

"We're going to take this bad boy out today." Kevin smiled as he wiped grease off his hands. Nate shook off his daze and looked up. Kevin slammed the hood down. With the view cleared, he could see Ericka coming down the alley.

"That's it?" Nate asked. His cousin answered by stepping back and getting out a cigarette.

Ericka walked up beside the van, carrying a car tape deck. She had her hair pulled back in a bun held together by two crossed pens. She was wearing her glasses that she really only needed for reading.

Nate thought they looked adorable on her, and caught himself staring for an extra moment. Kevin looked back and forth at the two of them before giving a harrumph. He put his cigarette behind his ear and grabbed the tape deck from her hands. "Can I set my backpack in your room?"

Nate nodded and watched her disappear into the garage. Kevin hit him on the arm with the handle end of a screwdriver. "Hey, idiot," Kevin shook his head. "She is in love with you, just saying."

35

Nate sighed and opened the passenger side door to the van. He put his hand out for the tape deck. "It's complicated."

"Not really," Kevin laid across the passenger seat to position himself to install the tape deck. "You like each other, but for some stupid reason you're ignoring your feelings.

Nate leaned against the door. "I can install that."

Kevin laughed. "No, you can't. I've never met a less mechanically-minded person in my life." Kevin continued to connect wires hanging out of the dashboard that connected to the speaker they'd installed last weekend. Ericka had found the last piece on Craigslist.

Nate nervously watched his cousin. He still felt a tinge of peer pressure. Kevin made fun of him for not being able to fix anything more than a flat on his bike. A part of Nate felt that same kind of unspoken judgment was happening between them about Ericka. Kevin couldn't understand why Nate wasn't going after Ericka.

He should have dropped the subject but Nate felt it was still out there just beyond the surface. "It would never work, dating and doing the band."

Kevin stopped his fiddling and gave his cousin the 'You can't be serious' face.

"I mean if we broke up or whatever, it would kill the band."

Kevin connected the last wire and started to slip the tape deck into the dash. "She ain't the only bass player on the planet, you know."

"We started this band together..."

Kevin slipped out of the seat and stood back. Scott and Denny were walking up the driveway. Kevin pulled out his cigarettes and offered them. Denny was the only other smoker in the band and shared one with Kevin.

"Have you started it yet?" Scott asked.

Nate shook his head. "I thought we should maybe go for the first spin around town together."

Kevin pulled the keys out of his pocket; the old worn original, and three copies he made at Bloomington hardware the day they brought it down. He threw the keys to Nate.

"Fire her up."

Ericka came out of the garage holding an old cassette tape. Nate knew she grabbed it from his collection and knew the case. It was a Fuckers bootleg off the soundboard at their gig in NYC. It was the only recording of some of the songs they wrote for the never-recorded LP.

The cover had the band name spelled The F*ckers, with a crude drawing of a penis spraying the name. She had read his mind. He thought there was something right about playing The Fuckers first when they got into the van for the first time. The Fuckers had driven to that show in this very van.

Nate opened the driver's side door and stared at the vinyl seat. It was cracked and worn, showing a little of the white fabric guts of the seat. Frank Fucker sat in that seat. The whole band did. Nate used the steering wheel to pull himself into the seat.

It was a different world when The Fuckers first set out in this vehicle. Nate thought about those times often. It was a glorious time for punk rock, fresh and new. No one had sold out to be on MTV. No one had a website. Everything was done with sweat and effort. Nate always dreamed of coming of age in that era.

"Holy shit," Nate whispered as he ran his fingers across the steering wheel.

Denny opened the first of the two side doors to the back. There was one long bench style seat that Kevin had replaced with a new plush seat. Denny felt the fabric and it felt like new. The two front seats were the original blue vinyl that would heat up like oven coils in the sun. The wooden loft was just a bit higher than the back of the bench and filled the back. Sitting in the bench, one would have to be careful not to rest one's head against the loft on bumpy roads.

Scott got in the van next and sat on the bench. He tested the leg-room and didn't look pleased at all. Nate knew he was the biggest hater of the old van idea. Ericka jumped in the passenger side and took the tape out.

"What are you playing first?" Denny asked.

Nate came around and sat in the driver's seat. "Guess?"

He put the key in the ignition but didn't turn it. Ericka pushed the cassette in the unmoving player. They all stared at Nate holding the key. This was the first test. Would the engine even start? Nate took a deep breath and saw Ericka crossing her fingers out of the corner of his eyes.

He twisted the key. The engine roared to life as he tapped the gas just slightly. Everyone cheered and clapped. Kevin pumped his fist and lit another cigarette. Denny climbed up on to the loft and acted like he was making snow angels laying on the cushion that Kevin and Nate had laid down just this morning.

"Whoa, this is a totally dangerous place to ride, but you bet your ass I am sleeping up here! Dibs!" Nate looked at him as the tape wound around to play the live Fuckers show recorded in the New York City of 1982.

Frank's tiny recorded voice echoed through the speakers. *"New York, if we can make it here...oh, fuck off. We're The Fuckers and we survive living in Indiana, so I suppose you could call that home. This one's called CARTER SUCKS AND REAGAN FUCKING SWALLOWS..."*

The recording was wretched, the punk raw and gnarly in ways that modern hardcore couldn't be. Scott pulled the doors shut. Nate put the van in drive, and they pulled out into the alley. Nate couldn't believe the band they were listening to toured in this same van twenty-four years before. The man screaming those vocals gripped this same steering wheel.

Kevin yelled at them "I told you, it runs perfect." Denny leaned forward in the loft as they pulled out into traffic on third. The second Fuckers song, was "Us Versus Them!" It was one of the songs from their released record.

"So, this is The Fuckers? I don't think I ever heard them before."

Ericka turned in her chair. "Don't you think his voice sounds a little like Nate's?"

Nate felt a little embarrassed, but Frank Fucker was one of his favorite hardcore vocalists besides Ian Mackaye and Keith Morris. Nate laughed a little. Denny slid off the loft back into the bench seat. They stopped at a few lights and took the bypass to test speed, sending them around campus. The van ran perfectly, almost like new.

They listened in silence for a few songs. Nate pulled the van up to the house, but didn't want to turn off the music. The sound of The Fuckers filled the van. Even with the front windows down, the music didn't seem to escape. It was like the van was absorbing the energy of the recording. They sat in the van listening until the next song ended. It didn't sound like many were clapping in the audience.

Nate turned off the engine. They sat there in silence for a long moment. Scott broke the silence first. "So crazy they toured right here. In this van."

Ericka nodded. "And that Frank dude died on the tour."

"What? As in dead dead?"

Nate shrugged. "Maybe, no one really knows for sure. For all we know he is living somewhere under another name doing a band. He could be doing anything. He just disappeared. The band showed up to their L.A. show opening for flag, but he was gone. They said he just disappeared after the Houston show. Everybody agrees he played that Houston and then poof."

"Didn't his family look for the guy?" asked Denny.

Ericka looked at Nate confidently. They'd discussed The Fuckers deeper the day he brought the van home. "Frank Fucker was the son of a hippie runaway who had him a couple of summers before the summer of love with a one night stand sperm donor on the west coast somewhere."

"His grandparents raised him in Indianapolis. They weren't very healthy or involved when he was getting kicked out of school. Weird guy, built like a football player, I think he played for a bit before getting into punk. Smart, angry guy, Way ahead of the times in 1982." Finally, she shook her head. "And he never played football."

"Depends who you ask." Nate shrugged.

Nate relaxed in the seat and looked at the odometer over the steering wheel. 235,023 miles. It was hardly anything for a van this old. No one said a word or moved. He thought about those miles.

When you move into a house, there is no count of the amount of days lived in the house. You know the years, but it's overwhelming to sit in a house with history. The stories float in the air like stink that hangs around. *This steering wheel... Frank Fucker held it, probably on the day he disappeared.*

"Nate?" Ericka shook his arm.

Nate felt light-headed for a moment. He looked around feeling dizzy, like he needed to lie down. Denny and Scott were out of the van, Scott already lifting the garage door. He swore they were still sitting behind him.

"Nate?" Ericka sounded worried.

"What?" He looked confused at her.

"Band practice."

Nate took a deep breath and slowly let go of the steering wheel. "Yeah let's do it."

"You OK?" Ericka asked as she opened the door.

Nate felt a sense of urgency to get practice. He didn't know where that feeling came from, but it was like a gust of wind hitting a sail under him. He just smiled at Ericka. She loved that look. He could feel her happiness. It was all going to work. They would go on tour and make this dream happen.

CHAPTER 5

With her last final over and summer officially started, Ericka made her way to Fort Flop. Even late in the morning, the neighborhood was quiet. Most finals were finished, and many students had already left town for the summer. Half the population of the city was gone when the university was on break.

Despite the quiet, the Fort hosted a show the night before. But it was a West Coast band she never heard of. Her Astronomy 100 final came first.

Ericka knocked. With the tour less than a week away, she and Nate were going to get out the atlas and Mapquest the whole tour, keeping a folder of print-outs with directions under the driver's seat. She had all the addresses written down except the Santa Fe show that Nate was still working on. Ericka knocked. No one came to the door.

Ericka was about to knock a second time. The door opened and Tick stood there, rubbing sleep out of his eyes.

"Hey, Tick."

"Hey." He left the door open for her, but started walking back to his couch. Tick was in his second month in Bloomington, mostly camped on the Fort's couch. He still hadn't asked anyone if it was okay for him to stay there. He talked about trainhopping out to Oregon at least three times a day, but still hadn't left.

The band that played the night before were sprawled in sleeping bags around the living room. All she knew about them was they were a mostly acoustic folk-punk band. Three of them stirred and looked up at Ericka. She kept walking down the hall and saw Nate's door cracked open. She knocked on it, and looked in. He wasn't there.

Tick was already using a blanket to block out the sun, peaking through the curtains. The three guys in the band

41

were sitting up and gathering their things. Ericka kicked the couch. Tick poked an eye out from around the blanket.

"What?"

"Where is Nate?"

"Fuck, I don't know," Tick pulled the blanket over his head.

One of the band guys pointed to the door heading out to the garage. "He's out there."

Ericka looked at the guy who was most awake from the band. "Where are you guys from?"

"Olympia," the guy said before falling back on his sleeping bag.

"Can you take Tick with you?" Ericka just gave a thumbs up and walked out to the garage.

Their band equipment was still set up from the last practice and the large door was open. The van was backed up to the garage that was never big enough to house anything but the smallest compact cars. Certainly the frame for this house built in the '40s wasn't meant to house a van. It was built more for storage.

The van blocked most of the sunlight. Ericka considered turning on the light. Nate wasn't in the small garage. She was about to turn around when she saw movement in the van. She walked to the side window on the sliding door and saw Nate sitting on the bench with his laptop. He looked up and smiled at her. She slid the door open.

"What are you doing out here?"

Nate had a goofy smile on his face. He pulled out an ear bud. She knew he was so happy about everything. The band and the tour was a dream of his being realized. She was proud of him.

"I booked the Santa Fe show, started saving the directions."

"In the van? You're doing this in the van?"

"I was using the neighbor's wireless."

Ericka got into the van and put her backpack down. Nate's faint punk playing in the single ear bud was the only sound. This van was about to be their home for a month. She was close to him now. They looked at each other, and she felt invisible.

She wanted to hold him, nestle down next to him. She couldn't look at him anymore. Nate had cleaned the van thoroughly. Ericka slipped off her running shoes and slid up on to the loft.

"Where is the Santa Fe show?"

"Punk house near the campus."

Ericka hadn't lain on the loft before. There was only a small space between her nose and the old musty fabric of the ceiling. She knew she would have to be beyond exhausted to feel the need to sleep up here. "Really think this old thing will make it?"

Nate shut his laptop with a snap. "If it doesn't, Kevin is picking us up."

They both laughed. Ericka ran her fingers across the ceiling of the van. The fabric hung down by her ankles towards the back doors. It looked like something was in it.

"The van's not what I'm worried about."

Ericka kept staring at the ceiling. Nate was almost positive to a fault. Outwardly she couldn't imagine him worried. She knew he kept most of his fears and concerns buried. It actually made her feel good that he felt comfortable talking to her. "Yeah, tell me."

"It's Scott. He doesn't want to go, because of Mel."

Ericka knew he was right. Mel was supportive of the band and wanted Scott to go on tour, but the guitar player was so in love with her, he didn't want to leave. Ericka could get a real deep sense of worry in Nate's voice.

"He'll go, he—." Ericka spun around ready to pull herself off the loft. Her foot hit something. Something was in the ceiling. She kicked it with her foot. It wasn't heavy. "Hold on."

She poked at the low-hanging fabric. Something square was up there. There was a spot in the fabric that had been torn and held together by tiny safety pins.

Nate had poked his head up and stared at her. "What is it?"

Ericka carefully undid each safety pin and pulled the fabric apart. Something slid out towards her. Ericka jumped back but it landed on her chest. It was a notebook. It had had expanded after years of getting wet and drying. Its pages were yellow and brown on the edges.

"What is that?" asked Nate.

Ericka opened the first page. And gasped. "No way."

Fuckers Tour Journal...

***

Nate grabbed it from her. Ericka slid off the loft to follow the notebook. Nate carefully turned the pages. Written in different handwriting styles, Nate could tell that all the members of the band had written in the book at different times.

Ericka was just over his shoulder. "Looks like Frank wrote most of it."

Nate barely heard her. He was quickly turning the pages as fast as he could without ripping their slightly faded and aged paper. He scanned the notebook. It contained stories, dates, scrawled phone numbers and addresses of people they met along the tour.

Driving directions to shows, contact numbers for legends like Henry Rollins and Harley Flanagan two and a half decades out of date, four digit illegal telephone codes for stealing long distance calls, unfinished lyrics and folded flyers stapled into the pages.

The historian in Nate was almost shaking when he shut it. "No way," he whispered several times.

"Did you see that it said their first show was in Bloomington?" Ericka opened the notebook. The first page was a list of all the tour dates. "The second show is Dayton. They were playing a lot of the same cities."

Nate pulled the notebook back and snapped it shut. "We should save this. I mean we should save reading this for the tour. Read as we go."

Ericka was surprised; Nate had a hard time putting down

zines from the 80's. She knew him too well, but after a few seconds she shrugged and gave him a smile. "Sounds like fun, but I have a hard time believing you won't peek."

Nate knew she was right. He smiled at her and waved the notebook in front of her before closing his eyes. "Hide it."

He could hear her get up and go into the garage. He opened his eyes just an inch, saw she was over by the drum set and quickly closed his eyes. He really wished he hadn't looked.

***

The band from Olympia was annoying. They didn't have a show to go to until Chicago the day after, so they hung around Fort Flop all day. Tick took them around town in the afternoon and Ericka saw them walking down Kirkwood Avenue checking out the sights. She had gone out only once to get a pizza for her and Nate to share. Normally Nate, the more picky eater, handled food.

It was dark when she returned and a light was on in the garage. The front door was unlocked and she walked in. She went straight for Nate's room where they hid from the house floppers most of the day, listening to records, talking about tour. Now the plan was to watch a movie on his laptop.

When Ericka came through the porch she saw the door to the garage was wide open. The light was off, and Nate was breathing heavy, sitting at the chair by his computer.

Ericka held the warm pizza box and stared at him, ready to laugh. He couldn't help himself looking for the notebook. Too bad she hid it in her backpack.

"Couldn't find it?"

He laughed. "Oh, come on, where is it?"

Ericka shook her head and laid the pizza on his bed. She kicked off her shoes and pointed at the pizza. "Eat!"

***

Nate had a feeling all night that the tour journal was on Ericka, that it was in her bag. He tried not to think about it

45

but the movie they were watching, a black and white Western starring Johnny Depp, was boring him. Ericka seemed to like it, and laughed a few times.

They sat next to each other on his bed, watching but being careful not to get their hands or arms too close to each other. Nate had fallen asleep, trying to follow the movie but losing track at some point of even what it was about.

He woke up holding Ericka, her head nestled right under his chin. He smelled her first. Then heard her breathing softly, feeling her chest rising and falling against his. He had an arm around her that held her there.

It felt comfortable, good in a way he had always admitted to himself it would. He was excited, and embarrassed that his excitement was impossible to hide. If she was awake she would feel it. He shifted trying to move slightly but a sensation of pleasure rushed to his brain.

Ericka stirred and looked up at him. She patted his chest, not apologizing for the first time. She smiled and Nate felt many waves of intense feelings. "I fell asleep." She pushed off him slightly but leaving her legs against his. "You want me to go home?"

Nate shook his head. Ericka lifted her eyebrow. Here came one of those moments. Everything inside him wanted to grab her and kiss her. Every cell in his body wanted her except that part of his brain that thought rationally.

It hurt as he formed the words. "I'll set up the sleeping bag."

Ericka shook her head. Nate squinted. In the darkness of the room, he hoped she missed him licking his lips. He did it when he was about to say something he was afraid to say. She watched him for it.

"Tour is in a week."

She smiled. "Yeah, it is."

He felt it. Had felt it every day since the first time he met her at the dorm but was always afraid to say it. He thought the words "I love you, Ericka." He had thought those words more times than he could count but never once said it. Again, he failed. The tour, the dream it was so close he could smell it.

"Can it wait till after tour?"

She sat up. She wanted to be offended. He could tell. "Sure," Ericka stood up and grabbed her backpack. Nate knew the journal was in there and felt a moment of panic. "It can wait forever."

Ericka pulled the Tour Journal out of her bag and spun it in the air. Nate caught it as she ran out the bedroom door. Nate followed her across the living room. The room was dark. The Olympia band was watching a movie providing the only light. Tick stood at the kitchen counter putting the last finishing touches on his sandwich.

"Ericka, wait!"

She was gone. Nate stood there feeling stupid. The guys in the band pretended like they were not paying attention, but they all watched. Tick slid his sandwich across the counter at Nate. "Want a bite, dumbass?"

CHAPTER 6

Nate sat behind the steering wheel of the van. He put the tour journal up on the dashboard and the shadow of the wipers darkened it under the intense light of the nearly full moon. He had grabbed the keys with every intention of driving down Second Street to catch up to Ericka. He never should have let her walk out the door.

He put in the key, and before he turned it he looked at the journal.

One little peek couldn't hurt a thing, could it?

Nate carefully opened the creaking pages. It opened like a pop-up book. The pages had survived water damage and been hidden in a dark dank spot for decades. The first pages were mostly unreadable phone numbers and dates written into June and July calendars Frank had drawn himself.

Nate was struck by looking at the numbers and addresses. He tried to wrap his head around doing a band without the help of the Internet. The task of putting together a tour without the help of Myspace and the contacts he had made seemed impossible.

Punk rock was totally underground and grassroots back then. In this day and age there was mainstream punk rock, and the scene had its own underground. Each individual underground circle, down to the smallest and most local bands, had a website or a Myspace page.

Nate stopped turning pages when he got to the first entry about the tour. The writing was clearer, less of the ink had run or faded deeper in the text. Frank's handwriting was surprisingly neat. He drew random band symbols like the Dead Kennedy's "DK" logo on various pages. Nate ran his fingers gently across the page. He wrote here on this page, probably sitting in this van.

Fucking Fuckers fucking tour!
Day one:
Our first show is in Bloomington for the college brats at
a house party. Address is 932 College.
He thought he knew the house. It wasn't far at all. Nate looked up from the page, to the key sitting in the ignition. Without thinking Nate turned the key and the van roared to life. Nate jumped in his seat, surprised by the power of the rebuilt engine. He buckled in and drove out on to the street before he could change his mind.

He reached over and pushed the power button on the stereo. The tape player snapped to life. The CD player above had been neglected for The Fuckers bootleg tape he bought at Tracks in Indianapolis before it became Vibes.

He didn't blare it. It was just louder than the wind. With the driver's side window rolled down, he drove slowly through the alley that lead to Third Street.

It was only two turns. In three minutes, he was heading towards College Avenue slowly to look for the house. The traffic was summer break light. He read the numbers. 926, 928, 930...

The white house was the biggest on the block, two stories and looked like it was built sometime before 1970, but Nate couldn't tell when by looking at it.

Nate pulled the van over into a parking spot behind a Volvo with a large Kerry/Edwards campaign sticker on it. Nate turned off the van and stepped out bringing the Journal with him. The house had a fresh paint job and fancy-looking deck added not too far in the past. Decades later, you'd never have guessed this house hosted a punk show. Nate opened the journal and thumbed through to find the entry about the Bloomington show.

Didn't want to play this show, we played Bloomington a
hundred times before, but Die Krusen from Milwaukee were
headlining. I like their shit so why not. It didn't feel like leaving
for tour. Indy kids came to the show, at least a car or two
of them. The show was in the basement, and we had to load
through this tiny basement door on the south side the house...

Nate walked down the short driveway on to a pristine cut lawn. He thought he saw the frame of the basement door when a motion-detecting light snapped on, and a dog barked at him from inside. Once his eyes adjusted to the light he could see a German Shepherd standing in the window, wondering what the hell he was doing. Nate didn't think he could explain. He turned to head back to the van when the front door opened.

"Can I help you?"

"Oh shit, I'm sorry," Nate said, his face beet-red. "I didn't mean to bother you it's just, uh, your house is kinda famous. I guess, I mean sorta."

The man was dressed in what looked like PJ's and holding the snarling dog back. Behind him a daughter, dressed head to toe in goth-tastic, Hot Topic-purchased MallPunk gear watched Nate over her Dad's shoulder. The man leaned down to calm his dog.

"We've lived here since before my daughter was born. Fifteen years now." He laughed. "I never heard that."

"It's true," Nate considered just walking away. "Nothing bad or nasty. In 1982 some punk kids rented the house, had shows in the basement. Some really great shows, cool bands I mean."

"Cool!" The young woman in the AFI shirt said, watching from the stairs. He looked back at her. "Go to sleep, Jessie." She shrugged and silently begged to stay put but he gave her that 'I'm Not Messing Around' look. Nate wanted to go inside. He felt drawn to the house, like he did the journal.

He just wanted to look around. He knew the house that existed in 1982 was gone now, filled with a family and the energy they brought to the space. He still felt something coming off the house. Inside a part of him understood that no matter what paint they put on the outside, he could feel the energy of the shows, the punk energy that never completely died. Something powerful happened in these walls, notes from songs that faded, but never totally disappeared. He wanted to step into that basement and listen for it.

A nervous-sounding wife called to the dog, whose name

was Pepper. The father stood up straight and looked angry now. Nate just felt bad for bothering them. It was after eleven. The daughter turned at the top of the stairs.

"Can't believe our house used to be cool," the young lady said as she disappeared.

"Sorry to bother you." Nate said and suddenly felt woozy. He looked up and stopped in his tracks. Two men were trying to get a bass drum through the basement door. The man backing in the bass drum had a green Mohawk and a sleeveless Black Flag shirt. Nate blinked and they were gone.

He could've sworn for a moment he saw them. Clear as day, a young Richard Abrams and his band mate Oscar trying to fit a bass drum into the basement. Just as clear as they were there, now they were gone. Nate stared at the obviously new door that looked like it never opened now.

"Young man! I would rather not call the police."

Nate turned back to him. The father looked worried. "I'm really sorry I disturbed your evening."

Nate turned around and heard the front door slam behind him as he walked back to the van. He got in and opened the journal to the page he held with his index finger.

The show was in the basement, and we had to load through this tiny basement door on the south side of the house. Oscar and Dickie had a hell of a time getting his bass drum in the door. Only 12 people were there when we first set up. We waited twenty minutes after the flyer said the show started. There were three times as many people drinking in the backyard. By the third song the basement filled up.

"Come on you fucking brats!" I yelled before we played Carter Sucks second.

Bloomington is weird. The towny Punks are cool, but the college kids can fuck off.

Nate closed the journal and put it on the passenger seat. He was about turn the key when he heard the sound of a band. He looked at the stereo, expecting to hear the gears of the tape playing. The van was off, the stereo was off. Still he heard music.

It was a totally different sound than a recording. It had a raw, live edge, the musical equivalent of the texture of very rough sandpaper. Nate reached across the passenger seat and spun the handle to lower the window. The music was gone. Then it reappeared just for a second. Like someone was turning the volume up and down.

It sounded like it was coming from the house. He knew that was impossible. Nate leaned forward. This time he turned the key and got out of there as fast as he could.

CHAPTER 7

Every time he sat in the van, he heard it. It started as whispers, multiple voices that were sometimes in the middle of long conversations. The first few times, he rolled down the window, thinking it was a conversation going on outside. When Nate walked away from the van he couldn't hear them at all. He tried to ignore them, but they were there every time he sat down in the van.

It was like music played in another room, or a ball that slipped through his fingers. He could sense the conversations, but never hear them. It had been that way since that night on College Avenue. He had a strange feeling whenever he got near the van.

Like being watched, but not exactly, like someone was behind him. He felt a little uneasy, and those voices were always there now. He felt stupid for getting nervous around it. It wasn't a big old run-down house. It wasn't a castle filled with monsters. It was a Chevy van.

He couldn't tell the band his feelings. Scott was looking for any excuse to cancel the tour and spend the summer with Mel. Denny was ready to tour, but Ericka had avoided talking to him since storming out. She didn't want to see him. He didn't think she would ever cancel the tour, but if there was a van problem maybe she would side with Scott.

The van was fine. It would make it, and they would make it. They would finish the tour.

***

Nate laid in bed thinking about the tour, unable to sleep. He was excited and terrified at the same time. This was it, go time. As long as he remembered punk rock was everything.

53

Touring and playing shows in cities he had never been to, in front of people he never met was his dream.

He jumped out of bed and looked out the window. The van sat in the tiny driveway off the alley backed up to the garage. The back doors were open wide. Ericka and Denny were already loading drums. The tour was now.

He tried to take a nap, knowing they were leaving around three p.m. He looked at his watch. He was late.

"Hey, I'm on my way!" Nate yelled out the window. Denny waved at him. Nate scrambled around his room looking for his shorts. He had packed the night before: five changes of clothes, a Stephen King novel, his iPod, and The Fuckers tour journal. He grabbed his backpack and ran down the hall.

Tick was on the couch reading a 'zine. He sat up and waved at Nate. "Hey you guys have room for me?"

"Fuck off, Tick," Nate laughed.

"Yeah, that's what Denny said. Just checking." Tick fell back on the couch and kept reading. "I'll carry shit and sell merch."

Nate stopped by the open door to the garage. "Uh, no, you won't."

Tick nodded. "Probably right, sounds like work."

Nate laughed as he entered the garage. Denny was backing the bass drum into a corner under the loft. Ericka had her back to him. Here came a moment of truth. How was she going to treat him? Nate cringed inside as she turned away.

"Hey," was all she said, but she smiled, and that was worth a lot more than words. She wasn't so mad at him that she couldn't smile. If Ericka wanted to be shitty, she could be pretty harsh. Nate waited until Ericka's hands were free and Denny was alone trying to squeeze the drum into place. Nate hugged Ericka. She tensed up for a moment hugged him back. He whispered close to her ear.

"It's here. We're doing it."

Ericka pulled back but didn't smile. Nate thought it was something he did but then he realized the problem. She wasn't mad at him. He spun around one last time to make sure. No Scott.

Denny jumped out of the van and sighed. They had been a band long enough to skip some of the obvious parts of the conversation. "I called both their cellphones and got voicemail. Mel's roommate thinks they went swimming at the limestone quarries."

"Swimming? Today?"

Ericka nodded, knowing that normally cool-under-pressure Nate was about to blow a gasket. It was after 3:30. They had to leave by four if they were going to make it to their first show in Dayton, Ohio, on time.

***

"Five-fifteen," Nate muttered. He couldn't stop pacing. Denny spent the time sitting in the van checking the time on his phone.

Ericka sat in the passenger seat, her feet on the dashboard watching Nate. One of the things she always liked about Nate was how easy going and unflappable he was. His roommate Tommy in the dorms took advantage of him, even eating his food. Nate made excuses for him, even joked that as long as he stayed away from his records, they were cool.

No matter what free-loading bullshit Tick or any the other train-hopping crusty traveling kids pulled at the Fort, Nate never got mad. She would get mad. Look at the man like he was crazy for not sharing her anger. It just wasn't his way. The only things that seemed to make him mad were political; the big picture.

Nate looked pissed now. They all were. Scott was two hours late already, but Nate looked like he was ready to lose his mind. Denny and Ericka shared a few silent looks, both surprised. They hadn't even left town, and they were all stressed. Nate's phone began to ring in his pocket. They all sat up.

Nate looked at the caller ID. "Not him," he said before he flipped the phone open. He stepped away from the van as he spoke on the phone. Denny turned and looked at Ericka. "Damn, Nate is pissed off."

"Yeah, it's really weird."

"I mean, I've wanted to him to get more backbone, but he needs to chill a little."

Ericka didn't get a chance to answer. Nate snapped the phone shut and walked back to the van.

"More good news," he said with a tone soaked in sarcasm. "The kid putting on the show is doing it at his parent's basement. They'll let us play last but the show can't go past 10."

Ericka looked at her watch. The math wasn't good. Dayton was a four-hour drive, even risking a ticket. When she looked up she saw Mel's Jetta coming up the gravel alley at a maddeningly slow pace. Ericka pointed. "There he is!"

Nate just pulled out the keys and jumped into the driver's seat. "Let's go!"

Denny jumped out and waved at the car as if to say *hurry your ass up.* The Jetta pulled up and Scott got out in Flip-flops, his Chuck Taylors tied to his back-pack. He still smelled like wet limestone. Mel jumped out. Her green hair was curly, and still a little wet. She was wearing a Sunny Day Real Estate shirt tied up to reveal her tiny waist. Mel grabbed Scott and pulled him into a kiss.

"Scott!" Denny yelled.

"Fuck that shit! You're two hours late!" Nate yelled over him.

Scott didn't give a shit. The second their lips parted, Denny pulled on his friend's arm. Mel laughed a little and mouthed the words *I'm Sorry.* Ericka jumped in the van. Nate was already in drive, when Scott crawled into the loft to wave and stare back at Mel until the very last moment.

Two hours and twenty minutes behind schedule, but the tour had begun.

***

"Can we listen to something else?" Scott broke the uncomfortable silence. "Anything else?"

Nate hadn't even noticed the music. They'd rounded

Indianapolis and started the main stretch of the trip to Dayton down I-70. He watched the time ticking down and hadn't noticed that The Fuckers tape had switched sides and started again. Every moment of recorded and released Fuckers material, both official and bootlegged, were crammed on to that 90-minute cassette. This was the third time they heard the song "God Hates Sports."

"Driver picks," Ericka reminded him of the sacred rule of touring bands.

"Well, then the driver needs to pick something else," said Scott.

"I don't want to hear it." Nate felt nothing but a simmering anger towards his guitar player.

"Minor Threat would be fine," Scott laughed. No one laughed with him. Ericka turned back from the passenger seat to give him the evil eye.

Denny had been reading a book until the sun dipped below the horizon. Scott shook his head. "All right, something to lighten the mood... like *The Muppet Movie* soundtrack. "Moving Right Along" is like a tour anthem. I think."

"Fuck you!" Nate shouted. A needle might as well have been pulled across a whole LP.

Denny woke up and jumped up in the seat. Ericka stared at him in disbelief. Nate gathered himself and spoke in a soft calm voice. "We miss this show, and there goes tomorrow's gas money."

"Easy, easy." Scott took a moment to compose himself. "Calm the fuck down, Nate. I'll pay for tomorrow's gas."

Nate switched the stereo off with a snap. The silence was powerful, only the humming sound of the new rebuilt engine. Scott leaned back on the bench. "You know I'm not seeing Mel for almost a month."

Scott must have thought that his bandmates would be sad for him. Missing his girlfriend. No one spoke again for another hour. Not until they hit the city limits in Dayton.

***

They pulled into the suburban neighborhood at a quarter to ten. Ericka was surprised by how big and nice the houses were. She had met Freddy, the crustoid political punk who set up this show, at Circle City Fest in Indy. It was his parents' house, and to see that they were well-off suburbanites shouldn't have surprised her. She and Nate both came from wealthy north-side families.

They were craning, faces pressed against the windows looking at house numbers on the mailboxes. They didn't need to once they saw several stickered punk cars parked on one street. Hardcore kids were streaming out of the house from two different doors.

They pulled into the driveway behind a van with Jersey plates. That had to be the Last Winter van, they were a mosh-core band from south Jersey near Philly.

"Hey maybe if Last Winter is still set-up we can use their shit to play a couple..." Scott stopped when he saw LW's drummer walking out with a snare and cymbal bag over his shoulder.

Freddy waved at them from the side door by the garage.

Nate had given Freddy's band Dis-Disown a show at Fort Flop on a Wednesday night. It had been the last night of their tour. They were haggard, broke, and at each other's throats.

Ericka was one of nine people who paid for the show. Nate put in fifty bucks to make sure they had enough money to get food and make it back on the last leg of tour. Ericka didn't expect that generosity in return. Last Winter was the band that everyone came to see, and as a band People's Uprising hadn't shown up. The first show of the tour and they blew it.

"Hey, man," Freddy walked up to the driver's side window.

"Sorry, we're late. It was crazy around Indy with construction."

"You know we only made like a hundred bucks." Freddy sounded uneasy, guilty even.

"Show ended like twenty minutes ago. I didn't think you'd make it, so I already paid Winter the money."

"It's okay," Nate said and forced a smile. He wasn't angry at Freddy. All his anger was at Scott. If thoughts could kill, they would've needed a new guitar player. Ericka watched him. "I understand it's our fault."

"Yeah, I mean I'd like to give you some. but Last Winter was the only touring band to play. You know?"

Nate did know. He just didn't know what to do or say. None of them did. None of their grand plans for tour included missing the first show altogether.

"You can hang out." Freddy smiled. "You can crash here. My parents are out of town. We dumpstered some bread, making French toast, totally vegan."

Nate was silent. Ericka leaned across him. "Yeah, we'd love that."

Nate shook his head. "Next show is in Muncie. I told Mark we would head straight there."

Mark was one of Nate's best friend's growing up. He went to Ball State and was now putting on shows up there. It was backtracking into Indiana, but not far. They played Dayton first so they could play with Last Winter. Ericka remembered that The Fuckers did the same thing. The only difference was they played a second Ohio show in Cincinnati before they backtracked.

"Maybe a little sleep and some food," said Denny.

"French toast sounds pretty good." Scott almost licked his lips. Ericka went to grab her backpack from her feet and undo her seat belt. Nate shifted the van out of park.

"Thanks for the offer." Nate waved and rolled up the window.

"What are you doing?" Ericka asked. It wasn't like Nate to ignore the opinion of others. Nate backed the van out into the road and drove them away. Ericka looked at the surprised Scott and Denny sitting on the bench in the back.

They sat in almost silence. A mix CD of 80's punk played softly in the CD player, but Nate kept the volume low. Normally she had to turn down his music. She preferred to talk on the road. Nate normally played music, often making mixes just for trips. Ericka didn't like it. The energy was weird. Nate wasn't being Nate.

Would you like me to drive?"

Nate didn't say a word, just stared at the highway rolling under the headlights.

***

The voices were a little louder. Nate still could almost make them out from time to time when one of them would speak up or laugh. It wasn't his band's voices, they had grown quiet. Denny was asleep on the bench and Scott was wearing headphones. Ericka hadn't said a word since they left Dayton. As Nate drove he listened to the voices over the music, turning the volume down a little bit at a time.

"Stop, man, I gotta piss," a male voice spoke up, clear as any sound in the van. Nate looked in the mirror. Both Denny and Scott were asleep. Nate took one hand off the wheel and rubbed his right eye.

"There's a gas station up there." That voice again.

Nate saw lights and a tall sign that read GAS MART at the end of a short exit. He turned the van slightly to head up the exit.

"You want me to drive for a little bit?" Ericka wasn't asleep, but she had her hoodie balled up against the window and was lying against it.

"No, I just need to piss," Nate answered her as they pulled into the lot. Denny and Scott stirred in the back. This could barely be called a gas station. Two pumps that looked like they were installed during the Carter administration were topped by rusted signs that proudly announced that they were supplied by Mobil gas.

The only thing that looked modern was an ATM chained to the wall. They didn't need gas, had more than enough to make it to Muncie. Nate pulled them up to the oddly designed convenience store that looked like an addition to a farmhouse.

With the van off, the only sound was a metal sign that wheezed and squeaked in the wind. It read "Short's Gas 'n' Go. Open 6 a.m. to 10 p.m. Since 1978." The house was darker than the bottom of a cave. The only lights in the store were light-up corporate soda logos which gave the store interior a strange glow.

"They're closed, just pee in the bushes," said that faint voice.

"Oh good I have to pee like a race horse," Scott said as he opened the door and stepped out onto the gravel lot. Nate grabbed The Fuckers tour journal off the dash board and stepped outside. He flipped through the pages until he found Frank's entry about the Cincinnati show.

Cincy blows. Two Skinheads, their girlfriends and one moron with green liberty spikes were the show, the entire crowd. They didn't give a shit about us so I don't care about Cincy. Got called a freak and faggot when we were in a McDonalds getting lunch. I thought that was just the way people treated us in Indy. I thought a bigger town would treat us better.

Freaks and faggots. That is what the world thinks of us I suppose. No different anywhere. I have had enough. No more bullshit, and taking hell from rednecks. Been saying it forever. We need to fight back.

My first test was a gas station off the highway not far from Muncie. Maybe I shouldn't talk about that...

A light came on in the house and several outdoor lights followed. Nate closed the journal and looked up.

***

Robert Short had fallen asleep watching *Orange County Choppers*. The empty KFC bucket was his only companion. The Taco Bell/KFC combo at the next exit closed an hour after he shut down the Gas Mart. Closing up often became a race to get to the drive-up window, but they normally had his bucket ready.

It wasn't good for him, but in the year since his wife

left him, he had eaten more than his share of the Colonel's secret recipe. Every so often he would switch it up and go to Hardees up by Muncie. They were open till midnight.

A motion light popped on and that was what startled him awake. The time on the cable box said it was 2:36 a.m. He knocked some crumbs on the floor to look.

It couldn't be his boys. They stopped coming to see him, after their mother told them how mean he had been. Robert avoided putting weight on his bad leg and lifted himself up. He hobbled his way to the window. Most people saw the lights out and the closed sign and moved on, but once a year some asshole would pull up, sometimes even honk their horn to wake him asking if they can buy gas anyway.

One time some rich Texan asshole driving to Chicago offered him one thousand dollars for a tank of gas. He wasn't all that lucky. The summer of 1982, the night his leg went bad was a night humid like this one, when Linda had shaken him awake and hissed, "There are some kinda freaks out by the station."

"Watch the boys," Robert answered as he grabbed his shotgun. On that night, he didn't stop to look, just stepped outside into the warm summer air. No shirt, just his boxer shorts, shotgun, and beer belly he walked out there to remind these people they were closed.

He couldn't believe his eyes. One of the freaks was already watering his poinsettia bushes. He had a goddamn safety pin stuck in his nose, with a chain that connected it. Behind him was a white boy with some kinda green colored Indian haircut.

"Station's closed," Robert said not bothering to raise his shotgun yet.

"Oh, sorry, just taking a piss," the safety pin guy said.

"I don't remember giving no freak permission to water my fuckin' plants."

A big man with a shaved head rounded the corner of their van. Robert didn't see him till it was too late. He didn't have time to turn off his safety. The big guy hit the end of the shotgun with a tire iron. Robert felt his funny bone vibrate like a tuning fork. He reached for the falling shotgun, but it slipped through his fingers. He didn't have time to react as the tire iron hit his kneecap. It broke into a thousand pieces.

"Freak?" the bald man said with a seething rage. All these years later, it haunted Robert still. "We're human beings, you fucking hilljack redneck piece of shit."

Robert still walked with a limp. He looked out the window and saw a nightmare reborn.

***

"Station is closed!" The man was in a robe, but limped out holding a shotgun. Ericka fought to hold in a scream. Scott did scream. He had his dick in his hand and was about to pee on some dead looking bushes. Denny and Nate put their hands up.

"We'll go, we'll go."

Nate was the last in the van, but they couldn't get to Muncie quickly enough. None of them could exactly say why they felt that, but in their own ways, they all surely did.

CHAPTER 8

Ericka sat and watched the second band play, feeling an urge to kick them off the small riser that was being used as a stage. The second night of tour and they still hadn't played a song. Nate leaned against Scott's cabinet and pretended to watch, his head bobbing a bit. She knew he couldn't focus on anything else right before they played.

The show was sponsored by the college radio station where Mark was allowed to spin hardcore at 10 pm. on Fridays. It was a cafeteria in a dorm called Studebaker. Some of the students complained, but it was a freshman dorm and most didn't want to look uncool.

Muncie had always been home away from home for People's Uprising. It was a college town like Bloomington, but the university wasn't as big and didn't dominate the town quite as much. Mark, Nate's best friend growing up, had become a big fish in a small scene. He was a wallflower back in Indianapolis and now he was the cool guy who put on shows.

He gave People's Uprising their first out of town gig, and every time a bigger band came through they opened up for them. A few months earlier they played a show with a Chicago pop-punk band called Hidden Journals who accidentally had a hit song.

Mark had booked them to play Muncie the week the video took off on YouTube. Today they wouldn't be caught dead playing the back room at a coffeehouse, but PU opened. The Muncie kids had supported them, buying shirts and the CD demo, even though all four songs were free on Myspace.

Mark assured them that this Muncie show would be big, and that kids had been asking him when PU would return. Ericka looked out at the crowd and was surprised. She knew lots of faces, some from Indianapolis, Bloomington, and even Louisville. She knew their faces from shows, but also they wore shirts for local bands that served almost as tribal markings.

The song ended and the young band awkwardly looked at each other. The drummer was the only member who knew they had exhausted their set list. He shook his head as the smattering of applause quickly faded out. The guitar player vocalist wiped sweat away. "That's it. Uh, thanks."

That was their cue. Nate turned and smiled at Ericka. She waved at Scott and Denny who were with Mark at their merch table. She felt jitters down to her toes as the young band cleared their equipment. Nate stepped down and leaned next to Ericka.

"Nice turn-out," Nate yelled over the sound of conversations that turned into a low-level rumble in between bands. Ericka smiled back but didn't feel like yelling or talking. She got nervous before shows. Her hands tensed up. Nate rubbed her shoulder and laughed. "You're going to be great tonight," he said, reading her mind.

Old Nate was back. The anger from last night faded away, although everyone was afraid to talk about what happened in Dayton. Scott, the one to blame, even relaxed a bit. Once they got to Muncie, got out of the van, stretched, and ate reheated dinner at Mark's house they all cooled off. The compassion and thoughtfulness she always loved about Nate had returned.

It took the younger band more time to clear their equipment than to play their set list. Scott was the only band member that failed to hide any toe-tapping. He breathed deeply, watching the young band stumble around.

It wasn't like they were old pros, but before the drum kit was half-broken down, Scott and Ericka had their cabinets set up and were tuning. Nate helped Denny assemble what he could of the drum set as they put the puzzle pieces together on stage. It took them eight minutes, while the PA played Propaghandi's "Anti-Manifesto" from the *How to Clean Everything* album. The nostalgia inherent there, too, made him smile.

Ericka looked up as soon as her bass was tuned and saw a little crowd had gathered at the edge of the small stage. They were talking to each other but clearly wanted to be in the front for their set. She knew their faces, could name most of them.

It was the intimate nature of hardcore, like she and Nate always talked about. The rest of the crowd had gathered at the back of the room. She knew when a band she was excited to see and had looked forward to for weeks was setting up. She got goose bumps.

Scott stepped on his distortion pedal for the first time and checked his levels with a loud e-chord crunch. Next he played the same riff every time, "Dethroned Emperor" by Celtic Frost. Ericka only knew the song from Scott playing it, but it meant a lot to Ericka now: Two-minute warning that the show was almost here.

Hearing that riff geeked her up. Adrenaline pumped through her. She hopped in place feeling enough energy building up inside her that could power a marathon run.

Denny hit the various parts of the drum kit while the far-off, impossibly young-looking sound man called out to him. "Snare." Pop, pop. "Floor Tom." Boom, boom. Ericka closed her eyes as the sound man turned down the CD playing in the background. Out in the crowd, she heard the various conversations come to an end. It was here. Her heart pounded.

Ericka opened her eyes, and watched Nate. He took the microphone off the mic-stand as he always did. He watched to get the signal from Denny. Denny played his all-kit check and gave a thumbs up.

"You ready?" Nate whispered, leaning over Ericka's shoulder.

"Go!" Ericka said and twisted the knobs turning on her pick-ups. Scott placed his fingers on the fret board ready to go. They just needed the word from Nate.

Nate used his thumb to turn on his microphone. "Hey, Muncie. We're People's Uprising from Bloomington. This first song is about surviving the Bush years, resistance comes in many forms, all made up of parts that look like me and you. The only way we'll survive is if we RISE!"

Nate held the mic out to the small crowd. Ericka cringed. He was betting that they had listened to their demo on Myspace. Betting they knew the song "And! fight!" The crowd responded in one voice.

Scott timed it perfectly, playing the opening cord. The crowd swelled and broke out into a mosh pit as soon as the band came in together. Ericka picked the strings and swung her hair. In some part of her vision she saw the swirling tornado-like movement of the pit.

It was more controlled than an outsider would imagine. No one could fall without getting picked up. If anyone got too wild or hurt anyone they would get glares that could freeze a person solid.

Nate squeezed the mic, shouted the lyrics and pointed at the crowd as he sang about the need for caring enough to get active. Ericka looked up and watched him for a moment, letting the bass line flow naturally from her pick and without a thought.

The chorus came quickly, and she looked up in time to see a wave of humans crush forward to the stage. Nate jumped off the stage crawling across heads and shoulders, several of the crowd fought him to grab and pull the microphone away. Together they screamed. "Rise! And! fight!" Their voices drowned out the band. Ericka looked at Scott. She wanted to see his reaction. He didn't notice her. He was thrashing around. She felt the breakdown coming. She knew the slower groovier mosh always set off the pit. Nate rolled back on the stage just before it came.

Ericka and Scott didn't plan it. They just banged their heads like a pair of metal guitar players. Nate slammed his fist on the stage before screaming the lyrics. "End this legacy of hate! We can't turn our backs!"

All the drama of the night before melted away. There were only the house lights in her eyes. Nothing but the songs could touch Ericka's spirit.

***

The show was long over before they were able to square money with Mark and load the equipment. It was close to eleven and they only had two hours before making the drive across Ohio to Pittsburgh for their next show. They all agreed driving at night would help keep the temperatures cool, and they could spend the day relaxing or whatever at Pitt University.

The van was parked in the small food service lot behind the dorm they had permission to use for loading and unloading. They were parked in a reserved space owned by Peggy, the assistant food service manager. Someone had written 'Hey Peggy Slayer rules!' on her sign.

Mark invited them to get Chinese food before leaving and everyone but Nate quickly agreed. Ericka hung back and pointed at the group with her thumb. She was happy, smiling like he hadn't seen in a long time. The show was good, and more importantly Ericka played great. He could see she relaxed and didn't overthink the songs. They were flowing.

"You want some take-out? On me?" she asked, backing up to follow.

Nate shook his head. He still had one sandwich left, so he didn't feel like spending money. More importantly, he felt like he needed a minute alone. He was still wet from sweat that hadn't completely dried. It took him a long time to calm down after a show.

After the show he sat at the merch table and lots of people wanted to talk. Now he just wanted a few minutes to himself. He felt a connection to the crowd that was hard to explain to anyone who hadn't experienced it.

It didn't feel any different being in the audience, or on stage. When live, it felt like a surfer catching wave after wave of spiritual energy. He knew that was cheesy, but that was what it was like. The sweat, the heat, all the sensations were ones he could still feel for hours after a gig.

"I'll just stay with the van. Probably a good idea to keep an eye out," Nate said as he waved her away. "Be back by one!"

"Yes, Dad!" Scott yelled from down the block.

Ericka laughed and ran a bit to catch up to Mark and the rest of her band. Nate watched her for a moment before unlocking the van. He sat in the driver's seat and closed his eyes. The ringing echo of the guitars, despite his thick ear plugs, echoed faintly. It almost blocked the sound of the voices. He still couldn't hear what they were saying, speaking just beyond. Beyond what? He couldn't say.

The journal sat on the dashboard. Nate opened it and stared at its faded pages. Flipping through, he looked for Muncie. The entry was written in Frank's handwriting. He had drawn the date in a rough version of Old English tattoo-style lettering.

July 6th 1982
The venue in Muncie is basically a cave. One orange light in the corner plugged into a splitter. All the other plugs have band equipment.

Nate could barely keep his eyes focused on the page. His eyelids felt heavy. He set the journal in his lap. He shouldn't be this tired. Then the sound of a grunt behind him. He looked at the windshield. In the darkness he saw himself and the backseat of the van, reflected faintly like a large rearview mirror. He looked at Scott's backpack on the empty bench and relaxed. He was happy to have this time alone.

"Dude, one shitty orange light down there we might as well play in the fucking dark."

The voice was so clear Nate jumped up in the driver's seat. It wasn't the faint mumbling that he could play off as his imagination. He turned and looked at the empty bench and loft. No one. He was still looking back at the empty van when he heard another voice.

"It's a show so I vote that you shut the fuck up."

Nate knew that voice from all the bootlegs introducing songs. Frank. Nate turned back to the front. He saw a faint reflection in the window, but it wasn't right. He wasn't alone in the reflection. He recognized a young Dickie Abrams and

69

Oscar the Crotch sitting on the bench. Feet he assumed were Gary's stuck out of the loft.

He almost screamed when he didn't see his face, but Frank's face staring back at him from the reflection of the driver's seat. Nate felt sick and gripped the steering wheel. That is when his world faded away.

A fading early summer dusk materialized around him. He turned and looked in back of the van to see Oscar and Dickie. Dickie had a safety pin in his nose, the hole looking like a self-injury that was slightly infected. Oscar had his green Mohawk spiked up.

"Well, I vote for me talking," Oscar said before opening the door to the van. "Come on. Neon Christ is almost finished."

***

Frank stepped out of the van. The summer night was humid. He would complain about it, but by the time the tour snaked through the sweatbox shows in the Bible Belt this weather would feel cool. The small house was spilling out punks, many carrying skateboards. As the band ended its set inside they would pile out into the street and the skateboards would clank and roll until The Fuckers started their set. Tim, the stupid bastard who rented this house and put on shows would try to beg the skaters to get out of the street, but it wouldn't convince them.

Dickie and Gary were in the basement, already setting up. They left Dickie's kit in the van, since it was almost impossible to see in the basement now. Neon Christ were an Atlanta band, but their drummer was willing let Dickie use his kit. As small as this basement was it had hosted bands like the Necros, Articles of Faith, and The Fix in the last few weeks of summer. Only once had the police come to shut down a show.

After drinking four Mountain Dews and two shots of whiskey, Frank walked into the dank basement, barely able to navigate the narrow wooden slats. Most of the non-skater members of the audience were waiting down there. In the small orange glow Frank could tell many were already in various stages of getting fucked up. One guy had already passed out and was rolled under the table where their handmade records and t-shirts were being ignored by the kids who used their last dimes to pay the small cover.

Gary was plugged into the other band's cabinet. Frank could tell the slight difference in sound. When he walked into the corner where the band was set up he saw Oscar in the corner with his back turned. Frank assumed he was shooting up, a last hit before they started.

The top crown of microphone was beat-up and dented. Frank found it sitting on the bass drum. He flipped it on and gave a "Check, one-two." There was no sound check, no nothing. This was like setting up in your garage to practice. The skaters piled in, and before a note was played the room began getting steamy. Gary looked at him and nodded.

"This is punk rock, not disco." Frank said without the mic to the room. He lifted the dented, cheap beer-scented microphone to his mouth. The PA amp he was connected to spit out feedback that sounded like a goose fucking a light socket. "I want to see some fucking chaos, Muncie!!"

At that point, Oscar played the bass intro to "Nun Bake-Off" and the whole band came together.

They never sound checked, and the guitars were loud. They took up the space like soap suds spilling out of an overloaded dishwasher. There was no room for a pit, just bodies colliding. Frank was glad. He hated stages, and wished they could play their sets in the middle of the pit. He liked being in the eye of the storm.

Boots stomped, arms spun around, fists were thrown. Frank felt the bare skin, leather jackets, and steel spikes slam into him as he sang. Dickie was driving their beat a little fast. He had to sing faster to not to lose his place.

Frank missed a whole verse when a moshing skater's head went right into his gut. Frank leaned over, almost puking on the shirtless kid's back. He put a combat boot on the kid's side and percussively helped him back into the pit.

71

The song ended and two idiots were still running into each other like rams head butting. He saw a younger one with blood coming off his forehead trying to crawl up the stairs. Friends took his shoulder and helped him outside.

"Hey, dipshits," Frank said into the mic. The audience laughed together. "Yeah, I am talking to all of you, listen close."

Oscar set a bottle of whiskey on the bass cabinet. Frank took a swig, it burned going down. He shouted in the mic and few of them laughed. "On our way here we had some shit kicker grit try to fuck with us. I know that happens to you. Walking down the street some redneck asshole in a truck yells out his window or calls you a freak, a faggot, whatever. Have you had enough? I know I ain't taking this shit anymore. This one's called, "US VERSUS THEM!""

The pit bounced off the walls as Frank tightened his grip on the microphone, then...

***

KNOCK! KNOCK!

Nate gripped the steering wheel with his right hand and jumped. The knocking sound surprised him. He felt the heat of the dank basement, even smelled the sweaty punks moshing, as Ericka stood there at the window of the van, smiling and holding a take-out bag.

"Open up, goofball."

Nate caught his breath, sitting at the steering wheel, feeling like he had been caught with his hand in something worse than a cookie jar. The sound of The Fuckers cut off like the power switch on a tape getting hit with a brick.

It wasn't a dream. He still felt like he was back in that basement. The side door opened behind him. Denny showed his copy of the key before jumping in the back. It was almost one a.m. They were ready to leave. Nate turned around and looked at Denny and Scott getting in. He was sweating. His head and eyes felt slow to match up that way they did when drinking, but he hadn't drank a drop of alcohol.

Nate unlocked the door and slid over to the passenger seat. Ericka got in the seat. "You okay, Nate?" Ericka asked. She set the left-overs in between them on top of her backpack. He leaned his head up against the window. "Fine. Can you drive the first shift?"

"Pittsburgh. Let's roll."

CHAPTER 9

They were entering western Pennsylvania as the sun came up. Scott was driving, after a two- hour shift when Ericka drove. Nate and Ericka took the bench. After stopping for gas and bathrooms, they moved around again. Nate moved back up to the front.

She noticed that without conversation, Scott and Denny kept letting the unofficial couple sit together. Ericka wished they were getting the right idea, but she knew she would have to talk with Denny and make her band mates understand. They were not a couple. Bottom line, she was driving again.

She took out the Dag Nasty CD that had already played a second time and looked at Nate, hoping he would wake up and help her change CDs. He was pushed up against the window sleeping on his hoodie as a pillow. Ericka reached down, and grabbed the first CD in the next page of the book. She held it up and smiled.

The white CD-R had "90s mix" written on it in Sharpie. Nate-made mixes were legendary, and this one of 90's hardcore bands was one of her favorites. It started with Born Against, the band they first bonded on. This was a sweet romantic touch that wouldn't mean anything to most young women. Ericka understood the moment she pushed play that first time.

Ericka had been tired since she started this shift of driving, and hoped the CD would do what her Mountain Dew had failed to do. The first song came on and she watched Nate out of the corner of her eye. He didn't wake up or react at all. That was fine. She didn't expect much.

Denny was the only member of People's Uprising with previous tour experience. He'd done two full tours playing drums, once for a metal band named Nocturonis and once in a hardcore band called Wasteland Tourism. He was the one that suggested driving at night as much as possible.

This old van had nothing close to an air conditioner. He knew that they would have free time here and there in the east and south. He warned them once they got out west it would feel like they were driving forever.

The whole band was basically vegetarian, but Ericka and Nate were the vegans in the band. They had a list of restaurants and bakeries they had found on a website called Happy Cow, places they wanted to eat at in each city. As soon as they got on the road, Scott's diet centered on kettle chips and Skittles.

Ericka turned the stereo down and reached over to slap the sleeping Nate in the passenger seat. He sat up, pretending to be wide awake.

"Hey, I need to talk or I have to blast this CD."

"Blast away," Nate said as he closed his eyes.

Ericka knew the music wasn't enough "I think we'll hear complaints from Tweedledee and TweedleBootToTheFace."

"Watch it," said the half-asleep drummer under the sweatshirt covering his eyes.

Nate shook his head, trying to cast off sleep, but his head leaned back against the window and his eyes were closed in seconds. Ericka looked back through the rear view and saw Scott had crawled up to the loft. Denny had already pulled his hoodie back over his head.

Ericka let the CD play, but kept the volume kinda low. She felt her eyelids get a little heavy but she was awake. The sun was already bright and the traffic was picking up. They would be in Pittsburgh in about an hour, so she wanted the boys to sleep.

The first song ended. The second song, one her favorites on the mix, an old California band, Downcast, was starting. In the pause between songs she heard Scott say something. She looked up in the mirror and thought it was strange. He was flat on his back, with his jacket still pulled over his face.

She swore she heard him, or maybe Denny. The song kept playing. Ericka reached and hit the volume knob that paused the CD. Nothing. The only sound was the engine and the road. She reached over to turn it off when she heard another voice.

Slightly distorted with the buzz in the speakers, nothing more than a mumble, she couldn't make it out. Ericka leaned forward closer to the speakers, her breasts softly touching the horn as she hugged the wheel.

Denny stirred behind her. He was the only one who'd heard the small toot of the horn. She looked back at him. He was shaking sleep out of his eyes. She knew it was a stupid question, but asked anyway: "Hey, Denny, can a radio accidentally pick up CB signals?"

"Huh?" He was confused. "You mean like truckers? 'Smokey and the Bandit' type shit?"

"Forget it." Ericka had no idea what he was talking about. She felt stupid now.

But she could have sworn she heard voices between the songs. She listened to the mix a thousand times and never heard that before. Ericka leaned back and almost forgot that she was driving for a moment. Denny stuck his head up. "What happened?"

Ericka felt stupid telling him because it sounded weird. "Uh, I'm not sure. I thought I heard voices but you were all asleep."

Denny raised an eyebrow. "Pull over. I'm driving."

"No, no I'm fine."

Denny laughed. "It's OK. I have somewhere I want to take you guys."

"In Pittsburgh?"

Denny smiled. "In Pittsburgh."

"You help keep me awake?"

Denny smiled. "Sure thing. What you want to talk about?"

Ericka gripped the steering wheel at little tighter. She wanted to talk about Nate; to tell Denny to stop treating them like boyfriend and girlfriend, which Nate had shown clearly that he didn't want. She wanted to ask him why Nate was so against it, really. At the same time it was such stereotype—

chick bassist in love with the lead singer—that it made her want to puke. Nate could wake up at any moment, so there was no way she could ask him any of that.

Denny didn't wait for her to figure out an ice-breaker.

"Got to hand it to Nate."

"Sure, what do you mean?" Ericka was confused.

"The van. I mean she's doing pretty good."

"Why is the van a she? Doesn't feel like a she to me."

Denny laughed. "I don't care. *It* is doing great. Smooth sailing. I have to admit I thought pulling an ancient tour van off a trash pile was crazy."

Ericka nodded. "Totally crazy."

Denny reached into his pocket and pulled out a wadded up paper. "I'll tell you when I see the exit."

CHAPTER 10

Nate woke up feeling hot. He knew they'd stopped, because he didn't feel the air coming through the vent. Realizing he'd fallen deeply asleep against the window, Nate also felt an embarrassing morning stiffness. His eyes adjusted slowly like a camera finding focus. The bright summer morning sun fought him.

He was surprised when he realized they were parked in the back of a mall parking lot. Denny and Ericka were already out of the van. Ericka turned to wave. She looked cute in her Crass shirt, sleeves long gone and the sides slashed open to the sports bra she wore under it. It showed off her curves in a way Nate hadn't seen before. He liked it.

Scott slid down on to the bench. He stared over Nate's shoulder. "A mall?"

Nate stepped out just as Denny and Ericka were leaning over and stretching. He shook out his legs as Scott poured himself out of the van.

"What are we doing at a mall?" Nate asked trying not to sound annoyed.

"Not just any mall," said Ericka giving him a pat on the shoulder. "A mall on the far side of Pittsburgh."

"Oh come on. It's not far from Squirrel Hill, which is where the show is. And this is not just any mall, it is the goddamn Monroeville Mall!" Denny put his arms up, expecting Nate to get it. He still had no idea why this was exciting. Denny dropped his arms in disbelief.

"Wait a second." Scott pointed at the mall. "No way! This is the *Dawn of the Dead* mall."

Nate got it now. As into record collecting as he was, Denny matched him on horror movies. For every issue of *Maximum Rock and Roll* he had collected, Denny had an equal stack of *Fangorias*. For every useless bit of old school punk trivia he had, Denny could equal him in horror movie knowledge.

As a band, they all once watched *Dawn of the Dead* together on a movie night. Denny, however, had seen the 1978 classic movie enough times that he could speak the dialogue from memory.

"You've been here before?"

Denny was hopping up and down. "Nope, but it's horror geek mecca. I tried on the metal tour, but we didn't have time."

Nate understood the feeling. He had it every time he sat in the van, or read the journal. It was a living part of history. He didn't give shit about the movie or this mall, but he would play along because Denny respected his love for punk history enough to tour in The Fuckers van.

"Come on, man!" Denny waved them toward the door. "Look, it's where they lined up the trucks to block the doors."

Nate reached back to lock the van door. "They won't be open yet."

"We aren't buying shit, anyway," said Ericka as she took off running to the door. Nate didn't have it in him to run yet. Too early for that.

He and Scott caught up and Ericka waited holding the door open. Once in the mall they saw a few mall-walking senior citizens and some Kenny G shit was playing on the loud speakers. Denny was pointing out stuff from the movie, but of course a quarter of a century had passed and it looked much different today than it did in the flick.

One group of the mall-walkers looked back at them. It was funny that they looked bothered by their presence. Nate was sure that these folks walked this mall every morning and didn't know what to make of an invasion of young folks. They didn't even look that punk rock besides a few streaks of green in Ericka's hair. None of them had wild dye jobs, no Mohawks or anything really off the wall.

It was something that had happened quietly in punk rock, but the need to make wild statements with the way you look just didn't have the impact it once did. Punk bands from Bad Religion, Green Day, and even Social Distortion had softened their sounds and mainstreamed punk rock. The true underground at this point was a lifestyle and they were proof of that. It wasn't a fashion statement. It was in how you lived day to day.

They walked up an escalator and looked out from the second floor deck by the Macy's that been a J.C. Penney in the movie. They stood on the second level looking out at the mall the same way the survivors in *Dawn of the Dead* did after they cleaned all the zombies out.

Denny pointed at the Hot Topic store on the first level. "My Grandpappy said when there is no room in hell, preps and jocks will buy Dead Kennedys shirts at the mall."

They laughed, all except Nate who didn't think it was funny. It was still closed, but even seeing Hot Topic just annoyed him. Its very existence was a sign of how things had changed since the era of punk rock that was his favorite.

Back then, no stores in the mall sold anything more punk rock than maybe a Clash or Sex pistols tape to a DJ. Now thirteen year old wannabes could just use Mommy and Daddy's credit card to gear up. It disgusted him.

"Mall should open soon. We should shop at Crotch Topic!" said Scott. Denny and Ericka laughed. Denny walked like a Zombie and growled "Do you have AFI and Fallout Boys shirts, sir?"

"Sure do, would you like a pair of these glow in the dark Green Day wrist bands to go with those?" Ericka replied.

Scott shook his head. "I would actually wear those."

Ericka was disgusted. "I wouldn't let you."

Denny pointed at his old friend. "Still likes Green day. Admit it!"

"Guilty pleasure," Scott laughed, "so I think I'll pick up some wristbands before—"

But Nate just put up his hand. It wasn't funny. It was everything that was wrong about punk rock today. It had no edge, it wasn't dangerous.

Punks back in the day didn't hang out at malls, they

got chased out of them. They got harassed by jocks and rednecks. Today they were lucky if they got a few shitty looks. Now getting a job with tattoos and piercings was no problem. Even his bandmates who he thought understood his feelings were just cracking jokes like the mainstreaming of punk rock didn't even matter.

Nate sighed deeply and walked towards the escalator. "Hey, what's your problem?" Denny called out, but Nate was already heading toward the bottom level. He could hear Ericka stomping after him. They got to the bottom and Ericka grabbed his arm. They were right in front of the Hot Topic. He could see the Marilyn Manson clone getting ready to open the doors.

Nate turned to see the confusion on Ericka's face. "What is your problem, Nate? We were just kidding around."

"My problem? You want to know my problem? Green Day and Nirvana are my problem. That was never supposed to happen. Bad Religion was never supposed to have a hit song. Green Day were supposed to play Gilman and basements, not football stadiums."

Ericka looked up to see if the rest of the band was watching this. They weren't. "OK, so what? We keep playing shows and we don't sell out. It is that simple."

"It's not funny."

"Nate, it is funny. A week ago you would have been joking about it. What is going on?"

Nate looked away. He whispered. He didn't mean too. It just came out that way. "I don't know."

Ericka rubbed his arm. Her hand felt good on his skin. He wanted to pull her close for a hug.

"Well, you're acting weird. Getting angry..."

"That's not weird."

Ericka shook her head. "Not for Denny or Scott, but you're different, Nate. Changing."

"Maybe it's overdue." Nate rolled his eyes as he pulled his arm free. "I'll be at the van when you guys are done being mall punks."

Ericka watched him walk away in disbelief.

CHAPTER 11

Pittsburgh was a basement show at a house venue called Squirrel Hell. The house they were looking for was off Murray Avenue, which they cruised up and down for close to an hour. The directions on the Squirrel Hell Myspace were terrible. They only found it because they saw two crusty punks turning on foot off the main drag.

A small crowd had gathered. The house was built in the '30s, when Squirrel Hill was mostly a Jewish neighborhood, and reflected simpler days. They were the opening band, so they were pushed into the corner where bands played right away.

Ericka couldn't move much during their set. Her legs were backed up against Denny's bass drum the whole time. Not that the show was crowded, only twenty people packed the basement.

Ericka had a feeling at least half of them lived here, even if it was only sleeping on a space of the floor. Twice as many were hanging out in the back yard all night. A carload drove down from Erie to see them and they were the only ones who seemed to know their songs or sing along.

The same set that felt like a heartbeat in Muncie dragged on that night. Ericka felt relieved when Nate thanked the crowd and Scott ripped his patch cord out. She could tell by the smile on his face that Nate loved the show.

"Awesome," said Jenn, who drove down from Erie. She'd been inches from him, singing every word of their songs during the whole set. Ericka had tried not to pay attention to her, but she didn't leave when they finished. Now she stood there invading Nate's personal space.

Kenny, who organized the show, despite living somewhere else in Pittsburgh also ran up to Nate. Ericka could tell that Kenny had a crush on Nate. They both did. Well, they all did. *How could she blame them?*

Scott was wrapping his cord around his fist watching it happen. He spoke just loud enough for Ericka to hear him. "Well, you're not the only one in love with Nate."

"Shut up." Not much point in denials with Scott. Denny was also flirting, with one of Jenn's friends that came in the Erie carload. She was a bit young looking to Ericka. Denny got the impression they had met before on tour or at show before.

Ericka tried to ignore it all. She put her bass away in its case. The basement felt like an oven despite an overworked, dust-covered box fan hanging in the back corner that just seemed to spread dust.

"Hard to breathe in here," she said to Kenny, but he only turned long enough to nod. "Suppose that is how this place got its name."

Everyone ignored her for the moment. Ericka stepped up the stairs and walked through the kitchen to a propped open back door. The back yard was twice as filled with people as the show was. More people had shown up since they started playing. The next band waited by their van for a signal to haul into the basement.

"All yours." Ericka used her bass case to point at the door. The band members waved and thanked her. They had two guitar players. She didn't envy them for that.

Their van was parked behind the house at the end of the drive way. Ericka felt a sense of relief at seeing it for the first time. It was starting to feel like home. It didn't smell to her anymore. She was feeling more comfortable.

They left the doors unlocked so they could load fast. She opened the back door, slid her bass in and waited. Normally she helped take down and load, but she didn't want to watch Kenny and Jenn flirt with Nate.

Scott came up with his guitar. He slid it under the loft next to her bass. "You played awesome tonight."

"No, I didn't." Ericka, who was self-taught, always felt inferior to Scott, who took lessons from the age of ten. He was a technically gifted musician who chose to play simple and powerful music. He got easily frustrated with her lack of skill early on, but always offered help. He wouldn't lie to her. One thing Scott could be counted on was brutal honesty.

Scott smiled. "You did too."

***

Wilkes-Barre was different. They were all excited to play with System Head in Philly the next day. The Philly show was a big one and a short drive away. They could have overlooked this show easily.

People's Uprising was on fire from the first moment of the set in Wilkes-Barre. The opening band was one they all wanted to see named Wasting Life from Santa Barbara. Wasting Life had played a back yard in Long Island and then cut across north Jersey to make this show. Ericka was sure no one from her band knew they would be playing.

It was an awesome surprise. They played with such energy it inspired them. The venue was in a pizza place that was host normally to jazz and Phish cover bands. The stage was as tall as a stair step. Wasting Life couldn't get off the stage fast enough. Ericka loved them, but she never wanted to play a show so bad.

She had to take deep breaths to concentrate on tuning. Nate had been quiet since the mall, but his smile returned as they got closer to playing. Ericka faced her amp and hit her high string, one she rarely used. She felt a finger tap her on the shoulder.

"Turn around," Nate whispered. The previous band had stowed their equipment and were set up on her side of the small stage. The room had filled in nicely. Then she saw what Nate wanted her to see: a young woman wearing a handmade People's Uprising shirt. Ericka smiled, liking to see that.

Scott played Celtic Frost and Ericka felt the energy spike in her. Nate grabbed the mic. The band knew what was coming. It was a little different speech every night, but the same song. One part of touring she didn't expect was seeing the reaction to the same songs in different venues.

"I hope you check out our stuff, we're People's Uprising from Bloomington Indiana. We're a punk rock band. I'm of how..."

That was a little weird. Nate paused. Ericka glanced at Scott over Nate's shoulder. He had his pick inches from the strings ready to go. Nate looked faint. It lasted only a few seconds but it seemed like forever. He shook it off."... sorry. I lost my train of thought." The small audience felt uncomfortable with the awkward moment. Nate let out a breath. "This one is 'Rise and Fight.'"

The set was a blur. Every moment was raw power. The audience sang along. Ericka watched Nate. He rebounded, drawing off the energy of the crowd. He dipped into the audience, grabbed the ones who knew the songs, and screamed with them face to face. He spoke on political issues that got the room cheering along with him.

Ericka wanted to kill him in Pittsburgh. As she watched him connect politically and spiritually to the songs they had written together her heart swooned. The love became power in her hands, it drove the pounding bass in the song.

***

Denny and Scott were inside still drinking beer and eating pizza with two of the show promoters. The hippie who owned the place made them an extra pizza because he was impressed by Scott's guitar playing. Ericka walked back into the joint after locking up the van and saw Nate talking to a local anarchist activist who sat behind a table with Xeroxed flyers. A banner made with spray paint on a bed sheet read, 'Wilkes-Barre Anarchist Black Cross.'

Nate turned and saw Ericka. He waved at her. Ericka shrugged her shoulders and stepped back outside. She shared a lot of Anarchist political views. She had a pin of Emma Goldman's face on her backpack but she didn't feel like getting a lecture; and, let's face it, that is what political tablers at shows are there to do. Nate could talk anarchism almost as long as he could talk vintage punk rock. She was too tired for that. The show was fun but exhausting.

She stepped outside and saw the red van with California plates pulling away. They were off to a show in Cleveland the next night. The guitar player who was extra friendly to Ericka rolled down his window, shouted, "See you later." Myspace friendship was on the way.

Ericka unlocked the door to the van, kicked her Chucks off, and crawled up into the loft. The cushion felt wonderful under her. She'd been sleeping propped up in the passenger seat, mostly.

She was sweaty and gross, and felt greasy from head to toe. She hoped there was a shower in Philly. Her hair was so greasy she felt a little squished as she tied it up in a makeshift bun.

Sleep came instantly when she got flat. Five minutes or an hour she didn't know. Her phone was buried in her backpack and she didn't have a watch. She woke to the side door opening. Nate stepped into the van and sat at an angle to look at her.

"Hey, you," Ericka said, so tired she was barely able to say the words. She rolled enough to look at him as he sat below her.

"You were awesome tonight." Nate smiled.

"You were the show tonight."

Nate shook his head. "I'm nothing. You guys play better each night."

"True," Ericka said, and laughed. He smiled a smile so big and goofy she had to look away. She rolled onto her back, already in love with him so much it hurt her daily.

"Ericka, can I tell you something?"

Tell her something? Fantasy topics flashed across her mind. She didn't expect any of those topics to be what he actually said.

"Of course..." She wanted to say *sweetheart*, but the word never left her heart.

Nate kicked off his shoes and slid into the loft next to

her. Ericka was shocked. He was so close she could feel how damp his shirt was from sweating during the show. Hers had dried faster. He was as grimy as her. She didn't care. She wanted him closer. He locked eyes with her.

"I'm not sure what happened back in the mall. I know I made you mad, but..."

Ericka leaned on her wrist. "Well, you were being a jerk, taking yourself a little too seriously if you ask me. Or Denny or Scott, actually don't ask them."

Nate nodded. He looked like he was trying to process what she was saying.

"OK, but I don't remember."

Ericka almost smiled. Assuming for a second he was messing with her, but she couldn't think of a reason why he would do that. "What do you mean you don't remember?"

"I don't remember being there at all."

Ericka let up a breath. "What?"

"I remember getting out of the van. You looked really nice..."

Ericka couldn't enjoy the compliment.

"...and then we were back in the van and you were pissed off at me."

"You blacked out? Because you were there, didn't shut up."

Nate shrugged. She saw past him through the open door. Scott and Denny both looked a little tipsy as they made their way out to the van. Nate would have to drive. She wouldn't last five minutes behind the wheel. He turned and looked at them and back at her. Without a word he slid down on to the bench, leaving Ericka feeling very alone. He threw his backpack up between the front seats.

Ericka didn't jump down. She needed the sleep.

"Hey, Ericka," Nate said as he jammed the keys in the ignition. "Can we keep this a secret?"

She wasn't sure what he meant. She wanted him to trust her. So even though she felt the need to talk about it, she nodded. She was asleep again before they left town.

CHAPTER 12

It was after midnight when they got to Philadelphia. The directions were solid, plus Denny had played a show there before. It was a legendary south Philly Punk house. Three years of shows and they'd never been shut down. They had one rent scare that was solved by a last minute show that raised the money they needed. Little else.

Stark House was a place Nate looked forward to playing the moment they agreed to tour. They had to cancel and book a smaller show in New York to be here on the same night as System Head, but they all agreed it was going to be one of the best shows of the tour.

The front door was unlocked and they walked straight in. You never knocked on the door of the house with the *'Property is theft'* sign on it. Only four crusties were in the house. One had a beer in hand and was cooking a pot of lentils big enough to feed an army. Behind him another crust Punk was digging through the fridge. He stood up straight and Nate couldn't believe his eyes.

Tick.

"Hey, you guys are a night early!"

"Oh, shit, Tick, what are you doing here?" It was a stupid question that Nate could answer himself. He knew Tick was doing the exact same thing he was doing in Bloomington. Rocking the couch, dumpstering food, and overstaying his welcome.

"I trainhopped to Pittsburgh, and got a ride with Kenny."

The back door opened and Kenny walked in, his backpack filled with out of date chips they must have found in a Trader Joe's dumpster. Kenny acted surprised to see Nate. Maybe he was. They were supposed to be in Wilkes-Barre.

Nate wished he didn't know why Kenny skipped the

last show. Too much drama with Kenny's ex-boyfriend who played guitar in the California band.

Kenny made rounds giving hugs. Nate noticed that Ericka was lukewarm on the hug but faked the best smile she could. When he got to Nate he lingered on the hug. Nate didn't mind. Actually a part of him liked Ericka's jealous behavior.

Ericka was exhausted anyways. It didn't help her attitude at all. "Hey is there a shower here?"

"In a house full of crusties?" Tick laughed. "Probably a lonely one."

***

Later, Ericka was up sitting in the corner reading a zine, her glasses at the end of her nose. Her hair was clean and tied up in a bun. Nate was glad she was the first thing he saw when he woke. Nate was still tired. A conversation about 80's hardcore kept him awake. He wanted to sleep, but also understood these were friends he almost never saw.

He talked until he was dozing between words. As a result, he didn't feel very rested. It was a cross section of traveling kids and band members they had met coming through the years. They knew people at each show but this one more than others. The night before felt like a family reunion as much as a slumber party.

"Well good morning." Ericka smiled, putting the open zine across her crossed legs. Nate sniffed the air. The smell was familiar. Mixed in with the musk of undershowered crusty punk that was soaked into the walls was Tick's famous tofu scramble.

"Tick cooked breakfast. Tofu scramble, of course," said Ericka.

"Yeah, I could smell it."

"Really?" Ericka lifted an eyebrow.

He understood what she meant. Stark House had a smell that could be detected as far as the curb. The house hosted sweaty hot punk shows, and since it was in the middle of a residential neighborhood, that required all doors and windows to be shut. Added to that nasally toxic soup were six to twelve people living under the roof that nightly picked dumpsters for food and didn't shower as a rebellious fashion statement.

Nate looked around the living room that was littered with bodies when he went to sleep, and it was empty now. "Where is everybody?"

Ericka dog-eared the page in the zine she was reading and put it back in her backpack. "Well, let's see. The woman Denny was flirting with in Wilkes-Barre showed up around noon and they disappeared for the afternoon."

"It's afternoon?" Nate couldn't believe it.

"Oh yeah. So, Denny took off with, uh, I don't remember her name. I think it's serious. She's getting laid for sure. Kenny tried to wake you up twice. He's totally in love with you, by the way. I think he went with Scott and Tick to hop fences at apartment complexes with pools. Everyone else I'm not sure."

They had a lot of hours in the day, and he didn't think he could stand the smell that long. "I can't breathe. You ready to walk?

"How far are we from Wooden Shoe?"

Ericka grinned. "Twenty-minute walk. I got directions."

Wooden Shoe was an anarchist, collectively-run book and record store since 1976. She was ready, and knew right where to go. "You're so awesome." He meant it deeply. He wondered if she knew.

***

The late summer morning breeze felt nice on his face. Nate stepped out of the house and sat on the step. Ericka went to the van and was searching through her bag for something. He just stared for moment. It was a miracle the van had operated as well as it had. He understood that it was just a shell and the new engine was doing the magic.

Ericka shut the door and pointed towards South Street. He smiled and walked down the ancient stone staircase that

90

lead to the sidewalk.

"Funny seeing Tick here, huh?" She said. Nate nodded but walked silent, his hands in his pockets. They were waiting at a light for a walk signal before Ericka tried again. "It's cool the Erie kids drove all this way to see us play."

He didn't feel like talking, but he was so glad to be there with Ericka. For just a moment he forgot about the tour, the band, the weight of the world. He was just happy to be here in this strange city with Ericka.

As they walked, he reached carefully over and slid his palm against hers. He slipped his fingers between hers. Nothing was spoken or declared. She just gripped his hand. And they walked.

***

At the next gig, Ericka played with a power she never felt before. Not once did she think about the songs. Her heart took over. The house shook as Nate reached into the crowd grabbing kids by the back of the neck and screaming together. "Rise! And! Fight!" Ericka had her eyes closed, but the second time they played the chorus it sounded like a stadium show. The sing-along drowned the band out.

Philly kids knew the songs, and they reacted like the crowds back home did. It was a show that felt normal to her. She felt more at home, and Nate had held her hand. The rest of the day was like any other but she felt such joy while she played. Scott and Denny enjoyed their days too.

Denny's new love interest hung out behind his guitar cabinet. They were all happy and playing with energy. Nate channeled the proper anger while shouting the vocals. The Philly set was a wonderful blur.

***

"Are you sure I can wait?"

Nate waved her towards the house. Ericka walked backward, torn between finishing packing the equipment and getting back to the basement. System Head had opened with a song called "Fury."

The blasting grind song was universally agreed to be their best song. Hardcore bands didn't measure hits by sales, but the crowd reaction. They were loud enough that Nate could hear what sounded like the version you would hear through thick earplugs. He didn't mind finishing the packing because Ericka, Scott and Denny were all rushing to get back inside.

Normally that would be him. They were a great band, and he had seen them twice in Indiana and twice at Fests. They played with an intensity live they had never been able to capture on a record.

"Go! I got this!" Nate smiled as Ericka bounced once then skipped the rest of the way towards the house. Nate turned to the open back door to the van. They were parked on the street just in front of the house. He just had a few parts of the drum kit left to fit under the loft. This was the first show on tour where he felt uneasy about the neighborhood.

There was a liquor store at the corner. What few customers the store had looked like they had begged for the money to spend there. A few seemed curious and looked down the street to see what was causing the noise.

This was also the first show where no one hung out outside the show. P.U. had packed the basement. He didn't know how, but the twenty or so that had been outside had somehow fit inside. System Head in the Stark house basement was probably packed beyond any legal limit. Thankfully, a house show didn't have fire codes.

He wanted to see the show, but didn't feel like squeezing into the basement. A part of him didn't want leave the van. He didn't feel safe leaving it here. Nate just put the last pieces in and shut the door. The first song ended, there was a split second and applause before the drummer snapped the snare three times, and then the band launched into their second song.

Nate opened the driver's side door and sat down. His mind was already on the drive to Boston. He wanted to look at the directions in his backpack. He leaned over the seat and looked through the backpack. Between his notebook and his laptop was the tour journal. He hadn't looked at it in a few days.

The voices were still there. Hard to make out over the bad playing up the stone staircase and in the basement, but the voices were heated. He could tell that much.

Nate pulled the journal out. He thumbed through the pages. The Fuckers had played Cleveland and then Philly. He opened the short, but not at all sweet Cleveland entry.

Cleveland Day 4
Fuck this town it sucks. Everyone here agrees. Show was all right.

Nate flipped to the Philly page. Much of it was scratched out with pen ink.

Philadelphia Day 5.
Philly show is in a warehouse. A fucked up crazy ghetto part of town. Philly has a cool scene. They have a couple bands that pooled their money to rent a empty warehouse in a old Irish neighborhood. The warehouse is a pretty fucked up place. The bathroom is disgusting, but Oscar loves it because he scored drugs. There is bar down the street that has an Eagles flag that the locals call the gauntlet. The bar smells like a giant ash tray and the people crawling out of that place are violent scumbags. They create serious problems for the warehouse...

The rest of the page was marked out. Nate angled the page to catch the streetlight just right. He hoped he could see marked out parts. Nothing, and the next two pages were torn out. He could see the nubs of the pages. The mystery interested Nate, but he was also tired.

He looked at his watch. 11:52 pm. He put the journal back on the dashboard and closed his eyes, feeling sleep coming, listening to the band through the walls of the house and the van. The muffled drone of it lulled him. It got louder

93

as if someone was turning up a volume knob.

System Head had a modern sound, somewhat metallic. What they were playing now sounded raw, old school. Nate liked it. Sleep overtook him like a wave slowly moving across a beach.

***

The Ford Explorer rumbled down the narrow Philadelphia street. High off the ground and re-tooled for power it shook the van as it passed. Sonically it was a match for the band playing in the basement, it probably woke at least one sleeping person on the block.

Nate slept through it. When it passed the only sound in the van was his stop watch. The second hand softly ticking down the moments.

11:59:55. Tick tick tick tick…

The key turned in Nate's hand. The engine roared to life. The gear shift slid from park to drive. Nate's foot pushed softly on the gas. The van pulled away from the house.

CHAPTER 13

The gear shift snapped into park and Nate's eyes shot open. His hand gripped the gear shift stick tightly. Nate felt a moment of panic. He was in the van, but asleep. Had he fallen asleep driving? He spun in the seat and looked around the van. Through eyes cobwebbed with sleep he saw it was empty.

The time on his watch read 12:35. He turned back around to look out front. The light from the headlights was so bright he couldn't see anything. He didn't remember turning on the van. The last thing he remembered was sitting in front of Stark House.

Nate opened the door and stumbled out. He was surprised he didn't hear System Head or the sounds of people from the show. He looked up trying to focus his eyes on the house. The van stopped in front of a locked chain-link fence.

The building on the other side of the fence was a rundown abandoned warehouse. A weathered for lease sign hung on the wall that had been there for twenty years. Nate looked down the road. A dimly lit bar had a sign that read Irish Pub under two spotlights.

His eyes got used to the light. On the sidewalk was a faded mural. Without the lights from the van Nate might have missed it. *Sandy Goldstein and Robbie Maddox Rip- July 1982*

"We can't ignore this, we have to fight back." A voice spoke from inside the ajar door of the van. Nate came around and looked inside. Empty and silent as a tomb.

Nate stepped back, sure that he heard a voice speaking in the van, different from the mumbling ones he heard before. Those he could accept were in his mind. Those he could discount. This voice was clear.

Nate leaned down and touched the mural. The face of a
man and woman, both stylized a little but clearly early-80's
Punk Rockers. There was a thick layer of dirt and grime.
Nate tried to brush it away, then it was gone. It disappeared
before his eyes.

The concrete was blank, no painting. He looked up and
the fence was now open. Music played distorted by walls, so
loud and raw it cut through. He knew the song. He knew it
well. The Fuckers—"Us Versus Them."

"What the fuck?" Nate looked around. The van was
shining its lights on him. He turned back to the factory and
the fence was gone. A crowd of Punk Rockers had gathered
in front of the building and the music got louder, and louder
until Nate heard it so loud he might as well have been on
stage...

***

...Frank spun the microphone around by the cord. The dented
silver head of the microphone swung just inches from the
edge of the swirling circle pit. Frank leaned on the edge of
the stage which was also a skateboard ramp with two holes
from water damage. A hole in the ceiling above them leaked
whenever it rained. Not that the salvaged wood was ever
the quality needed. The shows and skateboards had put them
through hell, now Frank had to watch his feet not to fall off
the stage.

The warehouse had been home to sets from hardcore
bands from all over the country. Tonight, The Fuckers were
sandwiched between White Cross from North Carolina and
SOA from D.C.

Two guys with multi-colored Mohawks and flannel shirts
tied around their waists were spastically throwing their fists.
They knocked into Oscar's bass. He lost his spot in the song
and was too doped-up to find his place. Oscar just dived into
the audience. No point in trying to play the song.

Frank pointed at the crowd "It's us versus them!" Oscar
was supposed to sing a backup, but he was lost in the pit. "To

the war again..." In Indiana the crowd would shout the lyrics back to them, but no one in this city had heard them before. They distributed the records themselves. The show booked by sending a record to the warehouse address they found in a *Maximum Rock and Roll* classified ad.

Dickie was beating away on the drums. He was on auto-pilot, unaware they had lost their bass player. Gary had his head down and was pounding away till the moment the song ended. Dickie pounded the fast beat and Frank screamed until it ended. "It's a war! You must fight!" The song ended and Frank could hardly stand. A few people clapped. One drunk guy in back of the warehouse howled.

"Fuck you," someone in the small crowd yelled.

"Yeah, fuck me," Frank laughed. "Maybe you'll like the next one."

Oscar was using his bass like a jousting pole to move through the mess of punks. "Thanks for nothing, Philly!" Frank said, pacing the stage like a tiger trapped in a zoo. He couldn't wait for the next song, pent up anger and rage built up like a bomb ready to explode. It needed to explode. Frank shouted into the mic. "Fuck, just play 'Conformity Factory'"

Gary picked the riff when the back door to the warehouse opened. Someone waved at the back of the room. Frank saw a black punk with dreds shaved into a Mohawk being dragged inside. The crowd had gathered around the man. Even from the stage at the front of the room he could see the black man's nose was crushed. His face was a blood-drenched mess.

People got hurt in the pit all the time. Frank shrugged it off and prepared to play on. Gary stopped mid-riff and stared. Oscar stepped on the stage and played the bass line one time through before he realized no one else was playing. He looked up, embarrassed.

"Keep playing," said Frank.

Gary shook his head in disbelief. Frank looked and the door opened again. This time Frank watched as the punks pulled a woman into the warehouse. They held her under her shoulders and dragged her feet. They sat her next to the injured guy. One woman who had come inside with them was bawling like baby.

"Wait here." Frank walked between the stunned members of the audience. They stared silently at the scene. As Frank got closer he saw that the man's injuries were worse than he realized before. No matter how tough he thought he was. No matter how strong he felt, that moment shook him.

Frank pushed through the crowd until he was standing over the man. The nose was mangled, the bones smashed. His eyes were purple, the right one the size of a softball. Neither looked capable of opening.

"What happened?" Frank asked.

"Somebody get help!" the young woman who shook the man bawled, dripping tears all over the floor. The woman who had taken a beating was wailing now, like a siren. She spit out some teeth.

"I'll go call the police," one of the skaters ran for the door.

"Wait, not the pub. Not Briars'. Don't call there." The woman over the bleeding man pleaded.

"Why not?" asked Frank.

"They did this. The owner, his goddamn bat."

"What did they do to him?" asked someone in the crowd.

"Nothing!" The crying woman was too distraught to be angry. "Just walking to the fucking show."

Frank felt like a spotlight was turned on him. This was what he was just screaming his guts out about. Fighting back. He heard about this bar, and the asshole owner before the show. The guy was a terror. Hated the punks that he felt invaded his street.

His customers spent hours drinking after work, talking about the freaks and faggots that plagued their working-class neighborhood. Frank knew how they thought. These freaks were useless, drags on society doing drugs, living on the streets, wasting oxygen. That is how they viewed punks; trash that needed to be taken out.

"We can't call the cops. You know they'll take his side." They were afraid of the police. The cops in the neighborhood had tried to shut them down. The last show they broke up they used clubs, broke more than a few bones. Frank had heard the stories earlier in the day. He saw fear in many of the eyes gathered around the beaten man.

"I don't care! Robby needs help now!" She screamed herself raw and desperate.

The skater ran out to get help, but the woman just wailed "Robby!" as she realized that her friend wasn't responding to anything. His chest stopped moving. He wasn't breathing.

The other woman's name was Sandy. Frank wasn't sure how he knew, but her name came to him. Frank felt his lunch twisting in his gut. Every ounce of his body burned with anger. Frank reached down and grabbed a loose brick. He pushed the door open and faintly heard Oscar call his name.

"Frank! Oh shit!"

Too late. It was time to act. No more talk. The brick felt heavy in his hand as he stepped out into the summer night. Frank heard grumbles, mumbles, and outright shouts behind him. He heard someone else call his name but he was locked in.

None of it mattered to him, reason or responsibility. None of it mattered. The image of that man with the twisted and distorted face, the woman screaming in pain. He couldn't ignore that. It was their tribe, his people under attack.

The rage grew as he saw the bar down the street. The front window was large. A neon Bud Light sign flashed in the window and Frank decided it was a target. He wound up like a pitcher ready to release a fast ball. The crowd behind him scattered as the brick hung in the air. The glass shattered and inside shocked customers at the bar screamed.

A man cursed inside. A few people cheered as an older gray-haired man stepped out the front door holding a bat that was stained with blood. Robbie and Sandy's blood. Carved into the bat, a sick joke: *'Peacemaker.'*

The man was huge and imposing, but mostly low-hanging belly and alcohol-poisoned red face. He bullied those punks, but Frank wasn't like them. The bar owner wasn't ready as Frank ran up on him. He was still lifting his bat when Frank tackled him. He let out a grunt and a deep breath as his back hit the pavement.

"Goddamn freaks!" he shouted. Frank heard the bat hit the pavement with two thunking sounds. Frank grabbed the bar owner's throat and looked into his eyes.

Terror and fear. It was all there. The man who had beat those punks and laughed about to his customers was afraid. He felt no sympathy. The song he had written played like a record in his mind. *Us versus them! To the war again!*

Frank gripped his throat like a microphone and screamed in the man's face. "This freak fights back!"

The man struggled to speak, spitting on Frank's hand. The bar owner's face grew red then purple. Now he had no air with which to speak. Frank wanted to kill him, but thought better of it. He loosened his grip a little.

A police siren came closer each passing second. He looked around, the crowd had mostly scattered. Only Oscar stood behind him now.

"Stop!" Oscar begged.

Frank loosened his grip a little more. The bar owner reached toward his waist. Under his massive belly Frank saw the pistol. A revolver, not a tiny one either, nestled in the man's belt. The bar owner reached for it. Frank finally let go of his neck and grabbed the pistol. The bar owner stared down the barrel of his own gun. Frank picked up the Louisville slugger with his other hand and stepped back. The pistol pointed directly at the man's face.

He wasn't calling anyone a freak or a faggot now. His lips were sealed, sweating buckets. A part of Frank wanted to laugh.

"Where are all the names, tough guy? This is a war, bub. It has two sides now."

Another man came out of the bar pointing a shotgun. This man was even older than the man on the ground. His hands were shaking. He pumped the shotgun, loading a shell. It was a stand-off.

"We're leaving, mister. We're leaving ain't we..."

Oscar stopped before saying his name. Frank nodded,

but kept his eyes and the gun trained on the owner. He got as far as his knees still holding his hands up.

"Yeah we are leaving, all right." Frank didn't see Dickie or Gary. He hoped they were smart enough to realize they should be packing the gear. Frank felt woozy suddenly...

***

Knock, knock...
Who's there?

***

...Knock Knock...
"Nate? Wake up!"
Knock knock...
"Unlock the door!"

Nate opened his eyes and saw Ericka in the window. He heard the sound of a key in the side door unlocking the van behind him. He didn't feel like he had woken up. He didn't feel groggy like he had slept. It wasn't a dream. He felt everything like he was there. A minute ago he was somewhere else.

He looked out the window. Confused, he saw the Stark house, now on the far side of the street. The van faced the opposite direction where he had parked the night before.

"Dude, where the hell have you been?" Denny asked as he slid on to the bench. "Don't drive off without telling us." Nate was ready to argue that he didn't drive anywhere. Ericka walked around the van and reached through the side door to unlock the passenger door. "We called your phone a hundred times."

Nate sat there, stunned. He didn't know what to say or think. A voice whispered softly. *Finish the tour.*

No one spoke it. Not out loud. That voice was right. *Finish the tour.* He had to. He had to calm them down.

"Gas, I got gas for the drive to Boston."

101

CHAPTER 14

"I'll take a turn."

It was Scott. Ericka turned and stared at her guitar player. She couldn't believe it. They were all shocked. Scott never offered to drive. The mood in the van was strange, quiet. They had made as far as New Haven in silence. The show they played in Philly was great, but everyone was weirded out by Nate's disappearance, and his refusal to talk about it.

"Next truck stop OK?"

"Word," said Scott as he woke up Denny.

"Fuck off." Denny was awake long enough to say that before his sweatshirt went over his head.

"We're stopping, I'm driving."

The hood lowered. "No fucking way."

Ericka laughed and stared at Nate in the dull light. The dashboard may have lit up twenty years ago, but it was hard to read speed, miles or anything now. Nate never complained. He seemed to be in the zone. He liked being behind the wheel of the van. He hit the blinker as an exit with two enormous truck stops appeared on the horizon.

He pulled them into a massive Flying J Truck stop. Denny had gotten them hooked on making suicide drinks, with a little of every soda in a self-serve fountain machine. He said he tried drinking them when he wasn't on tour and it didn't work, so it was a tour thing for sure. They didn't need gas, so he pulled up into a parking spot that was on the side of the building with a Subway sandwich shop.

It was closed but the convenience store on the far side was crowded. The middle of the night was a busy time in truck stops like these. The lot was filled with parked trucks. The place was crawling with truck drivers getting caffeinated, some taking long breaks.

Ericka felt a bit of tension at the idea of walking through it. A few days into tour she had seen this scene more than a few times.

She had to pee, and even though it was a humid night she put on her sweatshirt. She didn't want to go braless into air conditioning and draw every eye in the place to her nipples. She wouldn't be these men's first choice, but their eyes didn't discriminate. Ericka wrapped up in the sweatshirt before she walked inside.

Denny and Scott came in behind her. Denny had his plastic mug and headed to the fountain drinks like he always did. Scott followed her to the bathroom.

They walked past a lounge. A TV in the corner played some Arnold Schwarzenegger movie that had all the truckers' attention. Ericka breathed a sigh of relief and went into the bathroom.

***

Nate stepped out of the van and stood there with the door open. The rest of the band was already in the truck stop. The voices in the van had finally stopped. He listened to them get louder second by second as he drove. The whispers increased in volume like someone inched a volume knob up. He couldn't deny anymore that he heard them, like they were in the van.

Frank, Oscar, Gary and Dickie. He knew it was them. He couldn't make it all out at first, but it became clear they were all mad at Frank. He ruined Philly. He got them in trouble. They didn't get to finish the show.

The cops would be looking for them. It was only a matter of time. The tour was a disaster. They had to steal gas. They didn't have food. The argument was intense.

Nate shut the door, locked it and thought about their words. A part of him understood their concerns, but he felt Frank's words. He didn't take their shit for long.

This was a war. They retreat, again and again. More Sandys and Robbys will die. This was more than music now.

A large truck with a giant Wegman's grocery-store logo rumbled past him in the parking lot. It honked its massive horn at Nate when it passed. A group of truckers walked toward the front doors behind him. Here it was, Nate thought, the redneck patrol. One of them would call him a faggot, and the others would laugh. They just couldn't mind their business.

Nate stood up straight and felt them come closer behind him, ready for the commentary. They would read his Crass Anti-Christ shirt. It would offend them and they would make a crack.

He could hear their conversation as they got closer.

"I hate the fuckin' Patroits."

"Peyton is better than Brady, believe it."

"One ring," said the third trailing behind a bit.

"His first. You watch. He'll have four more before he retires."

They passed Nate, didn't even look up at him. They didn't even notice him standing there. Nate didn't know why he had expected it. He walked slowly into the store.

***

Ericka walked out to the van and saw the side door open wide. Scott waited in the driver's seat. She could tell the two old friends were having an intense discussion. Scott saw her first. He nodded, and the conversation stopped before she could hear what they were saying.

"Oh come on," She whined. "Really, secrets? We're living in a van together for a month."

Denny grinned. He looked around her shoulder. She turned around, and saw Nate was in line at the register. Three deep before he would pay, giving them some time to talk. She knew this was coming. She wasn't blind. Nate was acting weird, and eventually they would talk to her. It was the mechanism of the band.

"What the hell is wrong with Nate?" asked Scott.

Ericka shrugged. *What could she say?*

Denny sighed. "I know I didn't get friendly with Nate

until we started the band."

"None of us did really," said Scott.

"I did." Ericka rubbed one of her eyes, feeling frustrated.

"Okay, then, you ever see him lose his temper like he has been doing?"

Ericka shook her head. Nate was at the front of the line now. Their time to talk openly was fading quickly. She had questions too. She promised not to tell the rest of the band about the blackout. This became a question of loyalty. The loyalty to the man she was in love with, or the guys who made up the rest of their band?

"I'll talk to him."

"Tell her what Nettie said." Scott turned the key and fired up the van. Nate walked out and jumped in the back. Ericka took the passenger seat. Denny and Nate took the bench. She shut the door hard but made sure not to slam it. She didn't want anyone to think she was mad.

"You talk to Nettie?" asked Denny. Ericka wasn't sure she was asking her or Nate. Nettie was a good friend of theirs. The oldest living punk woman in Philly, a train hopper and hitchhiker, she came through Bloomington a couple times a year. She had been around almost as long as punk existed in Philly. Nettie had a grown son who grew up with the father, and he rebelled for a life of hip-hop. Ericka admired Nettie, a woman they all wished was their mother.

They all situated themselves as Scott pulled the van back out on to I-84. Finding your spot in the van could make the difference between sleep or not. The question about Nettie hung in the air. They were in the dark of the highway. Ericka's eyes were adjusting back to the dark when Scott asked again.

"So, either of you talk to Nettie?"

"Uh, yeah, I think so." Ericka was confused.

"About The Fuckers in Philly?" asked Scott.

"Hey, Nate, can I see the tour journal?" asked Denny.

"Why?"

Ericka was surprised by Denny asking to see the journal. He only looked at it briefly, never seemed interested in it as she and Nate were.

"I lost it, maybe in Wilkes-Barre. Not sure."

Ericka knew he was lying. He would never misplace it. It was in his backpack and she would have bet anything. She turned and looked at him in the dim light. She gave him the look meant to express that she saw through him. Denny didn't believe him either. She could see it on his face.

Nate sounded defiant. "What did Nettie say about The Fuckers?"

Denny raised an eyebrow. "Well, for one thing they are pretty notorious in Philly."

Ericka laughed. "Hardly anyone remembers them outside of Indiana besides total record nerds."

"In Philly they do." Denny shook his head. "Nettie about had a heart attack when I told her it was the same van. They played this show in the Kensington neighborhood. A warehouse show, it was one of the most famous shows in Philly history. Some guy owned a bar near the warehouse where they had shows. He hated the punk."

"1982, man, everybody hated punks," said Nate.

"Beat one of them to death and paralyzed the other. She died a year later."

"Sandy Goldstein and Robbie Maddox," said Nate in a matter of fact tone.

Ericka stared at Nate. "You knew this story?"

Denny looked at Nate. "Why don't you tell her what happened?"

"It doesn't matter. It was twenty-five fucking years ago, ancient history."

"Yeah the fucking glory days of punk rock, right?" Denny grinned. "Frank killed the bar owner. Brutally beat him with a bat."

Nate grunted. "Give me a break. He just scared the guy, is all."

"No, Nettie said she watched it happen. The punks got harassed by the cops for years about it. Some of them hung out at that bar. The Philly kids never gave up their names. It's been on 'Cold Case Files' before. Nettie said Frank started the whole thing. Threw a fucking brick through the guy's window."

"Bullshit, the guy beat one of their friends to death. He fought back, which is what he should do. When the tribe is attacked you can't hide in the corner. He wasn't going to be a fucking pussy and let them just—"

"Whoa, whoa." Ericka couldn't believe her ears. Politically-correct pacifist Nate never said a word like that in front of her, ever. Not once, not even a B-word.

"Let them do it over and over. They killed one of us. This is a war. Kill or be killed."

Scott laughed in the front seat. "Nate, come on man. It was 1982. We're not talking about 1882 in the Old fucking West."

"You have no clue," Nate pushed his shoes off and got ready to climb into the loft. "You grew up with Green Day selling punk records to teenyboppers at Hot Topic who saw them on TRL. Look at us. We are a punk band, but if you put suits on us we're ready to go out to a wedding. Back then, punks scared normal people. They were afraid of us."

Denny raised his hand like he was in class. "Can you explain to me what is awesome about that? People being afraid of us, I mean."

"You don't get it." Nate crawled up into the loft. "I'm getting some sleep."

Denny and Ericka shared a concerned look before she turned around to watch the sun come up over the New England highways.

CHAPTER 15

Ericka pulled out her patch cord and leaned over her amp. She crossed her arms and dropped her face just inches from the still-hot amp head. Her bass hung over her side and she just let the sweat from her forehead drain over her arms. She could hear applause happening behind her. She didn't have a shred of energy left.

She knew they had to take down, and get out of the way for the next band. The next band was toe-tapping stage left waiting for them to clear out. She tried to summon the energy. A hand rested on her back, moving to her shoulder. It was Nate's hand. She looked back at him. He smiled. "Go sit down. We got this."

The empathy and understanding was like the old Nate. The Nate that seemed to come and go each day. One minute he was there, the next someone else. The other guy had been hanging around more and more.

By the time they were ready for the show, the smile was back. She relaxed, and played the show of her life, watching the man she remembered perform the songs they had written together.

It was her first time in Boston. It was the first show that she didn't know anyone. It was a strange feeling for DIY hardcore, as small of a world as it was. Ericka handed her bass to Nate and walked like a zombie offstage.

The venue was a VFW hall. She found a spot along a wall and slid down on to the floor. She was too tired to feel guilty as the rest of her band scrambled to get their equipment out of the way.

"What do you think about Boston?" A boy standing over her asked. She looked up and remembered selling him a CD and shirt before their set. He was a younger kid; fourteen, maybe fifteen, wearing a messenger bag that had faded metal band patches, and a few newer ones from hardcore bands she recognized. He was young and transitioning from metal to punk rock.

She didn't know how to answer. She felt like she was barely there. In another hour they would be in the van headed back down to New York City. That is where they wanted to spend the day tomorrow. She hoped she could get some sleep, and she didn't really have feelings about Boston.

"Awesome." She hoped he liked the answer.

***

A few hours later they were parked in New York. Ericka watched Nate picking at his backpack. He acted like old Nate while they were at the show. Some older guy had set up his record distro. Ericka just sat back and watched the two of them talk old records. They talked mostly about records of 80's Boston bands.

The collector was impressed with Nate's knowledge and gave him good deals on rare Negative FX and SSD records. It was comforting to watch. It was like he had returned from a faraway place, even though he had been near her side all along.

Ericka had relaxed until they loaded up and got back in the van. Nate offered to drive and morphed back into Quiet Surly Guy by the time they left the Boston area code.

Ericka was first out finding a bench across from the van. Half-asleep against the cushion of her backpack, she watched him get ready to leave the van. She saw the old tour journal. Just the corner of it, but she didn't say anything. Nate had been Nate enough that the band tension had melted away.

They also had enough sales of CD demos in Boston to cause a good problem. They didn't have enough for New York, even. So Denny agreed to find a Kinko's, buy a stack of CD-R's, and make more. That was an all-day project. He put it all on his credit card, and everyone agreed the band would pay it back at home when money wasn't so important to keep their tour going.

They were all excited to play the famous ABC No Rio show space. They drove past seeing its famous spray painted design as soon as they pulled in to the city. She didn't want to sour the mood by asking him why he lied about losing the journal. *Why was he hiding it?*

Scott slept in the van most of the day, parked on a Lower East Side street near a park. Ericka and Nate walked for forty-five minutes until they found Vegetarian Paradise, a legendary all- vegan Chinese restaurant. They spent a long time just ordering, and by the time they were stuffed with lunch they were running out of time. Nate promised to watch the van in the late afternoon.

After eating, they walked to the park at Washington Square. It was full of people and activity. A street preacher hung by the fountain in the shadow of the large arch yelling at a crowd of students who had gathered mostly to taunt him.

Ericka was so stuffed full of food, the walk back to their van seemed impossible. She laid down flat on her stomach on a bench. Nate sat cross legged on the ground so he was at her eye level. A part of her just wanted to sleep.

He stared at her for an uncomfortable amount of time. "You look great."

She liked hearing it. *Who wouldn't like hearing that from their crush?* She hadn't showered in days. Only sponge bathed in a truck-stop ladies' room two hours out of Boston. Her hair was dirty and the last thing she felt was great. If he thought she looked good now, in this moment, maybe he did love her.

"Nate..."

She would rather talk to him about holding hands in Philly, but had to talk to him about the mood swings. His affection and moods were so up and down since they left. She had seen a new side of Nate; that side didn't have time for her or anything short of the mission.

The tour, punk rock, and justice were all that seemed to matter to him. She had to be honest with him. She loved him, but the mood swings scared her. She had to talk to him about it.

"Yes?" He said. He was close enough that she could feel his breath. She looked over his shoulder. It was a beautiful summer day. How could she ruin it?

"Nate, you know I love you, but—"

Nate cut her off. She didn't have time to think about the L-word she just used. He pushed in, touching her lips softly with his. It was gentle, soft and powerful at the same time. She had imagined this moment a thousand times. Just taste him. Savor. Stop thinking and enjoy. She told herself all those things. She forgot everything but the kiss.

***

Scott sat in the passenger seat, sweating. He talked to Mel back home until his phone started to die. Every time he talked her, he was ready to quit and take the first bus back to Indiana. The heat in the van didn't help his frustration. He felt like cold water splashed on him just seeing Nate and Ericka down the city block, coming closer.

It may have been the city summer heat that hung trapped between buildings, but it looked like they were holding hands. When they got closer they walked apart. Hard to know, hanging out in the van guarding the equipment was like sleeping in a sweat lodge. *Who knew what he saw?*

He had woken up just happy to switch out and get fresh air. Denny was still at Kinko's doing his thing. Zaya, the woman that was following Denny around since Pittsburgh, had shown up at Kinko's and was helping him. Great, he had two third-wheel options.

"Finally. I'm starving." Scott gathered his things.

Ericka pointed up the road. "There's a health food store down a few blocks."

"I'll take junk, thanks," Scott laughed, jumping out of the van. It was strange, still hot in the late afternoon, but being out of the van was enough to make the summer air feel cool.

Scott reached in and grabbed his backpack. Nate climbed around and piled stuff at the end of the bench, clearly setting up what looked like a nap station.

"Too hot to sleep, trust me," said Scott. Nate didn't seem moved by his warning.

Ericka had a foot on the inside of the van ready to climb in and hit the warm air. She turned back. "Yeah, too hot for me."

Maybe he wasn't a third wheel. "How about you show me where the store is instead of roasting?"

Ericka and Nate shared a look. He shrugged. Ericka then nodded at Scott. It was weird. Those two normally went out of their way to not look like a couple. It sure seemed like Ericka was silently asking him if he wanted her to stay. Ericka wasn't the type to ask permission from any guy.

"Okay, let's get coffee too." Ericka put her arm through Scott's and pushed him to walk. Scott looked back and watched the van door slide shut.

***

Nate was hot before he shut the door, but he wanted the time alone. He needed it. Ever since Philly, he felt like he had to work to put on a happy face. Everything was going fine, except the voices had stopped. Ever since Denny asked him about the journal, he worried about it. He didn't know why Denny suddenly wanted the journal. It was none of his business. Nate had found it, and it was his. So to protect it, he covered it in a zine and left it in his backpack.

He waited until Ericka and Scott were down the street and pulled the journal from his bag. He didn't even open it. He didn't have to. He understood now. He just laid there on the bench and hugged it tight.

It was Oscar he heard first. *"Fucking Boston man why is this city so fucking crazy."*

"What do you mean no show?" Frank's voice.

Now Dickie. *"We already left how could they tell us?"*

Nate closed his eyes and listened. He didn't believe in God, but he prayed in that moment, to the universe, to whatever power was affecting him.

Take him back. Take him back to that moment, like he did the other night. Take him.
He opened his eyes in Boston...

***

Frank stared at the van, feeling a moment of dizziness. He turned back to the house. It was a small white ranch house with peeling paint and a lawn that hadn't received care since before the winter. The right number hung by the door and on the mailbox at the sidewalk. He looked at his notes in the journal.

The contact was named Greg. They talked on the phone. He played drums in a Boston band called Wounded in Action.' According to Frank's own notes, the show was supposed to be here in this house's basement. The house was small, and couldn't have had more than one bedroom.

He had tried to book them at the Rathskeller, a bar that hosted hardcore shows all the time, but couldn't get anyone to call him back. Gary saw Wounded in Action at a show in Chicago and got his number. They promised to trade shows over the summer.

Frank walked through overgrown weeds and knocked on the door. Waiting, he looked back at the van. Oscar leaned against the side, smoking. Dickie leaned out and hung his head out over the gutter, dry-heaving, having nursed a bottle of vodka in the back of the van all night. The front door creaked open.

A blond woman answered the door. Her life story wasn't a big mystery as she stood in the doorway. All she was wearing was a small TSOL shirt. She looked like she might have been pretty, before the needle turned her into a junkie. Her arms were skinny, bruised and marked from the drugs. Her pants were MIA. She didn't mind if the neighborhood saw her beaver. Frank sensed Oscar walking up to the house.

"Greg here?"

"I'm Samantha," She spoke past him to Oscar. Junkies could tell a kindred spirit a mile away. Oscar offered her a

113

hand to shake. "Greg, baby. Some guys here to see you."

"We're The Fuckers," said Oscar.

She looked Frank up and down. "Yeah, so?"

"Touring band from Indiana," Frank added.

"Oh, shit, man!" A voice called out from deep in the house. Greg stumbled into sight, shirtless with his jeans hanging low enough to show the top patch of his pubes, quite a sight. It was the afternoon, but the curtains appeared to block out enough sun to make a vampire comfortable. "I tried calling, but you had already left for tour. Show is canceled. Sorry, man."

Frank knew getting angry wouldn't change anything. Oscar shifted nervously, not hiding the glances he made to the exposed vagina. Greg didn't seem to mind. He looked past Frank at Oscar. "I don't have a show, but you can score here."

Oscar walked right in.

***

The drive to New York City was long for Frank. Dickie didn't shut up for a minute, telling stories about Oscar while he slept off the Boston adventure. Frank and Gary stayed in the van. Dickie made sure that they all knew what Oscar did to score.

"Dude, he fucked that Sam chick twice. She was so wasted, half her weight was in her pussy, but Oscar nailed her like a champ."

"Gross, dude," Gary said.

"Oh, he was just warming up and shit." Dickie laughed. Frank looked at his drummer. "I don't know what's worse him doing or you watching?" Dickie was a follower, and even though that meant he worshiped Frank, it bothered him.

Dickie put up with everything, went along with anything. Dickie didn't pick up on Frank's disgust, he just kept babbling about Oscar. "So, like Oscar fucks her for a hit, but that Greg guy is lit in the corner jerking a puddle watching. So, he asks Oscar what he would do for a whole bag?"

"Shit." Frank didn't like the sound of this. Oscar with that big a score could end him altogether.

"Yeah." Dickie hit the sleeping Oscar. "He deep-throated that fag. I gotta say he looked like he knew what he was doing."

It went on like that until they made it into the city. Once Oscar woke, they found out that Dickie spent some of the night with Samantha the Junkie. Frank tuned it all out. It was stupid shit.

Every minute he spent on the road made him hate his band more and more. Gary was harmless. That was part of his problem. He was boring. Oscar started the tour a junkie, and was now turning tricks to get high.

Dickie was just a tub of shit. He never stopped complaining or trying to find food. He put up with all of it because everything was so right on stage. Oscar had a distorted guitar tone that sounded like a scouring pad on a cast iron pan, but he played tight.

He worked had to get that raunchy sound. Oscar was the best songwriter. He knew how to pace a song so it drove the crowd. Dickie was a drummer, and no matter how stupid he could be, being a drummer was valuable.

Frank listened to Dickie talk and felt the weight of the pistol he stole. Now that he had it, he couldn't imagine life without it. He kept it under his shirt and nestled in his belt loop.

He had a hard time booking a NYC gig. They all wanted to play Max's Kansas City. That club had shut down after Bad Brains played there over the last winter.

Peter Crowley was the man who booked the biggest shows from Max's to CBGB's. Frank talked to him several times before he told them they could play a place called Mother's if they got a local band to play with them. They called Regan Youth, Agnostic Front, and anyone else they had a number for.

The bands they ended up playing with were two bands called the Beastie Boys and the Cro-mags. When they unpacked their gear they were surprised by the size of the crowd. They were playing second. Frank wasn't impressed by the Beastie Boys, who didn't seem very talented but had a lot of friends they brought to the show.

The club was a gay bar, and the owner didn't really like the punk atmosphere, but the word was they had been doing shows here ever since Max's closed down, and CB's started passing on smaller punk shows. Crowley didn't show up. He farmed out promotion of the show to a lackey who introduced himself as Big Nicky.

Frank didn't like the guy. According to the guys in the Beastie Boys, Nick was a long time bouncer at CB's who hated the punks, an NFL wash-out turned bouncer after the Giants cut him in training camp. Big Nicky only talked to him once all night when he told the bands to keep the back door closed. While the neighborhood didn't seem that nice to Frank, he was told over and over the neighbors would complain if the door was open.

The Beasties took their time getting off the stage, and half the attendance of the show filed out. Oscar set up in a daze. Frank trusted him that as soon as he plugged in and started tuning he would be ready to play. Gary was already tuned up and noodling on the strings with pick-ups turned off, waiting as Dickie was getting his drum set put together.

Frank took out his marker and wrote the songs in the order he felt like playing them. He made two lists. He would set one in front of the kick-drum and then one next to Dickie, as he always did. They hadn't played a full set since before Philly.

The energy was building in him and he had never been so ready. It would be his first show with the gun on him. Something about it made him sweat a little. It was dangerous and he liked it.

Dickie nodded, even though he was still messing with his high hat. That was his signal to go. Frank took the microphone off the stand and wrapped the cord around his hand once. Gary leaked a little feedback as he flipped on his guitar.

Frank looked out into the club. Smoke filled the air.

He couldn't see the back of the club, but knew a lot of the crowd had stepped outside. "New York City. I'm sure we're a bunch Midwest yokels to y'all. We're The Fuckers, from Indiana." Gary hit a distorted heavy E-chord. Dickie played half a beat and rode his cymbals, building up for Frank. He knew he wasn't done talking yet.

"You have no fucking clue what it is like to be a punk where we live. This one's called "Us Versus Them!""

The song poured out of them. The crowd moved in quickly. Dickie played faster than normal just a bit, but with shitty monitors it took the rest of the band a verse to catch up. They were rusty after the night off. The crowd didn't care. Frank leaned over the edge of the stage and barked. Gary knocked into him as he screamed the chorus.

The pit swirled in a circle. Not quite a dozen slam-dancing punks looked a little weak. In the haze of the smoke Frank saw a lot of crossed arms, and shaved heads. When the song ended the only applause came from the dozen who had been dancing.

Behind the cloud of cigarette smoke voices rose together. "Cro-mags! Cro-Mags!"

"You pieces of shit probably voted for Reagan!" Frank had more to say, but Gary started the next riff. "Nun Bake-Off." They were already playing tighter together than the first song. Frank waited for his cue to scream. The guitars seemed a little loud to him.

He was screaming, looking to the back of the club when he felt a breeze. He waited for the break down when the song slowed down to look to the stage left. The back door was wide open. He knew the view was blocked by the PA in the room, so no one saw it but the band. When the song ended he thought about going and closing the door. He started to step off the stage and Oscar shook his head.

"Feels good."

Fuck it, let the neighborhood hear them. Punk fucking rock.

***

Fourth song. They only made it through four goddamn songs. Frank tried to keep screaming but Oscar pulled him back from the edge of the stage.

"Keep calm, Frank," Oscar yelled in his ear sounding generally scared.

The police entered the club together, four of them. The four cops, two white guys, a black one, and a white woman walked through the club like they owned it. Two of them held clubs in hand. Gary wasn't looking and was the last to stop playing. He only looked up when Dickie stopped.

Big Nicky stood in front of the stage and ran a finger across his neck. Some of the punks cleared out right away. A few shouted, "Pigs!" Another set ended, the dictators of social norm won again as these crypto-fascist pieces of shit ended the show.

Oscar was right to be worried. It took every ounce of restraint Frank had to not go after the cops. He slid his left hand under the shirt and felt the handle of the pistol. It was warm from the body heat he was generating during the show. In one motion he could pull the pistol, turn off the safety, and kill at least one of the pigs.

He could win this battle, but the war would end with his death. The war, the mission was so much bigger than tonight. He had to be smart.

"Motherfucker, not again." Dickie dropped his sticks.

"Let's get unloaded quick," said Oscar as he pushed Frank back. "Don't lose your shit, man.""I'm cool, let go of me."

Oscar looked unusually sober and rational. Frank didn't like being told what to do by his junkie bass player. Gary was already moving his amp back to the alley.

***

The cops waited until all three bands had unloaded every bit of equipment, every patch cord and every T-shirt before they left. Big Nicky talked and joked with them the whole time. Frank watched as they patted him on the shoulder. Great friends or at least it seemed. It was disgusting to watch.

When the club was clear only the bartender and Big Nicky remained. The local bands and their fans were long gone. No one had offered to pay them the promised amount. $30 bucks cash. It wasn't much, but they needed it. Oscar was worried about Frank. That worry lasted as long Oscar could wait before loading his next needle. He curled up in the loft leaving Frank and Dickie to walk back in the club. Gary wanted no part of this.

Big Nicky was at the bar talking up a storm. "You think these guys sound crazy, you ever hear those niggers the Bad Brains? They play this bullshit too, but they are some kinda Rastafar—"

Frank cleared his throat loudly. Big Nicky stopped and looked at Frank and Dickie.

Frank's size naturally intimidated most human beings. Not Big Nicky. He stepped off the stool wanting to remind Frank that he was a mountain of a man. He knew what was coming. Dickie let out a sigh. No one was pretending to be nice.

"We need our money." Frank stopped just inches from him. He was tall enough to look him in the eyes. Something Nicky wasn't used to. Frank knew this big man was surprised to see him.

Big Nicky smiled. "I have a boss, he tells me to make sure you freaks show up make that fucking noise for a whole set and then you get paid."

"They didn't play no full set, Nick," said the gum-chewing bartender.

"No, Jimmy I counted. They played three songs. I didn't pay the Cro-mags, neither.

"Four." Frank held up four fingers.

Nicky smiled and looked at his bartender friend. "That sound like a set to you, Jimmy?"

"Nah," Jimmy shook his head.

"Come on, man, we're on tour. Thirty bucks, we just

need to get to DC. It's not our fault the cops showed up."

Nicky shook his head. "I told you not to open that door. I know I shouldn't be surprised that you freaks are so fucking dumb."

"Freak, huh?" Frank thought about the gun, but that was loud. In his pocket he gripped his utility knife. The blade flipped out as Frank lifted it up. Nicky reacted slowly, stepping back, but it was too late.

Dickie and the bartender both screamed. Frank punched downward, the knife in his hand. Frank yelled as the blade point hit Nicky in his right eye. The blade would have disappeared into his skull if he hadn't fallen back. The bar tender fumbled for a weapon, picking up a bottle to throw. It sailed past Frank crashing next to Nicky squirming in pain.

Frank pulled out his pistol and pointed it at the bartender. "Don't you move." Frank nodded at Dickie. His shock was wearing off. Dickie laughed a little nervously.

"Oh, shit, Frank. You want me to get the money?" He sounded scared but Frank knew he would do it. He always caved.

Frank nodded. Dickie came around the bar slowly. Dickie started to protest, but Frank gave him the dirtiest look he had. Dickie nodded and went to the open register. Dickie held up stacks of money. He stuffed them in his pockets and came back around the bar. Nicky bled on the floor crying out in pain. He spit blood as he spoke. Dickie stood over him for a moment, he was feeling sympathy.

"Fucking freak."

Dickie's sympathy drained away. Frank leaned over the dying man. "I hate that word. You might not have died tonight had you not said that word."

"Just a word," Nicky begged. "I need help."

"Nicky you're right about that. It is just a word, and names will never hurt me but the problem is you and people don't stick to names. You always resort to sticks and stones. I'm fighting back now."

Frank stood up and looked at the bartender, hands raised. "Just another robbery in New York."

"Wait, wait."

Frank Fucker pulled the trigger, and the world shook with the sound of thunder...

***

"...Nate."

"Earth to Nate."

Nate shook his head. The voices sound like they were being spoken underwater. Scott and Ericka spoke to him. He shook his head and felt dizzy. He looked up and a crowd stared down at him. Hardcore kids, an entire room full of them waiting for his band to play.

"You ready?" A woman's voice asked.

Nate saw a set list taped to the monitor in front of the stage. The words written in Sharpie were fuzzy, and he couldn't read them. Nate leaned on the mic stand for a long moment. He used it like a crutch, holding himself up. All eyes staring at him. He didn't know how got to the show, but he had to pull himself together quick.

"Yeah, I'm ready." He took a deep breath. "New York City, we're the Fuck..."

He looked up and understood where he was suddenly. He had seen the white walls from pictures, the inside of the ABC No Rio. He was back.

Nate coughed. "I'm sorry, we're People's Uprising from Bloomington, Indiana."

No one seemed to notice.

CHAPTER 16

"What's more Metal?"

Ericka sat up and pulled her earbuds out so she could hear what Denny was saying. She pointed, to get his eyes back on the road as he drove. He'd been driving since they left Charlotte. Scott was neglecting his shotgun duties and trying to sleep. Nate laid down beside her on the bench.

Ericka kicked his foot playfully. "So it's What's more Metal time?"

"Play with them," he said not budging or sitting up.

The North Carolina highways rolled past them. It was a few minutes since they had passed a city and the darkness outside the van was complete. Denny really risked falling asleep and they had to do something to help him stay awake or they would be the latest band to flip a van and die. Scott had his head against the window, but sat and cracked his knuckles. He was always ready to play the game he himself invented.

"What is more metal? A pit of flames or an ice cavern?"

Ericka let out a thoughtful sigh. Denny tapped his steering wheel. Nate still didn't lift his head. He was quiet all day in Charlotte, even though they played with one of his favorite local bands. Before the tour he talked about this show often. It was one he was looking forward to. It wasn't like he put on a bad show, but it seemed like just another show to him.

"Yeah, see, it's a tough one." Scott rubbed his hands together.

Denny kept his eyes on the road. "Are we talking a mosh pit of flames, and does the ice cavern have frozen mummies?"

"What other kinds of mummies would it have?" Scott sounded annoyed.

Ericka wagged her finger. "Whoa, whoa the question

was a simple pit of flames. Don't start adding stuff."

"I don't know if you understand how the game works. Don't you need as much information as possible?" asked Denny.

"You want to know what I think?" Scott grinned. "I know it was my question."

"Don't make the tattoo argument. Getting tats of flames is just dumb and not very metal." Denny laughed. "Shouldn't "Trapped Under Ice" be considered?"

"No way." Scott pointed at him. "If we get into 'tallica songs you also have to consider "Jump in The Fire."'"

"The man has a point, not often, but he does today." Ericka laughed. The two continued to debate, but Ericka put her earbuds back in place. The Bad Religion *Suffer* album had gotten to its third song while she listened to the debate rage. She let the song play out and nestled in her seat.

Ericka saw Nate in the orange light that moved over him each time they crossed under a highway light. He wasn't sleeping. His eyes were wide open as he laid there hugging his backpack like a teddy bear. He wasn't asleep, but he wasn't present either. She couldn't tell if he was happy or sad.

This tour was their dream. They had done it. City to city, playing shows, seeing parts of the county they'd never seen before...Sure they were losing money and living off Nate's credit to fill in the gaps, but he should be happy. They were living the dream.

***

Nate listened to the song "Black Sabbath" for the fourth time on repeat. The bell and the droning doom of Iommi's guitar fit his mood. He stared out the window up into the clear night sky. He didn't remember so many stars back home.

He knew that the rest of his band was talking, joking as if the world wasn't full of pain, suffering and death. Nate always had trouble living with the knowledge of all the crimes and injustice in the world. The comfort he took was that hardcore gave him an outlet for the frustration and anger.

He didn't like the way things were going. Everything was becoming stale and computerized. Punk rock was accepted and mainstream. Anyone could go online and find a record. Back in the day, it took skill and luck to collect records. Worse, no one was afraid of them anymore.

They had less ability to change the world, mold it. They were just like anyone else. He hated it. The world that The Fuckers lived in was a perfect time. They were explorers finding new territory all the time. Everyone who saw them or heard them couldn't believe it. They were scary.

Even though it was in his backpack between the covers of a zine, he could feel the energy coming off the journal. It gave off heat like food fresh from a microwave. He felt it whenever he was in the van. The voices of the past spoke to him more clearly now, drowning out the members of his own band and their ridiculous game. Nate heard them all, and they kept getting louder.

"Fuck D.C. They think they are so fucking smart," said Frank.

"All their parents are like senators or work for people like that," said Dickie.

"They have the right to be punk too," said Gary.

"Shut up..."

***

...Frank hadn't meant for it to sound so harsh. Gary rarely spoke, and Frank probably shouldn't have told him to shut up. He had to pee so bad, his anger grew quickly under the bladder pressure he was trying to ignore.

He just couldn't listen to his guitar player explain again how those straight-edge, wannabe, goody two-shoes had a right to be punk rock. It was a tired argument they had whenever those bands from D.C. came up in conversation.

"You can't fuck with Minor Threat's music, boss. They rage." Oscar who couldn't go a day without shooting up, was a strange person to be defending the hardcore scene's drug-free do- gooders. He did dope the whole time they were in D.C.

"I hated that show." Frank watched Gary drive down the North Carolina highways from the back bench. They had to drive all night if they were going to make their show in Columbia, South Carolina.

"No drama was kinda nice," Dickie added from the passenger seat.

"Whatever." Frank took a drink of his Big Gulp that was filled with Mountain Dew.

"They make shows into drama." He sucked on the straw and got that slurping sound that came with emptiness. No wonder he had to pee so bad. His back-up pee bottle was already full. He had to get out.

"Stop."

Gary looked around. They had seen nothing but fields for a long time. Frank knew he was about to say next exit. He couldn't wait, that wouldn't cut.

"What happened to your pee bottle?" asked Oscar.

"Pull over right now!"

"Yeah, I could empty my pee bottle anyway." Oscar shook his half empty bottle up in the back seat, having used it just twenty minutes earlier.

The van pulled off the highway onto gravel near a farm field that came up just twenty feet from the embankment of the road. Only a thin dirt path separated them. Gary turned off the van and Frank was surprised by the quiet of the night.

A car zoomed past on the far side going north but the loudest sound was the wind blowing the tall corn stalks together. He could see empty highway and a nearby farmhouse.

Lights came on inside and in the front of the farmhouse. Whoever lived there knew they had pulled up. His bladder wouldn't let him think about it.

Frank ran to the edge of the tall fields, and dropped his pee bottle seconds before he started to piss. He was worried he wouldn't get his pants open in time. He heard the rest of the band walking towards the field.

He relaxed as his pee watered the dirt and grass. Relief was quick, but it felt like he was draining the lizard for a long time. His bandmates laughed as they lined up by the corn stalks and all let go. Frank kept peeing at the base of a sign that said,"McKenna Farms—No Trespassing Ever."

As he turned to zip up he saw what was making them laugh. Down the dirt path, a four- wheeler buzzed toward them with one bouncing headlight. A car zoomed past them. The bike stopped and spun out a little in front of them just as Frank took the cap off and turned down his pee bottle. The helmet came off and the man sitting on the bike was the spitting of James Best, better known to a whole generation as Roscoe P. Coltrane from 'The Dukes of Hazzard' on TV. A buffoon. A blowhard. But one with a large shotgun sat up easy to grab in a holder built into the four wheeler.

To this guy they looked like space aliens or worse. His eyebrow was raised and his hand hovered by the shotgun. Frank put the top back on his pee bottle. He stood in the middle of his bandmates in the direct light of the one weak headlight that flickered like a strobe as the bike idled.

"You boys didn't just pee on my crops now, did ya?"

"No, sir." Dickie was the first to tell the lie.

"I think you're lying, sure as shit is brown."

Frank dropped the bottle, wanting his hand free to grab his gun. He wasn't sure he could do it faster than this man could grab his shotgun. The man had fixed his gaze on Oscar.

"You got a goddamn ring in your nose, son."

Oscar tapped his nose ring and laughed. "Oh shit, how did that happen?"

Frank knew this redneck would get to mockery quickly. He probably didn't like anyone peeing on his crops, but a group of punks would take the situation up a notch. Good old boy truckers might get warning. His bandmates all had their hands up, looking as if they were being held up. It made Frank sick. The man hadn't even drawn his weapon, yet.

"We're leaving. You can go back to your house now," said Frank.

"My fucking farm. You don't give me no orders. You

ain't welcome. Get in that there van and get."

"Get and get." Frank shrugged and walked towards the van. Unafraid he passed right in front of the four wheeler's spotlight close enough it was on his chest. His bandmates followed beside him.

"Just get to the van," Oscar whispered to Frank.

McKenna laughed watching them. "You damn lucky I's found you first. Sheriff Musky don't like no hippies, freaks, or faggots."

Frank stopped.

"I should call the Sheriff, come lock your ass up. Probably have to take you to a goddamn zoo."

McKenna thought of himself as a hoot, laughing at his own joke. Frank seethed, the anger welling inside him like gamma rays in the hulk. Oscar hissed and tried to grab Frank's arm. Too late. Frank turned around. He watched McKenna's right hand twitch near the rifle.

"Shit! No!" Oscar hit the ground knocking Dickie and Gary down like dominos. Frank extended his arm pointing the pistol. McKenna had his hand on the stock of his rifle when the shot thundered through the late night. A huge chunk of McKenna's skull and brain disappeared into the field.

Frank had fired guns growing up in Indiana but this pistol was more power than he expected. The body tipped over the four wheeler and landed with a slop and thud inches from his terror- filled bandmates. Gas and blood mixed under the over turned bike.

The echoing thunder of the gun shot carried for miles. They were afraid to look. Oscar was the first to open his eyes. He meant to curse, but lost his breath when he saw the aftermath of the shooting. One glassy dead eye remained on the face.

"Get in the van," Frank said as he walked over to the man's body. He didn't feel remorse. This was a step he had to take. *They picked on us, beat us down. Only a matter of time before society tried to crush the Punks out. As we become more and more of a threat they will kill us. We had to strike first.*

127

"You killed him, Frank. What the fuck are you doing?" Oscar begged. Dickie and Gary just watched, stunned.

"I am fighting the war. He was going to put us in jail, in the South. They would kill us in there. Self-defense, really."

"Self-defense?" Oscar scoffed. His beady eyes shook from withdrawal as he tried to hold his gaze.

"Shut up and get in the van." Frank pointed at the van.

Oscar shook his head. Frank wasn't worried about him. He would forget soon enough, when he got out his needles. Gary ran back to the van. Dickie and Oscar watched as Frank got out his cigarettes and his lighter. He lit his cigarette and held the Bic down so the flame danced. "I would get back in the van."

Frank got into a catcher's crouch and held the lighter into the gas, then ran back as the flames burned to the bike and the farmer McKenna. Frank stood for a moment by the van and listened to the flames crackle.

The burning flesh gave off an instant rancid smell. He knew what his band was thinking: that it was dangerous, that he was losing his mind. They needed focus. The war had started and this tour was the mission. No matter what it took, or how long he had to finish the tour...

***

...Nate jumped up when Ericka shook his arm. "It's the van!"

Nate saw terror written in wall-sized letters on Ericka's face. He pulled his ear buds out and heard Denny and Scott yelling at each other. In the chaos he couldn't make out what they were saying. Nate leaned between front seats and watched Denny hitting the steering wheel.

"It's turning right!" Denny screamed, trying to pull the steering wheel back left with all his strength. The van pulled them towards the side of the road. They hit the gravel median full speed. The warning honks shook the whole van. Ericka screamed, and Scott covered his eyes expecting to die.

"The wheel!" Denny tried to pull the wheel back to lead them onto the highway.

"Stop!" Scott screamed.

The van halted, sending Nate forward into the stereo. The seat belt caught Scott, who grabbed Nate by his hoodie and kept him from hitting the windshield. Nate reached up and turned down the old Metallica album that was playing. The engine was humming normally.

There was suddenly silence as they all realized they were alive and safe. The gearshift rattled in place. They all stared at it. It continued to shake until it snapped up into Park.

Denny put his hands up before looking at his bandmates, his features drained of color.

"Holy fuck," Ericka whispered.

"You see that?" Denny said through heavy breath. "The brake pedal was already down."

"What are you talking about?"

Nate scanned the van. Everyone was fine. Scared, but fine. He looked outside and saw corn fields. A truck zoomed past them on the highway, shaking the van like a mini-earthquake before late night silence returned. He opened the door and stepped out onto the gravel.

The southern air was humid. He knew this scene. He had just seen it. It was no dream. He had felt this air and knew exactly where he was. He looked down the road and saw the farmhouse. It had suffered a few years of disrepair. He recognized it instantly. He scanned around and some things had changed.

A billboard for a truck stop was just a bit down the field but it was close enough to light the area. A new barbed wire fence was up guarding the corn crop. Nate walked across the dirt path toward the corn fields. A series of ribbons were tied to a fence post that separated the fields. The ribbons were faded and weather damaged, and had been there for some time. A sign read:

"Max McKenna 1939-1982 Farmer & Family man, RIP."

Nate pissed on the sign. He heard Ericka stepping out of the van walking toward him.

"What just happened, Nate?"

How could he explain it to her? She would never

129

understand. The van brought him here for a reason. A clear reason, connect him to the mission. The Fuckers never finished the tour.

Now he knew what he had to do. No matter the struggle. They would finish the tour.

Nate zipped up his pants. "Nothing happened."

CHAPTER 17

"Y'all put on a hell of show at circle city fest last year," Trent, the show organizer, said, opening the back door to the space. In the back of a coffeehouse, the venue was barely big enough for the sound system, and a few merch tables. The first band was already setting up.

"That's a local band, Scabella. They were excited to play with you." Trent's stereotypical hick accent made Ericka laugh inside. He had half his head shaved and a faded Conflict shirt with a circle A on it, but he sounded like the dad from *Beverly Hillbillies* when he spoke.

"Reckon you want to load in before they start?"

"I reckon we do," Ericka goofed. Trent smiled. He probably got it a lot from out of state bands.

Ericka and Nate walked in the room. The PA was blasting a hardcore record she didn't recognize. Ericka didn't know what to make of Columbia. The transition to the south was more of a culture shock than she had expected.

The shows all looked similar. It was the surrounding world that changed. They were mostly in the tour bubble, constantly hot and sweaty, couldn't smell each other anymore, the whole bit. They didn't have clean clothes or anywhere to shower. They were all working on disjointed sleep, and no one had slept in a bed since they left, the closest thing being the loft.

Everyone had been silent since the van's phantom freak out and emergency stop during the middle of the night before. "Why don't you grab the guys to load and I'll set up merch." Nate held the box of CD's and shirts and walked quickly to a table to set up.

Ericka shrugged and walked back to the alley where the van waited for her. Scott and Denny stood behind the open back doors, staring at the equipment stuffed inside. Even though they had it down to a science, sometimes just the idea of unloading and reloading the equipment seemed like torture. She moved between them. She was aware that were staring at the equipment, procrastinating.

"Nate is setting up merch. Let's get this over with."

Denny looked at the back door and back to Ericka. "He's inside?"

"Yeah." Ericka could see he was ready to talk about something weighing on him. "It's about the van."

Ericka knew at some point they would have to talk about the van. She could hardly believe the things she was thinking, and had wanted someone else to bring it up. "What about the van?"

"I didn't want to say anything. I thought I was going crazy."

Scott nodded. "Me too. It does weird shit, all the time."

Ericka felt the need to say the rational thing. "*The van* does weird things?"

"Come on, Ericka." Denny sounded desperate. "We all saw the goddamn gear shift by itself. The van wanted to stop. The wheel turned left, I swear."

Ericka sighed. She had seen weird stuff too. "I felt the pedals moving a few times. I thought it was me."

"No, I felt it too, a couple times." Denny shook his head. "The stereo turns itself up and down just phantomly."

Scott nodded. "I was listening to Pink Floyd last night, and the fucking thing shut off."

Ericka ran her fingers through her grimy hair. "Look we're a long way from home. None of us are getting good sleep. It's hot. It's probably in our heads."

"What about Nate?" asked Denny. Scott nodded, pondering the same thing. "He didn't lose the journal. He doesn't want us to read it. I know it's in his backpack. He protects that thing like Gollum and the one fucking ring."

Ericka wanted to understand too. She looked in the coffeehouse and saw a group of kids standing by the table talking to Nate. That would keep him busy.

"All right, here's the deal." Ericka pointed at Denny. "You two load in."

Nothing else had to be said. They knew what she was going to do. Ericka went to the far side of the van and opened the passenger side door. Nate's backpack was stuffed under the middle bench.

She heard the sounds of the equipment being unloaded. It was strange not being involved in that process as she always was. She looked out the window and saw that the door was still propped open. Nate might see her sitting in the van.

Ericka nestled herself into the spot on the between the bench and the driver's seat. She opened his backpack carefully. She saw it resting in the centerfold of a handmade zine. The old notebook had filled his backpack with a musty smell.

She slid it out and opened it, flipping past the pages filled with phone numbers and directions to shows, and parts she'd already read.

She couldn't understand what Nate didn't want her to see...until she passed the Philadelphia part of the journal. Frank wrote long rants about his emerging philosophy.

So much of the world today is corrupt. It has always been that way. The system rewards people for conformity. Punk rock is the answer to the system, and to conformity. The system rewards the conformers who lash out at punks. They call us losers, sluts, weirdos, freaks, and faggots. They tell us to get jobs and conform. Not always in those words but they shout it from trucks, they say it while pointing fingers at their children who dare to be different.

The gun changed everything for me...

Ericka was shocked, and flipped back the pages to see mention of stealing the gun from the bartender who harassed them at the show in Philly. She found her spot and kept reading.

The gun changed everything for me. The war was always there, but one sided. We didn't have the tools to fight back. I know what has to be done. I know who I am now. I am justice.

Ericka felt sick to her stomach reading the rants because she had feeling of where this was all heading.

***

Nate looked at his watch. It was fifteen minutes after the local band were supposed to be off the stage and even though their close friends were the only ones still watching they kept playing. They were a young band and not very talented. Most of the show had piled out to the sidewalk out front.

Nate breathed a sigh of relief when they mercifully announced that they had played their last song. It would be a challenge to find something nice to say to their bass player who had told Nate three times how much he loved People's Uprising.

Denny and Scott moved quickly to start getting the equipment up on stage. Nate quickly packed up the remaining shirts and CD's, carrying the case to the stage left. It wasn't till he was standing there that it hit him. He hadn't seen Ericka once since he came inside. "Where's Ericka?"

Scott and Denny gave each other a look. "I'll go find..." Denny started to say. Nate waved him off and walked to the van. He could see through the side window that the side door was open. He didn't see Ericka at all. He came around the corner and she sat on the edge, her feet in the alley, holding the tour journal.

Nate felt like a husband caught cheating. He also felt violated, knowing she had gone into his backpack to get it. "What are you doing?" He tried to grab it. She held it away at first, then just shoved it hard at his chest, knocking him back.

"I read through Florida, Nate."

Ericka watched his anger seethe. It looked to her like he was counting to ten in his head, trying hard to keep from blowing up.

"So what? You read it, whatever."

Ericka scoffed. "So what? Frank Fucker murders someone, and it sounds like he got away with it. Writing diatribes about guns and being justice against the conformity of society and you didn't think that was of interest to us? That's what."

"It has nothing to do with us." Nate put his hands up. "Come on, we have a show to play."

"Yeah, except you seem more like Frank Fucker than Nate lately."

Nate laughed. If looks could kill, Nate would have been dismembered.

"Don't laugh at me. The van is doing weird things. You said yourself you blacked out."

Nate cringed, and practically shushed her. "Just stop."

"You were defending his violence. Nate, you don't eat honey because it hurts bees, but now you are defending violence and brushing off murder like it is no big deal."

"Can we just play this show and talk about it later?"

Ericka shook her head. "We're all hearing weird things. You are a weird thing, Nate. Ever since you got this van."

Nate put up his hands. "Scott wants to go home, doesn't he?"

"I didn't say that. No one is saying that."

"We can't go home."

Ericka stood up. She knew they had to play the show. She grabbed his arm first. "What happened to Frank, really?"

He held up the journal. "You can keep reading if you want, but there are no answers to that question. Maybe if you kept reading you'd see he was fighting for us all."

Ericka sighed. "If we are going to finish this tour you'll need to get your shit together and start acting like yourself."

"Ericka!"

Ericka walked into the show leaving Nate standing by the van. She could hear his desperation, but she knew he was worried about the tour not her. She hit the humid air of the venue and saw her bass leaned up against her cabinet waiting for her. Scott was already tuning and Denny was drum-checking for the soundman.

***

Nate pushed the journal into his backpack, but realized they would just grab it from him again. She only read through Florida. He relaxed a little knowing that. He took the journal and put it under the passenger seat, hoping that was hidden enough. He heard her bass playing inside. She was tuning, and he would need to be in there in less than a minute.

The voice made him jump. He turned around expecting someone in the van with him.

"She's right about one thing. If we are going to finish this tour you'll need to get your act together."

The voice echoed in his head like a voice bouncing off a cave wall. He put his thumbs over his ears, but still heard it clear as ever.

"The tour has gone south, Nate. The war is just starting."

Nate felt tears forming, he couldn't control it. "Shut up. Just leave me alone."

"I wish that were possible, Nate. This is too important. We're going to finish this tour, Nate. This is why we were born."

Nate heard Scott's Celtic Frost warm-up riff. He slammed the van door shut and walked toward the show. The voice whispered now.

"Finish the tour, Nate."

CHAPTER 18

The Columbia show was small, but also energetic. Before they played, lots of the young kids thanked Nate for playing there. They often drove to Atlanta to see shows, because most touring bands skipped over them. The crowd knew all of the four songs from Myspace and sang along quite nicely as they played.

Nate focused on the songs, and forgot everything else. All the drama before the set melted away, at least during the show. Scott was still feeding back, looking at him as if he was ready to play more. They had played every song they knew. Ericka was already unplugged and wrapping up her cord.

Nate stepped off the stage, high-fiving a few people who waited to pat him on the shoulder and tell him he played a good show. He couldn't hear it. As soon as they were done, Nate instantly worried about the status of the journal.

Dripping with sweat, Nate walked out into what should have been hot summer air. After playing a show, it felt like standing in front of an AC unit. He should have helped, and normally he did, but they all took nights off from loading here and there.

He turned just enough to watch with one eye as they unloaded the equipment. He wanted to see if anyone went near his bag or looked under the seat. They moved quickly. They all wanted to start the drive to Gainesville.

They had lots of friends in Gainesville, as the scene there was filled with traveling punk kids.

The question was how many of them would be in town. Most left Florida for the summer, living there full time only in the winter months. When the van appeared packed Nate pointed at the bench. He often deferred dibs on it, but he had his reasons tonight.

The whole drive, he stared at the passenger seat. He wanted to read the journal. He hadn't skipped ahead before, wanting to preserve the mystery. To make the journey together.

The journal sensed his desire. He didn't understand how. He didn't care either but it was taking him back. The van or the journal probably both was putting him into Frank's skin, giving him the chance to relive that time. The era he was always meant to live in.

Now that Ericka challenged him, a part of him had to know what was there. The great mystery of what happened to Frank Fucker could have been there all along. They rode towards Florida and Denny started the conversation talking about the shows. How they could move songs around and keep the energy level up. His mind was on other things but Nate knew he had to act normal. So he engaged.

"We have to keep the opener and closer the same, maybe a cover song in the middle." He smiled and watched Ericka melt. He didn't remember her being so easy to manipulate. He knew what she was thinking: Old Nate, whimpy push-over Nate.

Ericka loved that version of him. She leaned up against him and hugged him. He put his arm around her. A few days ago this would have excited him. Now all he could think about was when he would see the journal.

***

The sky was purple with the coming dawn when Denny said he had to quit driving or fall asleep and kill them all in a rollover crash. Ericka woke up slightly and looked up at Nate. She rubbed his chest, looking at him with 'kiss me' eyes. He was surprised she would do this in the van, near the guys.

They had their eyes on the road. Scott put his feet up on the dashboard and cracked his knuckles, a nervous habit and part of his wake-up routine. No one remarked on it. They stopped at a quiet, abandoned looking rest area somewhere in Florida to make the switch.

***

Nate waited until everyone else had stepped out. The rest area was quiet. Two motor homes were parked at the end of the lot. A swarm of flying insects were in orbit of a lit-up but ancient- looking Pepsi machine. Nate watched his bandmates collect to talk to the right of the headlights.

"Scott, can you drive?" Denny asked.

"Sure, but somebody needs to talk to me."

"Uh, not me," Nate yelled from inside as he quickly threw the journal up into the loft.

"I'm sleeping in the loft for a bit."

Ericka backed up heading toward the small building with the bathrooms. She shrugged. "Okay, I'll take shotgun."

"Thank you!" Nate yelled as he kicked off his shoes and climbed into the loft. He positioned himself so the journal was under his back in case anyone looked. Denny sat himself in the middle bench for sleeping. When the sunlight hit Nate would try to finish reading the journal.

Nate stared at the fabric on the ceiling of the van, listening to the familiar sounds. The faint echoing voices of the past faded in and mixed with the sounds of the band loading up and selecting their spots to sit.

Scott started up the van again. Nate listened briefly to him and Ericka talk. It mixed in the soundscape with the voices of the past. He always heard them in the van. Sometimes, like now, they got louder, more insistent.

"So, what should we play? What's more metal? Or the Ahhhnold game?" Ericka asked. Nate cringed. The game went like this. Ericka would name a movie, like *Titantic* or *Gone with the Wind*, and Scott would imitate Schwarzenegger playing all the roles in the movie. It kept them laughing, awake, and alive during the overnight drives.

He closed his eyes and tuned it out even when Denny laughed just below the loft. The journal warmed under his back, like a heating pad. He heard the echoing voices getting louder with each mile they traveled down the freeway.

"It's just overheated. It is hotter than Satan's asshole here. A little water and time to cool down it will start again," said Dickie.

Oscar, sounding shaky, replied. *"We should just go home. We don't have money, food, and we have to steal gas everywhere..."*

"Stop the fucking crybaby act already." Frank was over it all. Nate heard the words like they came from his lips, echoing in his head like his own. He felt the urge to tell them to fuck off himself. The annoyance and fury swirled in his brain.

Nate opened his eyes to bright mid-day sunshine. He was back! He let himself go...

***

...Frank cursed the July afternoon sun that burned over Tallahassee. They made it fifteen minutes from the worst gig of the tour before the engine started coughing. Florida felt like an oven and it heated the van so much that the engine couldn't take it. Not after the miles they put in since tour began.

Cars zoomed by on the highway. A few slowed, but no one stopped once they saw who needed help. A truck looked ready to stop. Two big guys and a blonde with feathered hair sitting in the middle stared at them.

They didn't stop to help. They were staring and laughing at the sight of the punks stranded on the freeway. Frank made fists at his side and puffed up wanting to look scary. He would pull the gun the instant they stepped out of the truck.

A man wearing a Skynyrd shirt hung out the passenger window. "Lookie here! The looney-bin van broke down!" His friends laughed.

Oscar came around the van and flipped them off. "Your wife and sister are the same person! Eat shit and die, dirtbag!"

The truck peeled out, spitting dirt and gravel in the air.

Frank stood there watching the truck disappear, wishing they would come back. He imagined pointing the gun at them. The shock on their faces, the sudden fear. They were long gone.

"No one is going to help us, Frank." Oscar stood there, waiting for an answer.

Frank ignored as long as he could. "We don't need help. The engine just needs to cool off. Some water. We should have been doing this for days in this heat." Frank held up the now-empty jug for illustration.

Oscar breathed heavy. Every action seemed like a struggle when he was out of smack. He shared his bag of heroin at the Gainesville show.

There was a young lady he liked at the show. She was a junkie too. They connected right away. She invited her friends, and pretty soon Dickie got involved and they almost missed their show.

Tallahassee was worse. Only four people showed up who weren't in the bands. There was supposed to be a three-dollar cover charge. If they did pay The Fuckers didn't see one dime of that twelve dollars. They were paid two Tombstone pizzas and spots on a dirty rug to sleep.

The air conditioning was broken in the house, and even with fans and windows open the heat was unbearable. The show promoter (if you could call him that) was afraid of Frank but had nothing else to offer.

The Fuckers had lost their shirts on three shows already that month. Doing shows seemed like a good idea over the summer but most of the Punks in town went to FSU and were home elsewhere for the summer.

"Just get out of my face!" Frank pointed at the van, where the exhausted Gary and Dickie both sat sweating buckets. "We'll be in New Orleans tonight. Mackie has been selling the record there, and some guy is playing it on the radio. We just need to get to NOLA."

***

...Nate opened his eyes. The van hit a bump and it brought him back to the darkness. Now he was sitting up in the passenger seat. He felt the feeling of falling, even though he was sitting.

The disorientation of waking caused to him reach out. He looked up and saw a sign as they passed that read: 'New Orleans 10 miles.'

He turned and saw Ericka driving. She smiled. "You're awake."

New Orleans was two nights away. He missed The Gainesville show, and the day off they were taking there. At least he didn't remember it. *What the hell was happening to him?*

A familiar voice spoke inside his head. *Don't worry, bud, I took care of everything.*

Nate looked out at the highway moving quickly below them. He was afraid to look at Ericka as she drove. He felt nausea and the idea of the missing days. He opened his mouth, ready to confess what happened, to beg for help.

Don't do it, Nate. They'll want to go home. They will cancel the tour. Frank's voice spoke calmly inside his mind. His inner voice, however, was adamant.

I need to get help. I'm in trouble.

Nonsense. You're having the time of your life. You tell them and the tour is over, the band is over. Ericka will never speak to you again. Don't worry I am taking care of everything.

"Everything..." Nate whispered.

"What was that?" Ericka asked, turning down the stereo.

"Nothing." Nate smiled. Nothing was wrong, he told himself. "Nothing, just thinking out loud."

CHAPTER 19

Nate stared at the ghostly water line, just taller than him, marking the place where the flooding of Katrina happened ten months earlier. The city still looked like a wasteland. In fact, two Hollywood post-apocalyptic films had swooped in and were using New Orleans as their end-of- the-world backdrop.

As they drove in, they saw one of the film crews working. None of them knew anything about what neighborhood they were in, only that they were close to the French Quarter, which was spared from the flooding.

The insects were crazy, and here in the early morning, Nate was regretting the day they had to wait in this city before they played. It had grown quiet for him in the van. The voices of The Fuckers hadn't gone mute, but they were quieter than a whisper.

That whisper echoed just outside of his hearing range, but enough to remind him, taunt him. He wanted answers to what happened in the days he missed, but he couldn't trust anyone to ask. They would think he was crazy.

Ericka drove them to the French Quarter to look for a cheap motel. At some point, while he was out of it, they decided that it was worth it on this day to get a room. The network they booked the tour from had connections almost anywhere, but Ericka had booked this show. Nate remembered no talk of anywhere to crash.

They had friends in most cities but the only old friend he had here, Jay, had moved to Portland in the wake of Katrina. Ericka pointed over the steering wheel at a barely operating Motel Six with a neon "Vacancy" sign that was busted except the middle "A" that flashed by itself. "What do you think?"

"Is there, like, a park where we can chill?"

Denny pointed at the motel, and held up his emergency-only credit card "This city is depressing and we all need sleep."

Ericka pulled them up to the circle drive by the office. She turned the van off and followed Denny in. They hadn't yet broken down and gotten a hotel room. Nate expected they would not make it this far, so he didn't argue. It had happened before. They all shared a room on a road trip to play a fest in Toronto earlier in the spring.

Scott leaned up till he was in whispering range with Nate. "I'm super happy for you and Ericka."

Nate looked back at Scott and didn't hide his confusion. "What?"

Scott put up his hands. "Hey, man, we told both of you a thousand times to go for it. We're happy for you. It is more important than the band. And look, Gainesville was the best show you ever played."

"Really?"

Scott nodded. "Seriously, man, you were like an animal up there. All the more magical, I say."

Denny and Ericka walked out, both carrying key-cards. They walked towards the rooms. Scott jumped up into the driver's seat and drove the van to follow them. "Oh, wow, she got a room for you guys."

Nate watched Ericka open the door to the motel room and wave at him. He wasn't sure how she afforded it, and part of him wondered if Denny paid for it with his card too. "Bring my backpack, please."

Nate stepped out of the van and looked at the cracked-up door. Denny came out of his room and smacked Scott on the shoulder. "Don't get any ideas." They both laughed. Denny smiled at Nate as he gathered Ericka's backpack and his own.

He had to use his foot to push open the door. The room was a little stuffy. Ericka had turned the AC on full blast. He set the backpacks on the first of two beds and was surprised not to see her. Then he heard the shower come on.

The bathroom door was left open. Nate shut the front door, and stepped around the bed.

Her sleeveless From Ashes Rise shirt was a ball on the floor, the first piece in a trail that led to the bathroom, her shorts, bra and underwear all pointing the way. He heard her breathe a sigh of relief as the shower hit her.

He wasn't feeling what he should have been. His stomach knotted as he heard the echo of Frank's voice.

Don't worry bud, I handled it.

"You getting in or what?"

Nate stepped around her clothes into the bathroom. The shower curtain was clear. He could see the shape of her naked body. Early in their friendship he fantasized about a moment like this. He was always drawn to her sexually, then the band started. Then it seemed impossible. Sure they held hands, even kissed, but...

Ericka opened the curtain enough to show half of her dripping form. The water ran down her skin, giving her a sheen. Her breasts were perky, her hips just rounded enough to give her a curve. She was beautiful. He felt himself stiffen, but another part wondered what exactly Frank had handled.

She waved him in. He couldn't tell her what happened. That he didn't remember the last two days. Nate undid his cargo shorts, which had grown uncomfortable. He slid them and his underwear down. Ericka giggled at how firmly he stood at attention.

Nate flipped off his shoes and socks next. By the time his shirt hit the floor she had his hand and pulled him into the shower.

Ericka had a soapy wash cloth, and started with his back, then moved to his face and arms. He stared at her with nothing to say in the dim light from the main part of the motel room. Last, she cleaned his penis, stroking it with the soapy cloth as she kissed him. The fear and anxiety was gone as pleasure overrode everything in his mind.

The washcloth fell to the floor and Ericka turned facing the water. She was always a little taller than most women, almost as tall as Nate. She arched a bit, enough to direct the tip of his penis into her warm waiting skin. She braced herself against the front of the shower.

145

Nate grabbed her hips and pushed forward slowly, feeling her swallow him inch by inch.

Ericka groaned moving her hips back toward him. Nate felt his toes curl already, just seconds inside her, ready to explode. She reached back and pulled his hand up to her breast. Her erect nipple slid between his index and middle finger as he cupped her flesh in his hand.

It was too much at once. Too many fantasies coming true. He always knew it could happen. They loved each other, but he convinced himself that it wasn't possible. She arched her back and groaned out of pure pleasure. It was too much. He felt the rumbling sensation, he was about to cum.

He slid out just in time to spray her back, and made a goofy sound as he came. Ericka turned back and looked surprised. Nate felt stupid. Nate grabbed a towel and stepped out of the shower.

"Wait, Nate, I'm sorry.

"No, I'm sorry."

Ericka turned off the water and grabbed a towel. She started with the obvious clean-up and smiled. "It's OK. It happens sometimes."

Nate wanted to look away but the mirror in the small bathroom kept her in his sight even as he turned around. "It's just the first time should be special."

Ericka laughed and stepped out next to him. "First time?"

Oh, shit. Thought Nate. *Think quickly.* "First time in the shower. That should be special too."

Ericka smiled. "Yeah, in the shower. First time in the shower."

Ericka leaned in and kissed him. They lingered on the kiss. She leaned against his forehead. "You have nothing to be ashamed about. I love you." Ericka started to walk out of the bathroom. "Besides that, you were amazing last night."

***

With the curtains drawn and the daylight blocked out Ericka fell asleep quickly, given the power of a real bed to sleep in. She invited Nate to lie down. The bed, the covers, and the feeling of being clean was just as strange as post-coital Ericka lying next to him.

It had been almost two weeks since the feeling of a bed. Even the accommodations of an inner city Motel Six felt lavish in that moment.

Ericka fell asleep instantly. Nate couldn't relax. The van was parked directly in front of their room, and as irrational as it would sound to anyone else, Nate could feel it staring at the door, at him. As if the walls were invisible.

It watched him. He needed answers. Needed to understand what was happening. Slowly and carefully, he crawled out from under Ericka's outstretched arm and put on his shorts. He opened the door to the outside slowly, not wanting to wake her.

The instant heat and sunshine shocked Nate as he stepped out and shut the door. The van's headlights were like eyes piercing into him. He fumbled to get the keys out. He opened the driver's side door and stepped into the heat.

The NOLA air had turned the seat into an oven coil. The voices were gone. He could hear Black Flag's "Nervous Breakdown" softly despite the engine and radio being dead. Black Flag faded out, and the Circle Jerks' "Fortunate Son" faded in. And so on. Every few seconds, another band like the Misfits or Gang Green echoed softly in his mind.

Nate's eyes moved past the rearview mirror. He didn't see himself. He stared at it, as another face looked back.

Frank stared at him. Nate wiped sweat from his forehead. "What is happening?"

"We're finishing the tour. You and I, Nate."

"What happened to you, Frank?"

"I'm showing you. Forget the journal. I will take you back there."

Nate felt woozy and tired with the lack of sleep and the heat.

"Don't get weak on me, Nate. You were not made for this era. You belong back there. A trailblazer, someone who understands the power of that time. I belong there."

"Why?"

"Simple, Nate, I belong there because the mission is not over. I have to finish the tour."

Nate felt his eyes get heavy. The world was swirling like a surrealist painting in front of him. He was going back. For the first time, he didn't want to go. He shook his head.

"No, stop! I can't go." Nate reached up to the door handle and the lock snapped down. He pulled at the door frantically screaming. He felt the pull of that other time. This was the first time he resisted. In his heart, he knew he belonged in that time. He let go of the door handle and let it happen. The light of day faded away...

***

...Frank stepped into the small venue and was surprised that the pizza place with the beer-soaked carpets was packed. You couldn't smell pizza, only the near-solid cloud of cigarette smoke. Each table had a group of punks talking and waiting for the local band The Sluts to start.

611 Pizza was named for the address number where they were located on Canal street. Owned by an overweight, greasy-haired band burn-out trying to raise money to move away, the place was new and would never survive past the first health inspection.

Mackie was an old friend of theirs from Indianapolis, who they knew from working the guitar store on the north side. He'd moved here to join a band. He was an older acid rocker, but liked The Fuckers enough to get their 7-inch in stores and more importantly John G. had played them several times on the New Wave hour on WTUL. Each time he did he talked about the upcoming show at 611.

It was the first show on tour that The Fuckers were asked to headline. The tour had taken on a different tone since he killed the farmer. Oscar, while always having the edgy addict behavior, had become downright paranoid about the police. Anytime they even saw a police car, he overreacted, convinced that in every city that they would be arrested for murder, although Frank didn't allow them to talk about it. Dickie didn't care. Gary just wanted to play the shows.

Mackie was standing by Gary's amp and walked over to Frank. He was wearing the first hand-screened Fuckers shirt they sold in Indiana. They man-hugged, patting each other's backs.

"Welcome to NOLA, my man."

"Thanks, man. You really helped us out."

Mackie laughed. "The record is killer, dude. Better than any Indy band has a right to be."

"This place is pretty awesome, man."

Mackie shrugged. "You'll be lucky if you get to play, honestly."

"What do you mean?"

Mackie looked around, yelling over the warm-up music playing on the PA.

"Dude, so there is this diner owned by some red-ass named Eddie Whitman. WW two vet, with a limp and heart condition. His diner is across the alley. He calls the police fifteen minutes into the first band's set every night. If the French Quarter is slow, the police come and shut things down."

"What an asshole."

"He watches bands load and unload in the alley calling people freaks and clowns. People yell at him. It gets pretty ugly."

Frank listened, and realized something. *This Whitman was the enemy.* Mackie kept talking right up until the first band was ready to go. There was no stage. When it looked like a band was ready the crowd stood up and filled the small carpet. Frank understood now why the carpet was soaked with beer.

Several of the older folks held beers even as the small slam pit began to form. Mackie put a plastic cup full of warm lager beer in his hand. Frank took a swig, and it tasted flat and weak. He saw a young man with a purple spiked mohawk, couldn't be more that fourteen, nursing a beer. Frank cringed, knowing the young guy didn't like the taste, but was drinking it anyway. Just another sign of how conformity gets even the punks, he reflected. The crowd packed in.

The guitar player let out some feedback and the drummer clicked his sticks. Frank lost the second half of his beer as the pit broke out in the tiny confined space. The band was savage. Playing fast, grizzly-edged punk rock. Frank slammed into people and lost control. At some point he felt himself hit the edge of a booth and bounced off.

The band was loud, echoing in his ear after the song was over. The vocalist caught his breath after screaming. "Thanks, everyone."

Frank liked the feeling of the pit, always had. Feeling its energy and insane chaos in city after city, he loved it more. It was a celebration. To the outsider it looked like violence. To him it was a tribal dance. An expression of their culture. He thought about the asshole across the alley cursing in his kitchen, getting ready to call the police. His blood began to boil.

They would never play this show. The one he looked most forward to. The one they needed desperately to get out to the West Coast.

Frank ran to the back door. On the way, he saw Dickie banging his way through the pit. He opened the door briefly letting out the sound of the band. He walked across the alley. The diner's back door was open. Only a screen separated him from the kitchen. He heard Whitman cursing.

"Fucking freak show!"

Frank tugged on the screen door but it was locked on the inside. There was a tiny tear in the screen. Frank ripped and reached through to flip the lock.

Whitman stood in the kitchen slowly dialing his rotary phone. Frank waited until his waitress carrying a tray with three plates on it disappeared into the restaurant.

"Put down that phone."

Whitman dropped the phone out of shock and turned to see Frank in his kitchen.

"What the hell are you doing in my kitchen, boy?" Whitman looked around for a weapon. A large butcher knife was just beyond his reach. He lunged for it, but Frank got there first. In seconds the knife point was on a turkey wattle of his neck skin.

"I fought for this country, son. Who do you think you are, pointing a knife at me?"

"I am fighting for my country, my tribe. You make that call you're attacking them."

"Fuck you..." Whitman spit. Frank pushed the knife into his throat, cutting off the words.

Whitman grabbed his bleeding throat as he fell to the kitchen floor. Frank knew he should feel remorse, but he didn't, as the pool of blood gathered under the old man. He threw the knife into the sink.

He was across the alley stepping back into the show when he heard the waitress scream...

***

...Nate opened his eyes. He looked in the mirror. He was in the bathroom of the motel room. He was naked, and a soiled condom hung off his cock. He looked up and saw himself, sweaty but powerful, like he'd just played a show.

He looked into the room. Ericka was naked on the bed, her face bright red and her hair matted with sweat. She breathed heavy. "Oh, my god," was all she said. She rolled over, a smile on her face.

Frank was making him stronger. Nate smiled. He could do this. Finish the mission.

CHAPTER 20

Ericka adjusted the tuning peg slightly and listened to a heavy E-note. She nodded at Denny first. She was the last to be ready. She turned to the crowd that had gathered in the small New Orleans venue, a warehouse in the back of a record store.

Nate's pre-show behavior had changed. After Scott's Frost riff signaled the band was ready to go he became a different animal. He paced the stage like a tiger trapped in a zoo. The moment the first song started, he went Hulk like Bruce Banner on a bad day.

Honestly, Ericka had changed on the tour, too. They all had. She didn't turn her back to the audience or close her eyes anymore. Scott looked down at his hands less, and Denny was keeping their tempo a hair faster.

Tonight she didn't want to miss a moment of Nate. Scott let out some feedback, as Denny rode his cymbals to create a build-up. Nate jumped up and down a few times, wrapping the mic cord around his hand the way he saw Hank Rollins do at a show one time. The crowd ready for a blast of hardcore, already started pushing each other a bit.

"We're People's Uprising from Bloomington, Indiana!" At that, a few in the crowd cheered. Ericka knew that most of the kids at this show had never heard them besides a brief research listen on Myspace. Nate leaned over the edge of the small stage and leered at the crowd.

"I know a lot of you think we can find a solution marching in the streets. The solution might be in the streets, but it's time we fight a war ourselves. Crush the system that wants you to conform, don't be afraid to get a little blood on our hands too..."

Nate paused, then screamed the song title. "Us Versus

Them!!!!!"

Ericka couldn't believe her ears. It wasn't their song title. It was a Fuckers song. Not to mention the blood on your hands comment. *Nate the pacifist?* He had never explained any song that way before. Each night he said almost the same thing, like a political stump speech.

Scott was confused too. They both held their guitars and didn't move. A few in the crowd chuckled, as Nate clearly expected the song to start at that moment. He turned slowly to look at them. His eyes burned with a rage she couldn't make sense of.

"Let's go!"

Denny clicked his sticks four times. They hadn't needed that for timing since long before the tour. The song kicked in with its typical fury, sonically. Nate screamed the lyrics with a raw passion.

His throat pushed the vocals to the edge of dangerous. It was a wonder he could speak. Ericka loved being in his arms, entangled in his body, but she loved being in his band, entangled in the power of his songs even more. She played the songs and for the moment forgot all her concerns.

***

Nate had to push the edge of the guitar cabinet in and quickly slam the two back doors to make the packing job fit. It was amazing how the same equipment fit easily one night, and was a nightmare to fit the next. Ericka watched him from the side mirror, tapping a beat on the steering wheel. Scott was already laid out on the bench, and Denny was trying to get comfortable next to him with the small pace that remained at his feet.

"You ready?" She smiled. He nodded.

The alley behind the venue was still crowded with kids from the show. Nate waved at the show promoter, Gabe, who stood talking to a group of locals, all holding copies of their CD demo. A sure sign that they played well tonight. They would probably need to make more CD's in Houston.

Nate felt an odd tension thinking about Houston. The Fuckers played Houston too. Back in the summer of 1982,

153

they played their last real show in that city. That was the end of the line for Frank. After Houston, he was never seen again.

He wasn't sure what it all meant, but he was afraid his connection to Frank, to that time, would end after Houston. He didn't want it to end. He wished he could just be there back in 1982. He could save Frank, finish the tour.

He walked around the van to the passenger seat, running his hand along the side of the van. It was amazing that this white Chevy van had been where it all happened. The moment of truth was coming.

He stopped before he got in and nudged the side mirror so it pointed into the van. Then he leaned back into the passenger seat. Before Ericka reached down to turn the ignition, he heard the voices talking and the music of the past. They called to him through the years.

***

The 80's hardcore mix played in the CD player as they drove through the night. Interstate 10 was mostly trucks at this hour. Ericka kept the music just loud enough to hear and sing along.

Denny had crawled up onto the loft. Scott was asleep stretched out on the bench for most of the drive. They were going around or through Beaumont, Texas. He wasn't even sure. He just felt tension rising as he saw the sign that read, 'Houston 82 miles.'

Nate tuned out the music, listening to the debate that raged only in echoes inside the van.

***

"We don't have the money for that bullshit," said Frank.

"It's just a little bump. I said it was for all of us," argued Oscar.

"You have nerve, man. You put us all in danger again."

"I have kept this band going!"

"Fuck you, I know you killed that old man."

"Chill out, Oscar, we just played a killer show," said Dickie.

"No, no, no. I may be a fuck-up but I don't kill motherfuckers. We were lucky the cops were distracted with a murder scene, or we might not have played."

"Are you done?"

"You know what, Frank, I think I am, and if you guys were smart you would be too. Let's cut our losses, steal gas if we have to, but get back to Indiana now."

***

"Nate...Earth to Nate?"

Nate turned to look at Ericka and tried to tune out the voices.

"We need another CD. Pick something more modern, please?"

Nate was a little surprised to hear that, but picked up the CD book and flipped through it. CD after CD and nothing sounded remotely good to him.

"How about Walls of Jericho?"

"Uh, no. No modern metalized hardcore."

"We could just talk?"

Nate looked at her. A part of him was weary of the road, weary of the tour. A part of him just wanted to see what life would be like when they could be home together, really together this time.

Then he looked in the mirror and there was no reflection. It showed him the mission that was started so long ago, one he could finish.

"We will finish the tour, you fucking pussies."

Nate was confused. He tried to rub his temples. He wanted to agree with Frank, but knew he couldn't hear him across the years. Ericka took her eyes off the interstate for just a moment.

"Nate, what is wrong with you?"

"Wrong?" Nate sat up. "I thought we were good."

155

Ericka smiled. "We are. It's you I'm not so sure about."

"What are you talking about?"

Ericka looked in the mirror to see if the rest of the band was still asleep. She spoke just above a whisper.

"What was that stuff about waging war ourselves before 'Rise and Fight.'"

"The song is called 'Rise and Fight.'"

"It was always about non-violent resistance."

In the echoing soundscape, Nate heard Oscar raising his voice. *"Did you kill that man?"*

"Nate?" Ericka saw his distraction. "Where are you? Are you blacking out again?"

Nate felt frustrated with the competing voices. He was annoyed that Ericka was on to him. Anger bubbled under the surface. "That's rich. You and Scott made me look like an idiot out there, missing your cue."

"You called the song 'Us Versus Them.' That's not our song, Nate."

Nate felt caught, exposed. She knew damn well whose song it was

"You're a fucking murderer, Frank!"

"So what the fuck ever. What if they deserve it? Because they do."

He put his hands over his eyes, but knew that would only block out Ericka, not the voices he really needed to block, to at least act normal.

"What are you doing?" asked Ericka. "Are you trying not to block me out?"

"No, it's just something...I can't explain."

"Maybe we should just go home. Fuck the tour."

"No!" Nate yelled loud enough to wake the other bandmates. Just as he did, Ericka screamed.

Denny and Scott both jumped awake, expecting to be dying.

"What's happening?" Denny yelled from the loft.

The van's engine roared as it picked up speed. "The gas pedal!" Ericka shouted. "It's going on its own!"

Nate looked at her feet. Ericka pushed on the brake, but

it wouldn't move. She started kicking it. "It won't stop!"

They were getting faster each second, coming up quickly on two semi- trucks. Nate watched the steering wheel spin under Ericka's hands as the van weaved between the trucks. The chaos grew in the van. Both Scott and Ericka screamed. Denny reached from the back seat to try and control the wheel.

Nate heard laughter so loud that it hurt. He looked around to see who was laughing, but they weren't there. He sat back in the passenger seat and rolled down the window. Closing his eyes just for a second, he knew what he would see when he opened them again.

The intense motion was gone, the screaming tires and band members were suddenly quiet. He opened his eyes to look at Oscar in the driver's seat.

"We're not going home," he said calmly.

Oscar looked back at him stunned. "How can you be so calm?"

***

Ericka squeezed the steering wheel with strength she didn't know she had. Denny reached over her. She knocked him back. Scott whimpered in the back. Ericka looked over and couldn't believe her eyes. Nate was just staring at himself in the side mirror that was turned in. Cool as a cucumber, he seemed unaffected by any of it.

Suddenly the van stopped. Backpacks flew. Zines and records collected over the tour took flight in the confined space, and Denny spun in the air. Ericka and Nate's seat belts held, and Scott hugged the back of the driver's seat.

Ericka knew they were spinning, but they managed not to roll over. The tires made a screeching sound like a hundred Screamo vocalists in a chorus, before they stopped on the shoulder facing traffic. A semi-truck honked at them at as it passed.

She reached up to move the gear shift to park. It refused to budge at first. She screamed before wrenching it into place.

Ericka felt her dinner struggling to climb out her throat, and her nerves were like guitar strings pulled massively out of tune. She jumped out on to the highway shoulder, too dizzy to stand. She heard someone else puke. She turned and saw Scott on his hands and knees. Denny was out, trying to shake it off.

Another truck zoomed past shaking the van. Ericka looked at the big open Texas sky and saw the glow of the sun poking up in the east.

"Is it me or did the van just try and kill us?" Denny fell to his knees on the gravel, the exhaustion of fear overcoming him.

"Oh, stop it already," A voice came from the van. Ericka turned and saw Nate stepping out but he sounded different. "We just needed to stop."

"Have you lost your mind, Nate?" Denny stood up straight. "I mean you have been acting funny the whole tour."

"Everyone is safe. No one was hurt right?"

Ericka was stunned. He wasn't acting like Nate. As crazy as it all sounded, she knew exactly who he was behaving like.

"Nate, what happened to Frank after Houston?"

"You read the journal."

"It stops after Houston. It doesn't explain what happened to Frank after the tour ended."

Nate looked furious, like a hate was swirled in him like a storm. "It is not over. Not now, not ever."

"Can you even hear yourself?" Denny asked.

"Can you?" Nate shook his head. "Ready to just quit, run back home to Indiana."

"That van is fucking evil, Nate." Scott pointed at it. "I'm not getting back in that thing."

"Come on, the van is a fucking van. It's the system that is evil."

"Stop with the hardcore preaching." Denny walked closer to Nate. "Look I don't listen to Coast to Coast, and I don't believe in weird shit, but something is very, very wrong with that van."

"So if the van is so evil, how you gonna get home? Walk?"

"I will Greyhound it. I don't give a fuck."

"Go ahead, leave. I'll finish this mission by myself if I have too."

Ericka heard the word 'mission', one used often by Frank in the writings in the journal. She had to stop this. Calm everyone down.

They needed to help Nate. Something was wrong. She wasn't going to lose him, not now. Not two days after she finally got him.

"Everyone calm down. Look, I'm scared. We all are."

"Not him!" Scott motioned to Nate.

Ericka put up her hands. "Let's just play Houston. The show is with Die Young."

Denny sighed. She knew they were his favorite new band. Scott shook his head. Ericka helped him up. "Just play tonight and we'll talk after the show."

Denny looked away. Another huge truck passed them, shaking the van. Without saying a word he walked back to the van. Scott just shook his head. Nate's face softened a bit. He and Ericka shared a look. He pulled out his keys. Ericka shook her head.

"I'll drive, thanks."

CHAPTER 21

Nate felt funny. In the van the voices grew more heated. All the voices, the ones from the past in his head and the ones in his ears. No one was happy about being on the road. He stopped listening to the sounds of the debates. Everyone wanted to go home and quit. Everyone, except him and Frank.

They were at Daniel's house. Daniel was an old friend whose band they traded shows with. He lived a few blocks from the venue, and promised an air conditioned house. When they booked the tour in April, Nate didn't think that sounded that important. Now as they crossed the south the van became a rolling sweat lodge. Everyone was happy with the cool air.

The heat, the voices, the exhaustion all combined to churn inside Nate's mind. He was blacking out again. Waking up just long enough to realize the van was stopped on the side of the road and then the world faded away once more.

The next minute they were in Daniel's house. Ericka was snuggled up under his arm. She was crying. He had no idea why or how things were happening. The next minute he was on stage.

Ericka held her bass and looked at him, worried. He couldn't stop it. The world faded to black again. Nate opened his eyes. He was sitting in the van. Behind the wheel, he looked up and Frank smiled back at him in the rearview mirror.

"Let it take you…"

***

Nate opened his eyes as Frank. There was a confusing moment when the bright Texas sun faded in around him. The steering wheel became solid in his hands and the highway formed under them. He was holding the same steering wheel

160

but driving. Dickie was asleep in the passenger seat. Oscar was on the bench talking.

"Pull over. It looks pretty bad."

The storm clouds had formed a black wall against the horizon to the west, just beyond the skyline of Amarillo. Flashes of lightning danced in the air. The city looked small in the distance but the increasing billboards and signs told them Amarillo was the biggest thing in this part of the state.

"It's just a storm," Frank said taking a drink of his Mountain Dew. Dickie woke up and cleared his eyes. "Whoa, I don't know, Frank. That storm looks pretty bad. What if it's a tornado?"

"Just take it easy, okay, Dickie? We're almost to the show."

"They get fucking tornados here, dude."

Frank shook his head and kept driving. They had driven up north to Oklahoma and were heading across Texas towards Albuquerque with one more stop in Texas for a show in Amarillo. They heard through the grapevine that their New Mexico show was already canceled.

The bass player of the Houston band Really Red knew a guy who knew a guy from New Mexico. Ronny, who did all the punk shows there, was beaten so bad by a gang of jocks in his school that he couldn't keep it up. That or the show space was busted by the cops. They had heard both rumors. They kept driving, hoping neither was true.

"Dickie, get out the journal."

Dickie knew he was going to be asked to give the directions. He thumbed through the notebook until he found the page where all the Texas contacts and directions were written down. Frank saw him running his finger on the page.

"Take, uh, it says exit 21."

They had just passed exit eighteen. Frank relaxed a little guessing they would make the house where the show was at before the storm, no problem. He remembered booking this show. A guy named Kenny who wrote a scene report in *Maximum Rock and Roll*. They had a band called Wastedlands.

They hosted a few shows over the spring, a couple of Oklahoma City bands and a big show for MDC. He listed his number and Frank called. Amarillo was booked with a promise of gas money and nothing else, but it was better than taking the night off.

Dickie read the directions off the exit and they followed them into a middle class suburban neighborhood. Kids were racing big wheels on one street, and on another street a flag football game had to break up to let them pass. They looked upon the scene like an alien landscape.

"Oh, lord, this is where the show is happening?"

The van pulled up to the address Kenny gave them, a two story ranch house with a stereotypical white picket fence. The houses on all sides looked like they were made from the same cookie-cutter design. A man in a Dallas Cowboys sun hat was at the end of the next yard with a hose spraying a bed of flowers that lined the street.

He stared at them, his hose still running, as Frank turned off the van. Frank made eye contact with him as the side door opened. Oscar with his recently dyed brightly red Mohawk and safety pin nose ring stepped out first. Dickie was next with his green hair and his shirt that simply read Fuckers.

"What in the hell?" The man said as his jaw dropped.

Frank stepped out and looked at the shocked man. "Good afternoon." He walked up to the house and looked at his watch. It was just before five p.m. The show was supposed to be at six. He would expect some punks to be hanging around. His bandmates lit up cigarettes and lined up along the side of the van, watching.

Frank reached the door and saw an ornate-looking cover to the doorbell. He pushed it and listened as the bell rang throughout the house. A dog started to bark. Someone inside was holding the little yappy thing back.

"Mom! Somebody at the door! Looks like one of Kenny's friends!" A young girl inside yelled.

There was some rustling inside, then the sound of an older woman. "Get upstairs right now. Get!"

The door opened as much as the chain lock would let it

before snapping tight. Frank could make out one brown eye of a short woman staring out the door.

"I done called the Sheriff. I reckon you best get on."

"What? I just rang the bell."

"You ain't got no business ringing this here bell."

"Oh, Jesus," Frank laughed. "I'm just looking for Kenny. He gave us this address."

"That boy has the devil in him. You want to find him, you best head to Austin or Dallas. He ran away and I can't say I want him back."

Frank sighed. "You're a lovely mother."

"Step-mother!" Then the door slammed shut. Frank turned and walked back to the van. The lady was yelling, so he knew they heard all of it.

"This is such bullshit, man, no show." Oscar never stopped with the whining. "If we get to Albuquerque and there's no show, we're fucked. Hardcore fucked right in the asshole sideways *fucked*."

"Hey, watch your mouth, boy." The watering man in the Cowboys hat was pissed off. Frank pointed at the skies to the west. "You know there's a storm coming, chief?"

The man just stared at Frank, his hose still running water.

"Watering is kinda pointless, right...Oh, forget it."

"What do we do?" Dickie sounded defeated.

Frank was thinking about it when they heard the faint sound of sirens.

"Oh shit, man, we gotta go." Oscar jumped in the van. Frank shook his head.

"We didn't do anything wrong."

He was just sitting down and turning the key in the ignition when two Potter County Sheriffs' cars screeched to a halt in front of them.

Frank knew he only had five bullets left in the gun. He turned to look at the two cops as they got out of their cars. One was an old man with a pure white mustache, and the other one looked young and green.

Thunder rumbled in the distance. Lightning flashed across the sky. It looked to be rolling closer just beyond the horizon. Thunder shook the van rattling its metal shell. The storm was coming quickly bringing rain in buckets. Frank shifted the van in drive and peeled out backwards and around the parked police car.

"We were just leaving, officers," he yelled out the window.

"What the fuck?" Oscar yelled. "Are you crazy?"

"We didn't do anything wrong."

"Now we did!" Oscar screamed. "We can't outrun them!"

Frank almost tipped the van over taking turns to get them out of the neighborhood. He ran a red-light to get them towards the exit ramp. He could have gone on to the interstate. Signs for I- 40 were all around, but there would be more witnesses.

Frank passed the exit and turned on to a two-lane highway. It bordered empty fields. Oscar and Gary were looking back over the loft, out the one back window not covered in stickers.

"They're coming quick."

They all knew that the van didn't have the power to outrun a police car. The two cars, sirens blaring, followed them past the outskirts of the city. The older Sheriff slowed in front of him, and the young rook pulled up alongside

"What are you going to do?"

"Kill them," Frank said deadpan. He thought no one would believe him. The silent response told him otherwise. Frank finally pulled along the side of the highway. He left the van running.

"Turn off the vehicle!" A voice came from a loud speaker. Frank turned off the van. Oscar put his hand on his shoulder.

"Don't kill him, Frank. Please, we'll handle it."

The cops walked the length of the van. The older one stopped outside Frank's door and poked his head through the open window. The other cop stood beside him with his hands on his hips.

He looked at Dickie's spiked green hair and the small bone he had stuffed through his earring hole and his jaw dropped. He had on mirror shades. Until he saw himself in the Sheriff's sunglasses Frank had no idea how dirty and disheveled he looked.

"What the fuck have I found here? Must be some kind of Satanic circus."

"We didn't do anything wrong. Just rang her door bell."

"Why'd you run, then?" the younger Sheriff pointed out.

"Huh?"

"Have you looked in a mirror lately, son?" the older Sheriff laughed.

"You're doing something wrong by waking up in the morning."

His young partner laughed. "That's a good one, Dale."

Frank felt waves of hatred coming off the Sheriff and his deputy. Nothing good could happen here. The wind blew tumbleweeds behind him, and only a strap kept the older Sheriff's mighty tall shit-kicking ten-gallon hat on his head. He looked around the van again.

This time he saw Oscar's nose ring vibrating like a guitar string holding a note. He looked at Frank and took his glasses off. He understood Frank was the tough guy of the group, and they had a silent exchange of machismo.

"Indiana plates. What are you boys doing in my state?"

"We're a band."

"You think you're some kind of Elvis?"

"More like Johnny Cash, sir," Dickie said with a smile.

"Right." The Sheriff looked at Frank. "Except he is a God-fearing man."

"Are we done here?" Frank didn't bother hiding his annoyance.

"Why don't you fellas step on out to the road?"

Frank didn't budge. One by one the rest of the van doors opened and the members of The Fuckers stepped out. Frank was last. The Sheriff stepped back to give him room. The energy of the coming storm felt stronger in the open.

Oscar had an even harder time standing up against the wind. The cop pointed to the hood of the van.

"Put your hands on the hood."

The sun was gone. The black clouds sped by and lightning

stabbed the next ridge. Everyone shook when five seconds later the thunder rattled the desert floor. Dickie and Oscar already had their hands on the hood. Gary was a little slower, but Frank stood still watching the Deputy.

When the thunder died Frank heard the Sheriff's CB crackling with distortion.

He was out of contact. There was no way he could've called in for backup. Rain fell in the distance, coming quickly toward them. The Sheriff put his hands on his hips, but Frank noticed his side arm holster was still clicked shut. So was his partner's. They didn't even view them as a threat. Time to teach them a lesson.

"I said hands on the van, boy."

"I ain't your boy." Frank pulled out his hand gun from his pants. He aimed for the Sheriff's kneecap. Point blank range, the bullet exploded the knee cap turning it to soup. His leg basically snapped in half, and the Sheriff fell to the ground. His young deputy was still in shock when Frank pointed the gun at him and fired into his chest. The young cop died instantly. Frank leaped forward and grabbed the older man's hand gun.

It happened fast. Oscar turned immediately and screamed. "Oh, fuck!"

The Sheriff screamed in pain but all the screaming was drowned out by thunder and the echo of the gun blasts. Frank watched him squirm on the ground and felt satisfaction. The Sheriff turned purple from the pain and rolled to see his dying student bleeding on the ground.

The rain started to trickle on them, but the highway was already spattered in blood. Frank stood over the Sheriff, pointing both guns at his face. The man shook worse than Oscar now, trying to look tough and angry but failing. Fear overtook him as he looked up at his executioner.

"Wow, you were a pretty rootin-tootin pig a minute ago."

Dickie walked up behind Frank and spit on the Sheriff's face. Gary looked at Oscar who suddenly seemed more sober than he had in weeks. "Frank! This is fucked up, man!"

Frank ignored Oscar. The heavy rain was just a quarter

of a mile down the road, coming fast. Frank pinned the Sheriff's palm to the pavement with the barrel of his own revolver. The middle man aged tried to grit his teeth. Frank pushed the barrel harder against his skin.

"Come on, Frank, this is just torture now!" Oscar begged.

"So what made you think we were a circus? Is it because we don't look like some honky-tonk mother fuckers you have down here? I'm sure if we fucked our sisters and chewed tabbacy, like good ole boys you would've let us ride on."

"I didn't mean no harm, mister, just doing my job." The man struggled to say it without bursting out in howls of pain. He lost the battle and screamed.

Frank pulled the hammer back and held it with his thumb ready to fire.

"So, it's your job to harass people who are different. That's your job. Well, this here's my job."

At that, he held his breath and squeezed the trigger. The bullet ripped through the cop's hand like it was Kleenex, putting a hole in the pavement and shooting bits of asphalt into the air.

Frank was surprised by his hand blowing apart. His three biggest fingers blew off and only a skinned pinky and thumb held on. The Sheriff screamed in agony as the heavy rain fell so hard he almost choked on it. Nate stood as the shower washed the red from the pavement.

"Jesus, Frank! What the fuck have you done?" Oscar screamed from behind him.

The three band members stood in the rain staring at Frank.

"Get back in the van."

Gary pushed them back into the van. Frank wiped the bloody barrel on his jeans. Dickie had already started the van back up. The wipers wheezed to life for the first time in days. The headlights popped on, shining on Frank standing in the downpour.

The Sheriff begged for his life incoherently. Frank wanted to leave him to die slowly on the side of the road but couldn't risk him being found and living. Instead, Frank pointed the pistol at his head.

It would be over in a split second. Too quick, he thought. Frank pointed the pistol to the Sheriff's belly and fired a round. Lightning on the ridge flashed and the thunder harmonized with the pistol. The blood pooled under him but the massive storm quickly washed it away.

Frank turned and saw his bandmates watching from the front of the van.

He stuffed the burning hot pistol back in his pants. The heat of the barrel felt good against his abdomen. Frank jumped in the passenger seat and shut the door.

The only sound other than the rain was Oscar's heavy breathing and the windshield wipers. Frank reached for the radio and popped in a cassette. The SSD song "Boiling Point" blasted and Frank screamed. "Whoo! Fuck yeah."

Oscar freaked out, kept whispering, "What the fuck?" Dickie had his hand on the gear shift looking unsure. Frank shook his head spraying rain water around the cabin of the van...

"Let's go."

* * *

...Nate felt the steering wheel in his hands and was shocked by the bright Texas sun. He looked up into the parking lot and it was empty now. He could hear the band playing hardcore muffled by the walls of the club and the van.

Scott stood staring at him in the parking lot. He looked freaked out. Nate felt like smacking him. He had been standing in the way of their success and the tour since the moment they left.

Scott opened the door to the van. "Are you ready to pack up?"

Nate could still smell the blood on the highway.

CHAPTER 22

Ericka watched a few minutes of the opening band, but couldn't focus on the songs. She sat behind their merch table with Denny. They hadn't sold a shirt all night and only two CD's. Some shows, some towns, were just full of broke kids. Sometimes a good set could open some wallets, but for now they were bored behind the table.

Ericka watched as Nate stood in the front bobbing his head for the first song. She knew the band's modern sound would do little for him. She could tell right away they were too polished, and metal sounding for Nate. He wouldn't last long at all. So she wasn't surprised when he left and walked outside. Scott had followed him, and they were gone for a while.

The band weren't very good, leaving the crowd more interested in talking to each other than watching or listening to the music. They would be playing soon enough. Everyone was tense, and no one was talking.

Everyone but Nate wanted to go home. They needed the great eraser. A great set had the power to do away with all the negative feelings. Ericka had to admit to herself sitting behind the table, that she was done.

The tour was over, Nate was losing his mind, and they were not having fun anymore. Something was unexplainable about the van. They all knew it, but had as much trouble admitting it to themselves as much as each other.

Ericka stared at the edge of the pit, where an older white guy stood during the band's whole set. He had thick dreads that hung almost to his waist, brown and graying hair collected in ratty mats with an old looking camera taking pictures. He looked a million years old in contrast to the young hardcore kids standing around.

Daniel, the local promoter who put on the show, walked

past the table. Ericka waved him down and yelled in his ear so he could hear her over the band. "Hey, Danny, who is that guy with the crazy dreds?"

He looked over and chuckled before yelling back to her. "That's Greylock. Well that's what kids call him, not sure his name. Been going to punk shows in this town forever. He is a rock photographer. You've seen his pictures before, I'll bet you anything."

Daniel kept walking. The band finished a song, and told the crowd they had one more song. Denny and Ericka shared a look. They were on next.

"I'll find them," Ericka said with a sigh as the song started. She walked to the front of the venue by the bar that was closed during all-ages shows. She looked out the window at the parking lot and saw the van. Scott and Nate were unloading some last pieces of equipment. Most everything was on the side of the stage waiting for them.

"I've seen that van before."

Ericka turned to see who spoke in the voice wrecked by years of cigarettes and whiskey. Greylock stood tall, the punk equivalent of the grand old tree that had anchored a river for centuries. He looked out the window over her shoulder.

"You have?"

He smiled. "It was The Fuckers' tour van, sure. I've been taking pictures of bands in the mid-south since your parents were kids. I took their last picture as a band."

She knew that picture. It was on the cover of the 'Live at CB's' bootleg CD. The same photo Nate used to recognize the van. The insanity of him looking at it in this moment sent a chill straight up Ericka's spine. Another impossible thing connected to that damn van.

"Where did you find it? The van, I mean." There was true wonder in his voice.

Ericka gave him a curious look, not sure how to respond. "The drummer still had it. He sold it to our singer."

"Dickie's still kickin', huh. He was kind of a fuckup. You know Oscar got clean. He's a novelist now. Lives in L.A., I think. Changed his last name."

"I didn't know that."

Greylock nodded. "I think he wanted it that way. He never got over what happened."

Ericka's eyes got wide. "You know what happened?"

Greylock sighed. "I know the legends. I mean beyond the ones that are more common, the ones spoken of in whispers. The ones no one wants to believe."

"Well, I have seen some shit in that van, I believe. Tell me."

Greylock stared past her at the van. "Frank Fucker was a force of nature. He had some ideas about society."

"I know, war against conformity and fighting back to defend punk rock."

"They weren't just words. Frank cut a path of misery in his wake."

Denny was across the club trying to get her attention. While they were talking, Scott and Nate had gone to the back door and were setting up on stage.

Tell me quickly, I gotta play soon..."

***

Scott plugged in his guitar and started tuning. Nate was helping position the drum mikes and talking to the guy in charge of sound. Ericka walked on to the stage and saw her bass leaned against her cabinet.

"You're welcome," Scott said and returned to his tuning. Ericka ignored him and went straight to Denny.

"Hey, can I talk to you for a second?"

Denny looked up at her from positioning his floor tom, then to Nate and the sound guy. "Now? You need to talk now?"

Ericka knew it was crazy, but she had to talk to someone. Not Nate, it had to be Denny. The drummer sighed and slapped his stick on his floor tom. He followed Ericka out into the alley off the backstage area.

"I think the van is haunted."

"That is what you had to say?" Denny laughed. "That crazy talk couldn't wait."

171

Ericka grabbed Denny's hand. "Come on, we're all thinking it. You've seen the steering wheel go crazy, the radio, all kinds of weird shit. Scott's already said he's afraid. He called it evil. It's not just the van."

"Then what is it?"

"Didn't you ever think it was strange that Nate found that van, riding his bike in the middle of nowhere?"

"That was weird."

"I think," Ericka involuntarily whispered "The van found him."

Denny grinned. "Found Nate, the van - a vehicle found Nate."

Ericka nodded. "I don't know, I can't explain. It's Frank. Frank Fucker, the singer of The Fuckers. He was twisted, had very strong, very bad ideas."

"No one knows what happened to him." Denny stepped back. "Nate himself said he could be alive, he could be in Florida retired, or in prison."

Ericka shook her head. "He was a murderer, Denny. Remember that stretch of road where we stopped in South Carolina by the holiday Inn sign?"

"No, not really."

Cornfield in South Carolina. Nate was driving and he just stopped in the middle of the night. Frank murdered a man in that exact spot. The van wanted us to be there."

Denny remembered and nodded. Ericka kept going. "In Columbia I read The Fuckers' journal. Frank was obsessed with punks fighting back against people who picked on them."

Denny's eyes got narrow. "I thought it was strange mister super vegan anti-war was down with all that macho violent talk. Still, what does this have to do with Frank?"

"They killed him. His bandmates. They buried him out there on the highway, where we are supposed to be after we leave Texas."

"How do you know this?"

"That old guy with the dreds. He knew them. He was there. He and Oscar were a thing or something."

"He knew what happened to Frank?"

Ericka nodded. "Don't you think Nate has sounded more like Frank than himself?"

"So, what are you saying?" Denny tended to cut to the chase when he was tired of a subject. "That he is possessed? You know Scott hears one word of this and he'll be on the Greyhound. I've talked him out of going so many times. To be honest with you, Ericka, I don't like the new Nate. I like this band, I love being on the road, but I'm ready to go home too."

The back door to the venue opened. Nate poked his head out. "You guys ready?"

Denny put up a finger. "One minute, man."

Nate looked confused and a little bit angry. He ducked back in the venue. Ericka lowered her voice to a whisper.

"I want to go home too, but you heard how he reacted last time we suggested it."

Denny cracked up. "He said he'd keep going."

"Yeah, right, without a band. He is out of his mind. I think going home might make him snap."

"A little dramatic, don't you think?" Denny pointed at the venue door. Inside, Scott played his warm-up riff.

"I don't think so. I know I just have to say this. By this point in the tour, Frank Fucker wasn't as concerned about the tour as he was his so called war. He wrote these long diatribes about it. I'm worried about Nate. He's amped and I think if we call it all off now he'll lose it, like Frank did."

"What are you saying?"

"Say The Fuckers were cursed. Maybe we just need to make it further than they did. Play Santa Fe. Give Nate a chance to calm down. We'll deal with it there." Ericka was nervous about this idea, getting back in the van, getting even further from home, but above all she wanted to believe in Nate.

The door to the venue opened and Nate was looking at them. He could tell he missed some intense discussion. "What's up?"

Denny and Ericka looked at each other. Denny walked past him into the venue. "We were thinking about learning a cover before California."

Above all, she told herself, the show must go on.

CHAPTER 23

Nate shut the back doors of the van. He was alone, the last to work on getting equipment packed. A band from New York called Conserver was just starting their set. They had played with them in Florida, and the two tours were crisscrossing again in Seattle later this month. Scott rushed back in to watch them, since he was a fan of the guitar players.

Taking off his shirt, Nate then used it to wipe the sweat off his brow. Only twenty minutes had passed since their set, but he was still breathing heavy and perspiring. The heat and humidity of the South even at night was thick.

The set was quick. He didn't say as much as he normally did in between songs. He felt an odd paranoia while they played, unable to shake the strange feeling of watching Denny and Ericka being secretive.

They played well. They didn't go crazy just played the songs with a determination. The crowd was into it, and in the end that was the most important thing.

Nate walked around to the driver's side. He needed to sit, time to get his mind straight. He looked around and saw Denny and Ericka. They were sitting on a bench by the door, set up to be the smoke break area for bands and bouncers.

They were talking again. Nate stopped to stare at them, wondering if they would look up and see him. What happened that she trusted Denny more than she did him? They were lovers now, so why couldn't she talk to him?

Nate opened the door to the van and heard it right away. The Fuckers played loudly like speakers blaring. The keys were still in his hand. Nate shut the door and stood outside to cut off the sound. It didn't bleed through like real music would. It was different. He could feel it in his skull.

He opened the door slowly this time. The music faded

in. He turned to see if the people walking in the parking lot reacted. No one did. Nate climbed in, sat in the driver's seat, and rolled down the window. He positioned the mirror so he could see Denny and Ericka.

The music faded. Even though the van was off he saw the volume knob on the stereo spinning slowly on its own.

"You really love her." Frank's voice.

Nate looked in the rear view mirror and Frank's eyes stared back at him.

"We love each other."

"Ahhh, barf. She doesn't understand what we are doing."

"She is the most punk rock person I know."

"And yet there she is, conspiring against the tour, against us. Against you."

Nate looked in the side mirror and saw Denny's hand go up to Ericka's shoulder.

"You may have already lost her."

***

Denny looked at her. "You gonna be okay?"

Ericka took a deep breath. "Did you talk to Scott?"

"For about a minute. He wants to see Mel. He thinks we should be going home, but he's afraid to tell Nate, and he thinks you should do it. He'll play the next show."

Ericka rolled eyes. "Thanks, buddy."

"Nate loves you."

"I've lost him. We all have."

Denny put his hand on her shoulder. Ericka looked up surprised. She was never super-close to Denny and Scott. Liked them, she knew they would always be like brothers to her now. She could feel his sympathy and it felt good. She took his hand in hers.

"Thank you, Denny. I really think we might be saving his life."

***

Nate watched in the mirror as Ericka reached up and grabbed Denny's hand. She held his hand. Nate's jaw dropped slightly.

"I hate to say it my man."

"Then don't." Nate looked away from the mirror and stared at the steering wheel. The jealousy and rage battled in him and he fought an urge to lean on the horn.

"You see for yourself. Forget her, she doesn't matter. The mission is all that matters."

Nate felt a surge of righteous anger. He felt those feelings a lot, at the injustices of the world and the constant wrong he witnessed. Now he was just mad at himself. He loved Ericka but he put her ahead of the things that deeply mattered in this world. It was a mistake, one he needed to correct.

"Get us back out there, man. Get us back on the road."

Nate slapped the steering wheel in frustration.

***

Ericka let go of Denny's hand. "We need to come up with a plan. We haven't made a dime the whole tour."

Denny nodded in agreement . "We delay, that just means we'll be further away. New Mexico is a short drive from here, no reason to do that if—"

"What the fuck is going on here?"

Ericka didn't recognize Nate's voice, it was so full of venom that it sounded like another human being. She turned to see her sweet politically-correct Nate walking at them like a jealous redneck husband who caught his wife cheating. Ericka realized he saw the hand holding and got the wrong idea.

"Whoa, slow down, Nate." Denny put his hands up.

"It's not what you're thinking."

Nate looked at Denny. Scott walked out of the club and stood beside them, not knowing that he walked into the conflict. Denny put his hands up. "We're worried about you, Nate."

"Worried. Tour is going great, Ericka and I are..."

Ericka smiled. "We're great. I love you, Nate, You and

I are awesome." She grabbed his hand and looked into his eyes. "But the tour isn't awesome. We are hundreds of dollars in the hole."

"We knew that might happen."

Denny smiled. "Of course we did. Money is not the issue. Nate, you're the issue. You're changing."

"I'm growing, becoming what I was meant to be. I'm focused. If I am the issue then the only way to help me is to finish the tour."

Denny shook his head. "I don't think so. That van is weird, dude. And we know what happened to Frank."

Nate let go of Ericka's hand and walked backwards. "Get in the fucking van." He turned and walked with the keys out. "No one knows what happened to Frank."

"They killed him," said Ericka. "Dickie, Oscar, and Gary killed him because he was a danger to them. To everybody."

Nate laughed. "Those pussies? You can't be serious." He kept walking towards the van, they were still watching as he slammed the door shut.

Ericka turned to Scott and Denny. They stood there silent for a long moment.

"I think we better get in the van," Ericka said just above a whisper.

"Fuck that," said Scott. "I'll fly my ass home. He can't talk to us that way."

The van roared to life. The stereo was blasting, with the window down the sounds of old school punk rock carried through the parking lot. It took Ericka a second but she knew the song.

"Is that what I think it is?" Denny asked.

"Yeah, it's The Fuckers all right. Come on." Ericka walked first toward the van. "Being left in Texas won't help."

***

"I can't do it. They're my friends." Nate said as he watched Ericka walking towards the van in the side mirror. Nate started crying and held his face. The Fuckers song "*Us Versus*

Them" blasted, but Frank's speaking voice came through.

"Scott has been undermining you from day one. Now he's got Ericka and Denny turned against the band. This tour is bigger than us. It's bigger and more important than the bands. It's about punk rock, it's about the people victimized just for being themselves."

Nate wiped the tears away and nodded. "I know that."

"Do you? If you really do you'll take care of them. I know just the perfect spot."

Nate sobbed. "I can't."

The song played louder and louder inside Nate's head as it reached the crescendo. The song sped up its beat pounding. Frank's voice screamed over the last blasting beat. Nate had heard the song a thousand times, but in this moment Frank's screams reached through like a finger pointing at him. "It's a war! You must fight!"

The song ended and in the silence Nate whispered. "I will fight. I will end this tour."

The door to the van opened. Ericka sat in the passenger seat. She turned the stereo down slowly until it clicked off, bringing silence in the van. Nate felt an urge to slap her for turning it off, but the song continued on in some part of his brain like it was playing.

Us Versus them! To the war again... It sang in his head.

"You're crying?"

"I'm sorry," He lied. He had to get them back on track. Scott and Denny were at the edge of the van. "One more show, you'll see it will be fine. One more show."

CHAPTER 24

Nate drove across Texas and didn't say a word. Ericka sat awake in the passenger seat, staring out at the stars hanging over the clear Texas night. Scott and Denny whispered for a while in the back seat, but it seemed both had resigned themselves to the next show in Santa Fe. Ericka knew once they could get online and plan a way to get home, they would bolt. She couldn't blame them.

Nate played his personally compiled Fuckers discography twice through before she broke the silence. "Can we listen to something else, please?"

He gave her a *'This shit again'* look and pointed at the CD book. She opened to a Jawbreaker CD, that she would love to listen to, but didn't want the argument so she flipped to the old school CDs and put in MDC. That was old school enough punk rock that Nate wouldn't say anything.

That was the only time they talked until they stopped at a nearly abandoned gas station near the New Mexico border. The sun poked over some far-off mountains and lit the area in a strange orange glow. The desert was quiet and she realized they had left the interstate.

The truck stop was retro, like it was last remodeled in the 70's, and only three trucks were lined up in the big parking lot. The only thing modern was the gas pumps. Observing all this, he asked, "You need anything?"

"Coffee maybe." Ericka wanted him to go in the store and take a few minutes. "I should probably drive."

"No, I'll drive." Nate said as if there was no possible debate in his mind. He got out to pump the gas. He was still able to see her through the window. She didn't want him watching. She reached back and slapped Denny's leg waking him up but she kept her eyes forward. Denny sat up.

"Stay down!" Ericka whispered. He laid back. He tried to rub sleep out of his eyes. Scott woke up. He spun around in the loft so they could all talk.

"What did you guys talk about?"

Denny listened as Nate put the gas cap back on and waited until he turned to walk into the store. "We're not playing Santa Fe, Ericka."

She nodded. Not prepared on the lack of sleep to debate them. Denny sat up, and Scott slid down on to the bench next to him.

"He needs help or something." Scott shrugged. "I mean, he has lost his mind, right?"

"I know." Ericka didn't hide her disappointment.

"We told you we'd sleep on it, but if he won't go home were going to fly home from Albuquerque."

Ericka nodded. "OK, but we have to tell him now. Give him time to process it. We do this as a band."

"Agreed." Denny nodded.

"Fuck, OK," Scott relented.

The side door opened, Scott and Denny found bushes to water. She knew she would regret not pissing, so she ran to the building. She saw Nate in the store with two coffees on the counter.

She couldn't believe it had come to this. She was so close to having him, the man she wanted, having the band she wanted. Her dreams ready to come true.

Ericka needed to know more. She went back to Nate's backpack and opened it. The journal rested there. She checked one more time to make sure Nate wasn't back or watching and quickly put it in her bag.

Ericka jumped out and jogged at first toward the bathroom. She turned back to look at the van and felt like it was staring at her. The headlights were dark and the van sat silent, but she felt it.

"Don't you lose your mind, too," she told herself as she went into the bathroom.

***

Nate watched Ericka go into the bathroom as he walked across the parking lot. He stopped for a moment and thought about the time they spent together. A part of him wanted to knock on that bathroom door.

No matter how disgusting the room was, he wanted to steal a moment with her. He tried not to look at her, or think about her, even when he could smell her sitting in the van next to him. He got weak thinking about her.

At the same time he was disappointed in her. She of all people should understand the importance of what they were doing, and why they were doing it. He knew he had to stay on the mission.

Denny and Scott were out of the van taking a piss. Nate put a coffee on the roof and opened the driver's side door. He jumped as Frank's voice spoke to him before the door was even fully open.

"She's hot, I'll give you that."

Nate ignored the voice in his head as he put the coffee in the drink holder. He shut the door and put the key in the ignition. He didn't turn the key, and was annoyed that he had to wait for the rest of his band. He put both hands on the steering wheel and squeezed tightly.

"They're quitting the tour, Nate. Just said so while you were out."

"They can't."

"They are."

Nate looked at Denny and Scott walking toward the van. He turned back to see Ericka coming across the parking lot. He was disgusted at their apathy. When he and Ericka sat in the cafeteria first talking about their vision for the band it was that the message would always come first. Always come before everything else. They needed to all be on the same page for it to work.

"We need them."

"Bullshit. They just slow us down. Eat our food, drink our beer. Hell no, we can finish this tour. Just get me to L.A.,

Nate. Get me to the Black Flag show. The future of the band depends on that show."

Ericka walked in front of the van to go to the passenger seat. She froze as the engine roared to life and the headlights snapped on. She looked up like a scared deer in the road waiting for death. Nate's hands never moved from the steering wheel.

"She doesn't love you, not really. She was using you for the band. Don't you see if she loved you she would believe in you."

Scott and Denny opened and piled in the side door. Ericka made eye contact with Nate for a long moment. Nate waved her in. She took a careful step.

The van stayed in park, but the engine revved as she stepped. Again she froze, their eyes locked. Nate wondered who she saw in those eyes because he didn't feel in control.

Denny leaned forward "Come on, man, that's fucked up, not even funny."

Nate wanted to tell him it wasn't him, that his foot never touched the gas pedal. That he didn't even turn on the van. That would only make matters worse. Nate waved her closer again. She was angry, and didn't hide it as she came around the van. As soon as she was in, Scott slid the side door shut. Nate put the van in drive and headed back for the highway.

***

Ericka didn't know what to say. She didn't think Nate could ever intentionally intimidate her like that. So much of his behavior was out of character. In her most honest reflections, even when he made love to her, it was out character. (She didn't mind then.) The debate raged in her mind as she took her seat in the van.

A part of her thought it was the van that threatened her. She slammed the door as hard as she could getting back in, but Nate didn't seemed phased. He just pulled them out on to the two lane highway like nothing big had happened.

Now that the sun was up, she could see how desolate this

part of the country was. She looked out the back window and saw the gas station disappear.

"Nate, we need to have a serious talk."

Nate reached to the stereo and turned up the Circle Jerks song playing on the mix CD. There wasn't a more clear Fuck You available to him.

Ericka turned it back down. "You can't just ignore it, Nate. We told you last night the tour has got to end. We tried to keep a positive attitude, but it's time."

Nate gripped the steering wheel tighter but didn't say anything.

"Nate? Come on?"

He ignored her, just stared at the road. A long silent minute passed, feeling like twenty. The silence was brutal.

"Nate, this is bullshit, man," Denny pleaded.

He didn't say anything. After a few minutes he squinted. The van sputtered and suddenly braked. Denny and Scott were not buckled in and flew into the front seats screaming. If not for the seat belt Ericka would have gone through the windshield.

Zines and records flew around the van. Ericka screamed and looked up to see they had screeched to halt along the road.

"We're here," Nate finally spoke in a whisper. "I'm ready to do it."

***

Ericka leaned closer to try and hear what he said. Nate lunged at her and all she saw was a flash of silver. Pain radiated, and she heard her seat belt click off. A moment later the door opened and she felt herself fall.

The pain of hitting the gravel was nothing compared to the pain in her face. When the flash in her eyes faded she saw blood from her face drip on the ground.

She heard the sound of Scott and Deny yelling. Ericka tried to get up but her whole body was overtaken by dizziness. She looked up in time to see Denny drop next from the van. He had a large gash on his head. He wasn't out, but disoriented enough that he couldn't stand.

Scott stepped out of the van on his own, his hands raised. Ericka wiped blood out of her eyes but the morning looked like a film shot with a red filter.

Nate held a wooden Louisville Slugger bat inches from Scott's chest. He reached up the bat ready to swing it down. Nate was sweating part of him ready, to swing and something held him back. Ericka saw the struggle, the confusion.

"Don't let him do it, Nate!"

"Step back," Nate plead.

"Be cool, man," Scott begged.

Nate gripped the bat tighter. He shook his head.

"We don't need them. We can finish the tour." Nate sounded different.

"You're fucking crazy, Nate," Scott pleaded. "how you gonna tour without a band?"

Nate reached in the van and threw Ericka's backpack on the ground first, then with heartbreaking thuds she heard Denny and Scott's hit the side of the road.

"Nate, stop please," Ericka begged.

"Don't follow us." Nate slammed shut the sliding door.

Scott reached up and grabbed the door handle. The manual locks all snapped shut at the same time. Scott didn't even notice just kept rattling the door desperately. Ericka watched and reached out.

With effort to fight the pain on her face, Ericka yelled out, "No Nate stop! I love you."

The van tires spun kicking dust gravel in the air as it disappeared. Ericka let the tears come and wept in misery.

CHAPTER 25

Nate flipped the radio on and turned it up as loud as he could. Negative Approach, the old Detroit band, blared so loud the speakers ached with static. In the rear view mirror he saw Scott run onto the highway waving his arms, and for a second he felt guilty. He squeezed the steering wheel and kept his eyes looking forward on the desert highway

"Fucking A plus, man!" Frank said and slapped the dashboard.

Nate practically jumped out of his skin. Frank sat shotgun wearing the same faded Black Flag shirt he wore for the last week of tour. The same shirt he was wearing in the infamous last band photo taken in Houston. He was there bobbing his head to the song. Nate stared at him. Frank pointed at the road.

"Careful, man. Eyes on the road. You have things to do."

Nate turned back to the road and smiled, His favorite Negative Approach song, "Friend or Foe," came on and Frank sang along. They sang along together until the song ended. Frank turned down the speakers.

"That's the fucking spirit!"

Nate looked in the mirror. They had traveled far enough that he couldn't see Scott anymore. He felt waves of guilt, disbelief at his own actions. He hit Ericka in the face, Denny with the bat. He remembered it happening now but didn't remember the decision to act. He wouldn't have done it. He couldn't hurt Ericka. What had he done?

The van rattled. He looked at their speed, close to eighty-five MPH. The vision of Ericka's bleeding face flashed in his mind.

"What did you do?" Nate pleaded but when he looked to the passenger seat it was empty. Nate turned down the stereo to a whisper. "Frank?" He hated the sound of desperate fear in his voice.

"They wanted to ruin the whole tour," said Frank in a soft voice. Nate wasn't sure if it was in his mind. Nate looked into the rear view mirror. He saw his own face. He heard his own voice but it wasn't his words.

"That's right." Nate didn't recognize the smirk on his own face.

"Don't feel bad, Nate. I was ready to kill 'em. You saved their lives. It's over now, time to seize your potential. They don't see like you do."

Nate wanted to hit the brakes, but his foot was suddenly lead on the gas.

"You see, Nate. You see me for a reason. Hell, you're the fifth fucking Beatle man! You always were."

"Me?" Nate grinned. "For real?"

"Hell yeah, man! You were meant to be a Fucker all along. You think it was an accident you found the van?"

"No, I don't." Nate squeezed the steering wheel. "Where we going?"

Frank's finger pointed forward.

"You let me worry about that. The tour is booked."

***

Ericka was afraid to open her eyes. The sound of the occasional passing trucks and cars were nerve-wracking. She lay on the ground, crying. He had finally lost his mind, completely and she was the one that had tried to convince them to stay. This was all her fault. She didn't look up in shame as much as in fear of the situation.

Finally, Ericka did an upward dog yoga pose to push herself up. Scott and Denny were trying to wave down a car that passed, filled with a very nervous looking family. They sped on, leaving them alone in the quiet New Mexico desert.

All Ericka could hear was her own breathing. Her nose wasn't as crushed as she first feared, and the blood had quickly dried and crusted in each nostril. She had no idea how long they sat there. Denny leaned down in a catcher's stance to look at her nose.

"I bet it feels worse than it looks."

Ericka would have laughed, but that would have hurt. "I don't give shit how it looks."

"You're going to have a shiner. You have any water in your bag?"

She looked over to her backpack and knew that her water bottle was still on the floor of the van by the passenger seat. She reached for her backpack and unzipped. She dug through the extra pair of clothes and didn't find the bottle. She almost laughed looking at the Fucker's tour journal.

"No water, but..." She held up the tour journal.

"Doesn't really help us, Ericka."

"Going to help me find Nate."

"Oh, fuck that, fuck him," Scott said standing in the road. "I think I see a truck."

Ericka put out her hand, and Denny pulled her up. The morning was still chilly, as the sun was still climbing. They didn't know where they were besides generally in New Mexico. She looked west and assumed that was their best bet.

"You have any ideas?" Denny asked, putting on his hoodie. Ericka shook her head, and didn't want to think about walking. She and Denny both had emergency credit cards from their parents. If they could get to a town, they could rent a car. Maybe find a Greyhound station. Denny and Scott wanted to fly home.

Scott stood in the road. Untouched by the violence, he seemed the most angry of the three of them. Ericka stared to the west, all of her thoughts and internal prayers focused on seeing the van, and minute after minute passed with nothing.

"Come on, Nate," she whispered, admitting to herself that he wasn't coming back.

Scott didn't shut up. "I'm going to kill that fucking motherfucker. When we get back to Bloomington, I swear to god..." and on it went.

Denny waved him off. He walked back to Ericka. "There

is a part of me that's relieved," he laughed.

Ericka looked at him and around to the open desert. She gave him an evil eye, but a part of her understood. He had given up on Nate. He was just happy and felt safer to be away from him.

"I can't give up on him. You know that wasn't him acting. Our Nate would never do that."

"I know that, you know that. I am not sure I can convince Scott or anyone else."

Ericka felt the stabbing guilt. They should've never gotten back in the van in Houston. This was her fault. Scott started jumping up and down, pointing.

"A truck, for real this time!"

"I'm really scared for Nate."

Denny had sympathy on his face, but just a little. "I think you should be a little more worried for us."

"We get to safety and then I'll figure out what to do."

"You still love him?"

Ericka nodded. "I've wanted him since the first moment I met him. I had him, Denny. I know it was just a moment, but I had him. I can't let go now. I also can't let him hurt himself or anyone else."

Scott waved wildly, as a large semi-truck slowed and stopped just down the road. They picked up their backpacks and walked toward the eighteen-wheeler as the brakes blew off steam. Ericka felt nervous about who was behind the wheel of this massive truck that had a Safeway grocery store logo on the side of the trailer.

The door kicked open. The person driving stepped down and out of the truck. Ericka grinned and almost laughed in surprise. It wasn't a big burly redneck guy, but a middle aged Mexican woman wearing a ten gallon hat, which she now tipped gallantly at them.

"What the hell are you doing out here?" she barked in a thick Mexican accent.

"Long story," Scott said.

Ericka stepped forward. "Ma'am, if you could get me into town, I can come back for my friends."

Scott shook his head ready to climb aboard. Denny pulled his old friend back. "Chill out."

The driver lady looked closer at Ericka and the wound on Denny. "Looks like someone hurt you folks."

Ericka nodded. They were in a bad spot anybody could see that. The driver looked closer at Denny. She pointed at his forehead.

"I'm Pat. Come on, I got room. I can get you all to Santa Fe. You need help right away."

***

Nate couldn't drive anymore. After arriving in Albuquerque, he pulled into the first park parking lot he could find. He put up the sheets and thumbtacks they used to close up the van for privacy and day sleeping.

It was still hot outside, but the dry desert air was a relief, compared to the deep South. He didn't and couldn't think about what he had done. It was best he decided to forget about his life till this point. The mission was everything now.

He hadn't slept in almost twenty-eight hours, and he knew it was Frank driving in every sense, the last few hours. He wanted Frank to just take over and he knew what he needed. To just be a passenger in his own body, or to go back to that simpler time.

Nate was confused, and wanted to finish the tour, but a part of him knew he should resist. He needed the journal. It would take him back away from here. Away from this time.

He reached into his backpack to grab the journal and felt around. Zines, records, a plastic laundry bag with his dirty clothes but the journal wasn't there. He felt a moment of panic, and tore up the trash and stuff on the floor in front of the bench. Nothing.

"Ericka," he said as he leaned back on the bench. He was too tired to be angry. He just laid back and closed his eyes.

He felt that weird feeling of time passing as dreams swirled around him. He saw the desert highway. It rolled in front of him like a film rolling backwards.

The sun reversed until he was standing over Ericka's body. She was naked, beautiful as he had seen her in New Orleans, her hair longer than normal but it spread out on the highway under her. Scorpions were crawling up her legs covering her quickly, like an army of ants discovering a picnic blanket. She screamed until it was impossible to speak his name. The scorpions overran her face drowning the screams.

Nate opened his eyes in the back of the van. The sun had nearly set in the western sky. He hadn't slept long. He looked around and saw that he was alone. He felt a split second of guilt before Frank appeared in the passenger seat. He had his legs up on the dashboard.

"Time to move on. I can see you're not sure about this."

Nate felt the anger flowing through him. Frank had a way of making him feel whole.

"You can't be real."

Frank grinned. *"When did I say that I was?"*

Nate shrugged. "I gave myself to you."

Frank put his feet on the floor of the van and leaned in closer. *"I need you to understand, Nate."*

***

...The van disappeared around Nate. He could feel the engine starting, but it felt far off. It came to life. He felt the movement, but it was invisible. He was swimming in between places he couldn't explain.

He saw a house, a white ramshackle one. The toys in the yard were simple, old school. He didn't know them at first, but then he recognized the Tonka truck and the red and blue Spiderman Big Wheel plastic trike. He wheeled it around the yard until his butt was sore on the plastic seat.

The low rider was his favorite toy. The pebbles in the wheels made a sound as he peddled that was enough to pretend that he was behind the wheel of a Harley like the last temporary Dad who had driven in and out of their lives last year. They moved yet again, and Frank was scared that Mom had forgotten the Big Wheel.

Frank wheeled it around the house that the new temporary Dad gave them. He didn't like the new Dad, but once summer came he liked the house. There was a sidewalk path that went all the way around. He stopped under his parents' bedroom window for a second. He would keep going but he heard his Mom screaming. Frank jumped, startled by her voice, thinking she was yelling at him again.

She wasn't. Frank jumped off and hid under the window so he couldn't be seen, and he listened. Mom was yelling at his temporary father. New Dad had moved them out of their grandparents' house to this Southport house, which meant another new school. Frank knew that, even if they tried not to talk about in front of him.

Mom could get pretty mean. Temp Daddy ignored it for a long time but it wasn't often long before arguments like this one happened. This often meant going back to Grandma's house.

Frank wanted to go back to Grandma's, and didn't want to listen to another temporary Dad punch his mother. He knew there wasn't a thing he could do for her so he got on his big wheel and peddled. The last Dad almost killed them both. He rolled away from the house heading to his grandparents' house.

He could hear Mom screaming down the block. Lightning flashed in the clear sky, stopping him in place. Frank had no idea that was the last time he would hear his mother's voice.

Grandpa and Grandma said she had to move to Ohio for a job. No more temporary Dads, but that meant school in Greenwood with his friends. So Frank didn't complain when she didn't come to visit.

It wasn't until Frank was thirteen years old that he found out the last temporary Dad, a man named Harold, had beaten her to death. He made a clumsy attempt at trying to make it look like suicide. Mom's face had been smashed before Harold put a pistol in her dead hand and shot her...

***

...Nate woke from the vivid memory for a moment and swung his head back and forth. Frank's childhood home faded into the desert highway coming toward him under over the van. Lightning flashed, not in the sky but it seemed to flash in the windshield.

The van faded away. Nate watched as an office formed around him. A man with greased-back grey hair and wire-rimmed glasses sat across a desk from him. The room felt real enough that the smell of hair grease and brand new basketballs piled in a trash can in the corner filled the air. The man tapped a pencil and lectured.

"This is a respectable school. You come in here dressed like some kinda carnival freak, and I can't protect you."

Frank had heard this lecture twice already this year. He leaned back in his chair.

"That's crap, I don't threaten people just cuz' they wear Izods."

"People feel threatened by you, Mister Huff."

"Mister Miller, I didn't do anything. I was just walking and they tried to—"

"Push down your, uh, Mohawk."

This was a full year before Frank shaved his head. His Mohawk was as tall as most of Greenwood high school's trophies. Two seniors from the varsity football team had bet a dollar they could get his spikes to collapse. The dumbest part is Frank would have let them touch it if they asked nicely.

But when the exchange begins with, "Come here, freak," it is harder to feel helpful. Frank's right eye was black, his nose bleeding, and worst of all it happened to him in the hallway near his fourth period biology class.

Bio was taught by Coach McCall, coach of the football team. He was mandated to have a teaching job, if he wanted to coach. He didn't want to teach Biology, so every day of the year he came in angry. Day one, he told Frank not to come to class until he got a haircut.

Principal Miller couldn't wait to get his grandmother on

the phone. They all wanted Frank to cut off the Mohawk. Eventually McCall had to let him in class. But on this day, the Thursday before the big homecoming game, he couldn't lose two key players. So, the story changed.

According to the coach, his players were minding their own business when Frank slammed one of them against a locker and threatened him. Roth and Lucas hadn't even been taken out of class.

"My grades are good."

"Doesn't matter if you're starting fights."

"That's bullshit. Lucas grabbed my hawk, that hurts—"

"Language," Mr. Miller tapped his pencil on the table harder.

Frank turned red. He burned inside with anger.

"Are you even going to talk to Roth and Lucas? They don't have a scratch on them."

"It is not my fault, Mister Huff that you chose to wrestle with a bear. They bite, you know."

"What the hell are you—?"

"Frank Huff, I am suspending you pending an expulsion hearing with your Grandmother..."

***

...Lightning flashed in the window behind him. Nate saw the desert highway lit by the van's headlights. The lightning streaked back and forth across the windshield. The memories flashed before him like channels flipping past, settling on a bright summer day.

His eyes opened wide on a Burger King parking lot. The bright light of a summer day shocked Nate. Through Frank's eyes he was rolling towards it on a skate board.

Frank pushed his skateboard through the parking lot towards the Burger King. He needed a drink. His Mohawk was wilting in the heat, and the Indianapolis summer afternoon was humid enough to cause sweat sitting still. Stepping into the air conditioning and the smell of flame-grilled cows gave him a second of relief as he wiped the sweat off his forehead.

When he stepped into the restaurant, he saw a group of rednecks in various Skynyrd and Crue shirts drinking milkshakes. Male and female hicks looked him up and down, like he was a naked sasquatch. He sighed. It was 1981 get the fuck over it.

They laughed and kept making jokes to themselves while Frank waited in line. When he got to the register, the woman working seemed nervous as he ordered a Coke. She brought him his drink and Frank carried it out quickly.

Skateboard in one hand and sipping on his drink, Frank relaxed when he stepped out into the lot. After his first drink he saw what looked like the Alpha male hick walking toward him.

He wore a sleeveless Bad Company shirt and walked back towards the Burger King from his giant monster truck. Frank had already been kicked out of school and beaten up several times. He wasn't in the mood to take any shit. The giant looked at Frank and shook his head.

"What are you? Some kind of faggot?"

Frank stopped and smiled at him. "Why, you looking for one?"

The man turned red with embarrassment and got in Frank's face. Frank was tempted to blow him a kiss, but he knew he had already pissed him off.

"Don't get smart with me."

"Yeah, that is not a challenge—"

The huge lumbering man blew his top and swung slowly at Frank. He was slow. Frank dropped his soda and grabbed the back wheels of his skateboard, swinging the board like he was hitting the game-winning ball at the redneck's ugly face. The metal trucks of the skateboard slammed into jaw and skin. The man fell to the parking lot.

Frank swung the skateboard twice down on the man's head, keeping him down. Frank was celebrating inside when he should've been running away. He turned around just in time to see a swarm of faded black shirts jump him. Before he hit the pavement, his skateboard flew out of his grip.

Like a samurai losing his sword, Frank was defenseless. Frank hit the pavement on his back and felt pain everywhere. He endured kicks to his side, his face, punches to his stomach, and a kick to his balls.

"Fucking freak!" They screamed over and over. "Freak, Freak, Freak..."

***

...Nate watched the beating unfold as a reflection in the windshield as it faded back into the desert highway. An older, stronger looking Frank sat in the passenger seat. He turned up the speakers playing a Fuckers bootleg from the last tour. Frank smiled. Nate looked back at him with a grin that he recognized. He had seen it in the mirror many times.

"I'm glad we're on the same page, because without you I can't be in this world."

Nate turned back and watched the white center dashes pass under the van.

"You're my vessel of wrath, Nate."

Frank held a single finger.

"I just have one more thing to show you."

CHAPTER 26

Pat was a truck driver for Safeway and delivered to stores all over the Southwest. Thankfully for them, she was delivering pallets of soda pop to a store on the outskirts of Santa Fe. She was happy to give them a ride, but didn't say much. There was almost a full apartment in the sleeper-cab, which every bandmate envied.

She was grumpy about having to drive the truck into the old narrow downtown of Santa Fe and dropped them off at a Whole Foods. Ericka hugged her and they stumbled into the deli area and sat at a table. Scott put his head down and almost fell asleep.

Ericka walked around the store with her basket getting food and dialing Nate's cell. Every time she got his voicemail.

"Hey, this Nate..."

"...And People's Uprising!" The whole band yelled on the outgoing message."We might be out of range, but we are making our way to your town so please leave a detailed message if this is about a show and we'll call back when we can! Go Vegan! Peace!"

His voice made Ericka break out in tears, standing by the self-serve bagels. She composed herself, rubbing her eyes dry, and got back to shopping. She knew that to the yuppie shoppers she looked like warmed-over hell, but she didn't care.

She used her emergency credit card to buy them all juice and bagels. Denny had Ericka's laptop out, and had found a weak wireless signal. Scott and Ericka cut up the bagels, and Denny worked the Internet despite the slow connection.

"Well?" Ericka chewed on a bagel.

"There's a bus at five we can catch to Albuquerque, three hour layover, and then it's just two more days on the bus we'll be home."

"Two days." Scott looked at his phone. He had already explained everything to Mel best he could. "Dude, fuck that. Mel offered to buy me a plane ticket."

"Well, good for you," Denny said chewing on his bagel. "I can't afford that."

"Use your credit card," said Scott.

"I still have to pay it."

"Fly home, Denny. I'll put it on my mom's card. We'll figure out a way to just pay it back."

Everyone knew Ericka's mom was loaded, a fact she wasn't very proud of.

Her mother was forever upset that her daughter cared more about music than flying to New York for shopping trips. Her step-sister ended up playing that role and never shied away from letting her mom buy her anything.

Denny clicked away at the computer and smiled. "We can fly Southwest and be back to Indianapolis by eleven a.m. tomorrow. Five a.m. flight, we'll just sleep at the airport."

Ericka nodded. She didn't think about home. Indiana seemed to her like it was on another planet, exiled to another lifetime. She could only think about Nate. She felt his touch on her skin like a phantom limb. Denny saw her welling tears, and he held her hand across the table. It was a nice gesture, but it wasn't the hand she needed. Scott didn't know what to say.

"I'm not going home." Ericka wiped a tear away just as it left her eye.

Now Scott knew what to say. "What? Ericka, he hit you."

"I know how this sounds, but I can't leave him."

"Wait a second." Denny dropped his bagel. "I hate to agree with or give credit to anything Scott says, no offense, dude, but Nate left us to die in the fucking desert. You don't owe him shit."

"Exactly," said Scott. "And offense taken by the way."

Ericka ran her fingers through her hair. She needed a shower, sleep, and time to think. She didn't have a single luxury.

"Come on, Denny, it's not him and you know it. He needs someone to believe in him. He is in trouble, really, really bad."

Scott was confused, looking back and forth between them like he was watching a tennis match.

"Say I believe you; I'm not saying I do. How would you find him? He hasn't exactly been taking your calls."

"That's a good question, but I have an answer."

Ericka opened the front pouch of her backpack and laid The Fuckers tour journal on the table.

"Whoa." Scott was still confused. "You stole that from Nate."

"The van wants him to finish the tour, so we have the information. I'll get a rental car, follow the information. There is all kinds of info in here about the other members of The Fuckers. Plus that Greylock guy in Houston, he knows how to find Oscar. I'll call them. They have never talked about what happened, but maybe if we tell them..."

"What do they have to do with this?" Scott shook his head.

"Scott, shut up." Denny kept his eyes on Ericka. "If we go, your mom will pay for it?"

"Money doesn't mean anything to her. She probably won't notice."

Denny looked at Scott and leaned back in his chair. Scott saw it coming before he said a word.

"I'm staying with Ericka."

"You guys are fucking nuts if you think you can just catch up to him and make nice. Finish the tour. As far as I'm concerned he stole my guitar, my cabinet, and left me to starve in the desert. So you better find a new guitar player."

Ericka waved at him and started cleaning up her stuff. "It's not about the tour or the band anymore, Scott. It's about Nate. He is in danger."

"Good." Scott smiled. "Fuck him. I hope he rots."

Ericka slid her chair away from the table with a honk. As she walked away, Denny closed the laptop and got ready to follow her.

"Ok, on that pleasant note I'll see you back in B-town, dude."

"Ericka, you're crazy, dude, just like him," Scott said.

Ericka waited for Denny. He looked at his oldest friend. They had known each other since they were little. They made fun of each other and picked at each other's personal scabs in ways no one else could. At this point he still loved Scott, but he didn't want to try to explain or argue with him, he just wanted him to go home.

"We'll talk when I get home," Denny said, running after her.

***

They got a motel room, because they were both exhausted. Denny watched a little TV before falling asleep, but Ericka was out. When she woke up she walked out onto the staircase of the motel and called her mother.

She didn't want to explain, and just said she was going to be running up the card. She told her not to freak out, but Mom was worried. The call was over quickly without argument.

She tried calling Nate and got the voicemail again. She clicked the phone off and watched the sun dropping down. The New Mexico sunset was beautiful. There were rocky-looking mountains off in the distance, and she felt a chill coming with the night. Nate was out there and he needed her.

Ericka walked back into the room. Denny was up and on her laptop. He had the journal open, and had been reading it. "I reserved the car in your name," He waved her mother's credit card. "We have about a fifteen-minute walk to get the car."

"Awesome." Ericka smiled. She couldn't believe Denny was sticking with her. It made her want to hug him. The bond in the band was pretty tight before the tour. Denny could tell what she was thinking, but he stayed focused.

"The journal stops in Houston, but the contact info and directions for the rest of the tour are all still there. They had a show in Albuquerque. I Mapquested the directions to where it was supposed to have been, and the next show after that was in Phoenix."

"What else have you learned?"

Denny laughed. "For one thing we have it a hell of a lot easier now than when these guys did punk rock. I Googled the band members. Not much luck there. Hairy Gary–they all had hilarious names by the way–died about a year after the tour."

"How?"

"Drug overdose at home alone. His landlord found him a month and half later. Pretty gruesome shit. Oscar the Crotch..."

"The bass player. He was a big junkie, too."

"Yeah, he was but guess what? Greylock was right. We would never have found him without that tip. Not many people are aware of this. Have you heard of the thriller writer Ozzy Hill?"

"Yeah, cookie cutter serial killer mystery novels."

"Same guy."

"Ozzy Hill is Oscar the Crotch." Ericka couldn't believe it.

"Oscar Hill, yep Ozzy Hill's website says he grew up in Indianapolis. Didn't mention the band but why would he?"

Denny swung her computer around so she could get a look at Ozzyhill.com. He was older, clean-cut, but the face was there. It was him.

"I sent him an e-mail telling him that we had the van and need his help."

"He's a best-selling author. I doubt he reads them all."

"He lives in L.A. Maybe we can look him up when we get there."

Ericka laughed at the craziness, and then a moment of sadness hit her.

"What about the drummer? Dickie Abrams. He sold the van to Nate."

Denny sighed. "The weirdest part yet. I called his house. Phone is disconnected, but I got a hold of his parents. They had a lot of stuff to say. I'm kinda shocked they were so..."

Ericka sat down, waving him on to continue.

"His mother said he hung himself in May."

"What? That's when we..."

"Yep, that's when we bought the van. That's not all, his note that he left..."

Ericka could have hit him for pausing like that.

"Well, it was short," Denny gulped. "Frank's coming to get me, to finish the tour."

"The note said finish the tour?" Ericka leaned back.

"Yep, they were hoping I knew what the note meant. It's the only reason they talked."

Denny had his backpack on his shoulder and was ready to go. Ericka closed the computer and looked out the window at the sunset.

"We better find him quick."

CHAPTER 27

Like an ant under a magnifying glass, Nate sat and cooked in the driver's seat. It was eleven a.m. when the sun was high enough over the ridge to shine directly on the windshield. He woke and looked around.

He was parked on the shoulder off of a desert road. It was a dead looking two laner, not an interstate. To his right the view out the passenger window looked like it was pulled straight out of a Western.

He didn't know how long he had slept. His phone rang in his backpack again. It rang almost every hour since yesterday morning. He reached into his bag and flipped it open. Thirty-two missed calls. Most of them were from Ericka.

He didn't even have to look or listen to the thirteen voicemails. He wanted her to stop. Maybe if he answered just once to tell her to go home, she would. Nate looked at the battery symbol.

It was low. One call would kill the power and he didn't know when he would be able to charge it. He saw her name on the caller ID and it triggered something in him.

Nate felt a full wave of remorse washing over him. A moment of disbelief crept into his mind. He looked up and saw Frank in the passenger seat, anger framed his face. His eyes cast judgment on him like a restaurant heat lamp.

"Don't answer it. She just wants to weaken your resolve."

Nate shook his head but clicked on the green button anyways. He put his hand over the receiver and whispered to Frank. "Don't question me, not now." There was a pause on the other end. Ericka wasn't expecting him to answer.

"Nate?"

The sound of her voice was comforting. Nate wasn't prepared for how the sound of her voice made him feel.

Frank slowly shook his head.

"Nate where are you?" The tiny voice came out of the phone.

"Next she's gonna tell you she isn't mad. Its bullshit," said Frank. *"You know she is angry it's a trick."*

There was a pause on the other end.

"What did you say, Nate? Oh come on, I'm not mad, I just want to talk."

Frank raised his eyebrow. Nate put the phone up to his ear.

"You told me punk rock mattered more to you than personal comfort." Nate nodded at Frank as he spoke. "You fucked over the band and me. Worse you lied to me about who you were. You used me."

"Nate, you have to get away from the van. It's doing something to you."

"Tell her not to call again," Frank said pointing at him.

"Don't call again," Nate said. He pulled the phone away from his face. He could hear her call his name as he clicked the phone off. He held the button down turning it off completely and he threw it out the window into the desert. They both laughed. Frank stepped out of the passenger seat and walked around the van to open the door for Nate.

"Come on, one last thing I have to show you..."

***

The phone line was dead. Ericka wanted to smash the phone into the rental's dashboard; she still couldn't accept that he was gone. "Nate!"

Denny kept his eyes on the road and over the steering wheel, but he felt the frustration too. Ericka looked away from him at the rolling New Mexico desert off I-40. She dropped the phone in her lap. Denny nervously tapped the steering wheel. "At least we know he's still alive."

"But where?" Now she cried. Denny gave her a minute to calm down. "What did he say?"

"Nothing," she whispered between sobs.

"Come on now, anything helps."

Ericka thought about his voice, it was deeper, scratchy, barely sounded like Nate anymore. Like someone else speaking with his mouth. Stranger, it sounded like he was talking to himself, telling himself what to do and then responding. Ericka knew in her heart what that meant. She had been suspecting it all along.

"Frank's controlling him."

Denny sighed. She knew how crazy it sounded. It could be mental illness? Could be the stress? But to her it was the only thing that explained what was happening.

***

Nate could feel the heat of the desert floor under the faded soles of his old New Balance sneakers. The sun beat down on them as they walked together off of the road. By his third step into the desert, the clear blue sky changed.

He could see black and grey clouds forming out of nothing just over the ridgeline. A scorpion ran away from the crunching sounds of their footsteps. Snakes burrowed deeper as they passed. The ground rumbled. Far off, thunder pounded from the heavens.

They had only gone about a hundred feet. Nate stopped to watch the unnatural storm forming. The wind picked up and chilled the air.

Frank laughed. "Looks like we got here just in time."

Lightning flashed across the sky. Another rumble of thunder followed shortly. "Maybe we ought to go back?" Nate was almost whining.

"You consider yourself more than just a fan of The Fuckers, right?"

Nate nodded, trying to stand still as the wind pushed him around. His skin goose-fleshed in the sudden cold air. "Sure. Maybe we could talk about this later or in the van."

"No. The time is now. Let me ask you, Nate, when was the first time you heard one of our records?"

Nate sighed. "Eighth grade, I think, I was hanging with

Danny Ewing my neighbor. His sister was into punk, and we liked Green Day and shit. But, man, I never heard anything like The Fuckers."

"What did it sound like to you?"

"It wasn't like the shit now, it was raw. Wild and untamed, just fucking crazy. When I heard 'Dear Congressman, Fuck You' it spoke to me. All the old stuff, Bad Brains, Minor Threat, or 7 Seconds. It was like they were speaking for me."

"All those other bands were famous in the underground, but The Fuckers were almost lost. Not to you. That's because you were meant to hear it, Nate."

Nate understood, and nodded.

"How long have you wondered what happened after Houston?"

"Oh, man, that's like the biggest legend in Indiana hardcore. I mean, there are all kinds of theories. I guess since that first time I heard the record."

Thunder rumbled and the wind picked up again. This time it felt even stronger. Frank stood there unaffected, but Nate looked like a reporter covering a hurricane.

"You lived with the mystery all these years. I'm going to give you the answers."

He wasn't yelling to be heard over the storm. Despite the roar of the wind, Nate heard his voice clear inside his mind. They were one, after all.

Frank kept walking out into the desert, until they stopped at a small rock outcropping. A hand stuck out of the desert frozen in a grip. The skin had long ago decayed down to bone. The wind came across the desert, straight for the spot where the hand rested.

It blew the sand away with enough force to reveal the shape of a skeleton. Nate stepped back knowing exactly what he was looking at.

"This, Nate, is where the tour ended."

Lightning flashed across the sky and struck the van. Nate screamed, between the wind and the thunder he knew was coming, he covered his ears and closed his eyes. The howl of the wind was gone. The thunder never came.

Nate heard his rapid breathing. He was afraid to open his eyes.

"It's okay, Nate." Frank's voice was soothing, inside him. He felt safer just hearing it. *"Open your eyes. I want you to see this."*

Nate opened his eyes and the desert was gone. He was in the van.

The Van hacked and spat like a cat trying to cough out a hairball. After thousands of miles in the short two years of the Chevy van's life, it was already pushed beyond reasonable expectations. Frank was white-knuckling the steering wheel, trying to will the engine not to die. Smoke rose out of the hood from the overheated engine. His bandmates were waking, putting down magazines, and realizing the danger they were suddenly in.

Dickie reached up and turned down the mix tape that was blasting the Zero Boys so all the cursing and pleading could be heard. He had been nervously playing with the safety pin he put through his nose after he lost his nose ring.

Oscar rolled around in the loft that housed the bed over their equipment. He looked out the window and squinted at the desert sun. His Mohawk had sagged and flattened since he fell asleep in the van.

Nate floated inside the van, his skin glowing. He looked at his luminous hands. He was right between Oscar and Frank. He waved his hands around, and it was clear they didn't see him.

Just watch, Nate.

The van came to a stop.

CHAPTER 28

"It's a parking lot now," Denny said as he turned off the rental car. Ericka stepped out into the unbearable Phoenix mid-afternoon heat and looked at the cars lined up in the rows outside of the Rite Aid. She looked at the old yellowing notebook. This was the street where The Fuckers show was supposed to be held in 1982.

The Jamba Juice next to the drug store was just two numbers off the address for the warehouse where punk shows happened, according to the tour journal. An older man in a` Rite Aid uniform and massive sun hat pushed a bunched set of carts past.

His sleeve lifted slightly to show what looked like a faded Misfits skull tattoo on his arm. Ericka smiled at the luck. She walked beside, having to yell over the loud rattle of the rolling carts.

"Excuse me," Ericka yelled louder. "Excuse me!"

The man kept pushing. "What?"

"Can I ask you something?"

"I'm a little busy..." He stopped when he saw Ericka. He didn't hide the fact that he was basically stopping because she was cute. Ericka knew he was old enough to be her father, but ignored the creepiness for the moment. He wiped sweat from his forehead on to his short sleeve. "How can I help you, ma'am?"

Denny walked up behind her. The aging rocker looked like the wind had been knocked from his sails.

"I was wondering if you remember a warehouse that used to be around here. They used to hold punk shows, back in the day."

He laughed. "Way back in the day. Yeah, the Metal Factory. All the greats played there." He lifted his sleeve and pointed at his tattoo. "Even the Misfits."

"Rad." Ericka acted impressed, smiling as big a fake smile as she could muster. She waved at the expanding strip mall with Home Depot and Wal-Mart.

"It was right here by all these stores."

"Nah, none of this shit was here till the '90s. In the '70s and 80s this whole area was abandoned metal works. Who wants to work metals in Arizona, right? Most of the factories were condemned. Kinda creepy, but awesome shows. They built a stage right in the middle of a skate ramp. Hotter than hell in there, but shit it is Arizona."

"So they rented out the place to have shows?"

"I think they were squatting the place. The police shut it down. Got ugly."

Ericka looked around tried to imagine the scene. Old dusty dirty factory with skater and punk kids breaking in and building a stage. It was right here on this spot decades ago. Now all traces of it all were gone. All of it, lost in the suburban sprawl.

Ericka pulled out her digital camera and scrolled to a picture of Nate and the van. She held it up for the guy.

"Have you seen this van or this guy?"

She scrolled to a picture of the van and back to Nate.

He looked at it. He shook his head. "Nope. I notice punks. I mean ones with old school stickers and shit. Around here, it's Hot Topic-ville, so I would have noticed a van like that."

Ericka put the camera away and pulled out a piece of scrap paper. She had written a brief description of Nate and the van. The picture of Nate was of him smiling in front of the van before the tour. Looking at the picture the night before had sent her off into tears. Seeing Fort Flop and their practice space in the background was gut-wrenching. She wanted so badly to be there with him now. "If you see him, will you please call my number?"

"Your number, sure."

"If you see him," Denny added speaking for the first time.

"He owe you money?"

"Don't worry about it, just call us if you see him. It's important. We think he is looking for this old warehouse like us."

He didn't understand what she meant, or why anybody would give a shit about seeing the parking lot that had been a punk venue so far back in the day hardly anyone without grey hair would remember. Ericka could read it all in his face.

He started pushing his carts again.

"Hey, you mind if I show the picture to some of your employees?"

He didn't even turn around. "We're busy working, honey."

He disappeared into the store. Ericka dropped her cellphone into her pocket. The afternoon was ungodly hot. Denny, who was never a fan of AC, blasted it in their rented Prius. He turned the car back on, moved the seat back, and turned on the laptop.

He was already on his phone. Having the brand new car felt very odd to them both when they left New Mexico, after driving a burnt-out crazy old van for three weeks. Even the wonders of fully-functional power steering felt strange.

Denny was online from a signal coming out of a Starbucks in the Wal-Mart, but since she started walking back to the car he was on the phone. She opened the door and smiled at the relief brought by the AC.

"...no my name is Donald Nilsson. I'm with, uh, *People* magazine. It's just for a website column, but I assure you I'm well read."

Ericka laughed, and Denny waved at her to stop.

"Yes, I'd be willing to meet with Mister Hill in LA."

Ericka shook her head and mouthed the words 'Phone number.'

"Actually, a phone interview today might make the print edition."

Ericka waited while he listened; she was worried they wouldn't get it. Denny smiled and gave her a thumb up.

"Twenty minutes would be great. Thank you."

Denny hung up the phone. "You ready to talk to Oscar?"

"*People* magazine?"

"Hey, it worked. If Frank is sending Nate after him, I think it's our best bet."

***

They moved into the Starbucks to give the car a rest. Politically and ethically speaking, they both hated Starbucks. Even just for Starbucks, they felt underdressed. Denny got a rooibos tea and plopped down in a fancy chair. They stared at the cellphone, waiting for Denny's ringtone sampled from a Dead Prez song to ring. When it did he let it go for a few seconds before answering.

His number came up blocked on the caller ID. Denny cursed that as he answered the phone. Ericka got up beside Denny so she could listen.

"Hi, Donald Nilsson, please?"

"Speaking, and you must be Oscar Hill."

Denny cringed a little, maybe it was too early. He got nervous that he had overplayed his hand. There was a pause on the other line.

"I suppose that's what my birth certificate says, but, uh, no one, not even my folks, calls me Oscar anymore."

Ericka spun her finger encouraging him to go for it. She whispered "This may be it."

Denny nodded. "I would like to ask you about Frank Huff?"

"Who are you?"

"I'll be straight with you. I'm not a reporter. My name is Denny. I play drums for a hardcore band from Bloomington Indiana..."

"Uh, hardcore? Look, I'm a mystery author and I'm very busy. I don't do fanzine interviews."

"Our singer bought a van from Dickie Abrams. He was your drummer." Silence on the other line. Denny cleared his throat. "We took the van on tour and—"

"Look, I'm gonna tell you what I've been telling Dickie

for twenty years and then I'm hanging up. I know what Dickie says that van does, how it fucking behaves. Get rid of that fucking van, drive it off a fucking cliff if you have to."

The phone clicked off. Ericka fell back on the couch. Denny dropped the phone and fell back next to her. She looked at him. "Okay, the first call was slick, but that last one was fucking dumb. Try to be subtle next time."

"What was this shit?" He mocked her spinning her finger. "You told me to go for it."

Ericka got up and stormed out the door. Denny looked at the time on his phone.

"Where are you, Nate?" he whispered to the universe.

CHAPTER 29

"Band meeting!" Frank shouted as he put on a clean(er) Black Flag shirt. Nate walked behind him. He wasn't really there. He couldn't feel the desert heat or wind whipping in the air. He wasn't a passenger with Frank like his past trips. No one could see him now, not even Frank. He followed him but tried to stay out of the way.

Gary had the hood up and poured water into the radiator when Frank tapped him on the shoulder. Oscar and Dickie stepped around the van. They were both rail thin when they left Indiana, and now skeletal. Dickie had left his mohawk flat since Florida and he looked broken. Oscar had a kind of determination in his eye. Despite his near-deathly visage, he had a serious expression on his face.

"Good idea," Oscar said and sat down on the ground by the van. Frank sat across from him, Gary beside him, but Dickie remained standing. Oscar gave him an impatient look. Frank gave him a moment to sit, but he didn't. A semi-truck zoomed past and Frank found his focus.

"We're finishing the tour..."

Oscar shook his head. "How exactly are we going to do that?"

"The van is just overheated," said Frank. "It will be fine."

"We're playing L.A. with Flag. We can't miss that," Gary added. Dickie and Oscar were worried that Frank had invented the Black Flag show in L.A. just to convince Gary to go on the tour. It was the summer before he started at Indiana University. His parents didn't want him to go on tour and the only thing that would make it worth the arguments with his parents would be sharing the stage with his favorite band.

Gary, who started the tour a light drinker, had been drunk almost every night for the last week. He wasn't the only person in the band to do almost as many drugs as Oscar. Dickie had taken every free hit he could.

"We're in trouble now, deep shit. I'm not talking just the van or money—"

"Fucking pussy." Frank cut off Oscar off "You want go run home to Momma. After all we've seen. We've got things to do."

"What is that, Frank? What do we have to do? Kill more people."

"Everything I did was justified. People who meant to do us harm."

Nate watched Oscar go to the back of the van and open the back doors. He was searching for something. He couldn't make out what it was.

"We're finishing the tour!" Frank yelled in his vocalist voice.

Oscar stopped and turned around. "Yeah, we are, right now." Oscar came back around the corner. "That Sheriff didn't have to die."

"Oscar, you are so fucking naïve. That prick was ready to throw us in the fucking clink. Because why?"

Oscar took a deep breath. "What about the farmer in South Carolina, or the diner guy. Frank, you are a fucking serial killer, and if we ignore it that makes us guilty too."

"Fuck, man..." Dickie's face showed that he hadn't thought about it that way.

"I didn't hurt nobody." Gary's voice was filled with dread.

Oscar started with a stunted laugh. "You know what, Frank? I am sick and fucking tired of your bullshit. Nobody but you believes in this Grand War On Jocks crap. I'm tired of your disrespect. I'm tired of your speeches. It's fucking music and clothes. Nothing more. It's not worth killing for. It sure as hell isn't worth prison or dying for."

"You didn't answer the question, Oscar. Why was that fucking pig going to arrest us? What had we done?"

"I think everybody needs to relax and take some, like, yoga breaths or something," Gary said, sounding slightly drunk.

"Oscar is right, dude. We're in fucking deep shit." Dickie walked over to Gary and patted him on the shoulder. "Frank, it's your fault, man."

"Listen up, you goddamn pussies." Frank stepped closer to Oscar. Frank seemed surprised, as they stood face to face, that Oscar held his ground. "We are on a fucking mission. This tour will end when I say it does. Any motherfucker out there who gets in our way has to pay. Plain and simple. If they don't want to die they just have to act civil."

Oscar shook his head in disbelief. He looked at Gary and Dickie. Even Gary looked a little more sobered up. "Fuck you, Frank," said harmless, milquetoast Gary. It was strange, hearing anger from Gary's lips. "Seriously, fuck you, man."

Nate watched helpless. He could see all the anger swirling around Frank. He knew Frank didn't take any of his bandmates seriously as a threat. Nate moved behind Oscar and saw a pistol stuffed between his back and his pants.

"Frank!" Nate yelled. He couldn't be heard. He was a ghost watching history unfold. "Frank!" he shouted again, knowing it was useless.

"You're crazy, Frank," Oscar said as he reached behind him and pulled the Sheriff's stolen revolver out. He held it out pointed two feet from Frank's chest. Frank took small careful steps toward Oscar.

Nate stepped closer, watching unnoticed. He wished he could step in and help Frank. He was afraid to watch, but had to keep his eyes open.

Dickie stepped behind Oscar. "Do it, man," he whispered. Gary stepped closer, but was afraid to get in front of the gun.

"Let's talk about this. We're almost to L.A." Frank had his hands up but was just inches from the barrel now.

Oscar squeezed the handle of the gun. His finger wasn't even close to the trigger. He was afraid. The barrel bounced slightly in his hand as it shook. Frank got a step closer. Oscar used his thumb to pull on the hammer. He was so weak from the heroin he could barely do it. Oscar lifted the pistol higher towards Frank's head. His arm got weak quickly.

Frank walked until his forehead was on the barrel. He

stared through hate-filled eyes at Oscar. "You're as bad as the fucking pigs, all of you."

Oscar gulped. He felt like pissing himself. Dickie was behind him whispering, "Do it."

"That's what I thought, pussy." Frank stepped back and turned around. Nate felt relief. Watching this was awful. Why didn't they understand what was happening? Hadn't they seen Philadelphia, hadn't they lived through the struggles of their own being different in the world? Frank opened the driver's side door and got back in the van.

"Quit your fucking whining and get back in the van," Frank yelled as he put the key in the ignition. He was just turning it, to see if it would start. The engine sparked to life just as Oscar ran up to the open driver's side window. Frank saw him huffing and puffing like a wet and angry dog, for just a split second. Oscar pointed the gun in the van.

Nate screamed "No!" hearing his own voice echo in the other realm.

Oscar looked unprepared for the power of the blast. He squeezed the trigger, aiming the heavy gun at Frank's skull. He was knocked back on to the empty road and the bullet hit the metal frame of the van. Dickie turned away and covered his ears.

The blast would echo in his hearing for hours and his hearing was never the same. Nate watched the bullet burst through Frank's neck and land in the passenger seat, sending little pieces of foam into the air. He had sat on that hole in chair a hundred times and never once thought he would learn how it happened.

Oscar fell back onto the pavement and screamed. He couldn't hear anything. His ear drums felt like a small person had a fist up each one. He had never fired a gun, and he wasn't prepared for the raw power. Dickie tried to help him up. Nate moved to the driver's side door and helplessly watched Frank. He held on to the steering wheel.

His neck was spitting blood like a knocked-over fire hydrant. Frank opened his mouth to scream, but spit up even more blood. His throat was torn apart. Parts of it were now resting on the passenger seat, the horn, and the windshield. His body shook violently as he bled to death gripping the steering wheel.

"Finish the tour," he said in a garbled voice that his wrecked throat struggled to make.

Dickie tried to prop up Oscar who couldn't hear him screaming in his face. He saw his mouth moving but he heard nothing. He looked up at the van and saw blood everywhere. Oscar began to laugh manically.

"Finish him off, goddamn it!" Dickie yelled as he grabbed the smoking gun from Oscar's hands. Dickie stood up and pointed the gun at Frank's head. He shook as well. Now standing with a gun pointed at his friend's head, fear gripped him. Fear of Frank, fear of the blast, fear of the sound of the blast.

Frank turned to him. His throat was gushing, but his hands were gripping the steering wheel. His eyes were wide, burning with intense hatred, the kind that Dickie imagined you came home from war with.

"Finish the..." Frank tried to speak, but a mouthful of blood poured out of his mouth down the driver's side window. Dickie closed his eyes and pulled the trigger. Nate turned away, unable to watch. He felt the anger sparking a massive flame of hatred deep inside him. They were the ones who killed Frank. They ended his life, they ruined the band, destroyed the mission.

Nate wanted to hurt them, wanted to make them pay.

***

Gary accidentally hit the horn as he wiped a chunk of Frank's brain off of it. Across the desert floor the sound of the horn startled Oscar. He kicked the sand back over the trail of blood that had followed Frank's burst-open head. Dickie held on to Frank's ankles and dragged his body. He couldn't look at Frank's destroyed head, or the halo of flies that were following them.

"Dude, it's totally your turn." Dickie dropped Frank's legs with a thud.

Oscar looked back to see what Gary was honking about. His heart raced, positive it was a cop pulling up. A few cars zoomed by, mostly trucks along the road, but the traffic was light and if anybody saw what happened they must have assumed it wasn't their business. Thankfully no one was feeling helpful enough to stop them.

Gary leaned out of the van holding one of Frank's shirts covered in blood. "Sorry, I was cleaning the steering wheel."

Dickie breathed hard and looked around. He needed to pull Frank a few more feet behind a rock so he could not be seen from the road.

"Dude, what are we going use to dig?"

Oscar shrugged. "We don't have to go deep. No one is out here, and no one is looking." Oscar waved him on. "Come on, before another truck goes by.

Dickie pulled the body a few more feet, around the rock outcropping. "What are we gonna tell people, back in Indy, I mean?" Frank's open wound seemed to catch on a stone firmly in the earth. A chunk of his brain stuck on the stone.

"He ditched us after Houston, met some chick, and took off," Oscar said as he used the heel of his combat boot to push the brain piece into the sand. He kicked sand over it to give it cover.

"I don't know, man. That doesn't sound like Frank. I mean that dude loved punk more than pussy."

Oscar looked back. They were probably a hundred feet from the van. Nobody would see Frank if they weren't looking for him.

"I guess he met someone special." Oscar reached down and started digging with his hands. The ground was soft sand but it was hard work doing it without tools even though they weren't going deep. Dickie grabbed a large stone and soon they were both digging as fast as they could.

"You think you could play bass and sing the songs?" Dickie mumbled the question while digging. "I mean, maybe we could still play with Flag."

"I don't even know all the lyrics." Oscar couldn't believe he was thinking about it. "Playing shows is the last thing on my mind."

Nate walked up behind them in his ghostly form and watched as they made their hole. Frank's body was getting purple and stiff. His ghost came up beside him. They were two spirits watching the final indignity of his murder. The ridiculous half-assed attempt at burial.

"You see what kind of dipshits I was dealing with?"

"If we don't play the show, how are we going to get money to get home?" Dickie sounded defeated.

"We'll see how it goes." Oscar stopped and looked at Frank's head. He felt like puking, he held it in. "One show then I'll sell my bass and my cabinet in L.A. I'm going home."

Frank's ghost turned to Nate and looked him in the eye. *"You see now? They killed me. Cold fucking blood, they killed me. They killed The Fuckers, the tour, and worst of all, man, they killed the mission."*

Nate felt woozy as he stared at the rock outcropping. The sky turned dark and the skin and bones gave way to a skeleton. They barely hid the body, not even deep enough to keep it covered over the years.

Nate was back in the real world. Lightning flashed in the sky and thunder rumbled. It shook Nate and brought him back. The transition shocked him. The wind blew like a major storm hitting. The sky was almost black in the west, but in the east the sun shone.

The wind had been blowing so hard the sand was flying away from him in giant swirls. He saw it now, just as it was laid to rest twenty-four years earlier. The skeleton supported a few pieces of decaying fabric stained in blood, but the Black Flag symbol was still there. It was Frank's body, what was left of it.

You see now. You are my vessel. You must finish the tour.

Nate looked around but Frank's ghost wasn't there anymore. He felt him in every fiber of his being. He would never be alone again. He flexed his hand. He felt stronger. He felt more will and determination. Nate walked back towards the van.

"I see, it's my duty, they must pay."

Frank was happy and amused. Nate laughed for him.

CHAPTER 30

They made the best of their time in Phoenix. Denny knew he had to make up for screwing up their contact with Ozzy Hill. They got a motel room with Wi-Fi and got to work on the laptop doing research. Denny went to message boards and chat rooms devoted to Hill fans. For a bestselling author with a rabid fanbase, there were many, including a thread for his L.A. fans.

One interesting tidbit he learned was that every day at three, Hill quit writing for the day and walked to a Coffee Bean and Tea Leaf near his Beverly Hills condo to read the paper and eat a Danish. The word was that he was currently working in L.A. on a tight deadline for a novel whose film rights had already been sold.

They planned on following The Fuckers' tour journal to the next show on the tour. Ericka decided that was where they needed to be. Oscar was there, and the mythological Black Flag show was to be held somewhere there. The information for the show was strange and cryptic. The journal said they were to meet the show promoter at a golf course. That was it. It didn't seem possible that the show was with Black Flag.

Denny barely slept, and when he did wake he saw Ericka's face lit only by the glow of the laptop screen. They had spent hundreds of dollars of her mother's money. Ericka uploaded tour photos to her laptop and posted pictures of Nate and the van to the People's Uprising message board.

She registered and signed up for all the local punk boards in Phoenix and L.A. asking for people to e-mail her if they saw Nate or the van, to keep their eye out for him. Every stop along the way she looked for an Internet signal to check for responses.

As they were nearing L.A., someone had e-mailed them a

219

picture of the van parked in Los Angeles. They Mapquested the directions to the spot and sat still in the City of Angels' legendarily horrible traffic before finding it.

The van had been parked by a Burger King in Torrance just south of the city line. They pulled into the parking lot just before noon. Ericka jumped out of the Prius and stared at the doors to the fast-food place. Denny stepped out happy to be free of the Arizona heat.

"What was Nate doing at a Burger King?"

Ericka walked to the sidewalk by the busy road that led into south central Los Angeles. She pointed at what looked like a park. "The golf course."

Denny sighed. "Doesn't make any sense. What are we going to do? Play a round of golf to look for him?"

"Just let me think." Ericka didn't know what to do. She avoided making eye contact, afraid she would tear up.

"It's a dead end. We have to talk to Oscar."

She said nothing, just stared down the road at the golf course.

"He was here," she whispered. Denny got in the car. They had two hours before Oscar was due to take his break at the Coffee Bean and Tea Leaf in East Hollywood. They might need every minute in L.A.

***

At 2:53, they sat down at the coffee shop and waited. Ericka tapped her Chuck Taylors nervously. "If we talk to him, he'll just walk away."

Denny had already considered this. "According to the woman in the chatroom, as long as we're young and attractive to him, he's a sucker. He sleeps with anyone with a pulse. So use your charms and maybe he'll talk to you?"

"Me?" Ericka smiled. "Why not you?"

"I was told he always makes conversation with cute young girls, real trite stuff."

"He sounds gross."

"Just talk to the man," Denny said and set himself up at

220

another table. Ericka sat on the couch and she felt ugly. She almost never worried about how she looked, even around Nate. But now his life might depend on if she looked cute enough for a creepy old man.

It was a strange feeling, one she hated. Even though she had showered in the last day and her black and green hair was brushed and bobbed over her shoulder, she suddenly felt very dirty.

Twenty minutes passed and she started to relax and feel more like herself. He probably wasn't coming. Then the door opened. He looked even older in person. Not like Keith Richards or Iggy Pop's warmed-over death look, but old after all the young photos she had seen.

He wore thin glasses and three-hole oxblood Doc Martens. They were worn-in and stylish. He looked around as he walked in. If the word got out to his fans that he came here, and he kept coming back he must not have minded. He must have enjoyed the ego stroke or he would go somewhere else.

He looked at her as he walked to the counter. His eyes lingered on her. Nate once told her that she had a charming and radiant smile. *'Don't smile while were playing. It's too cute for punk,'* he joked with her in a rare early sign of flirtation. If Nate thought her smile worked, why not? She smiled at Oscar.

His eyes stayed on her a second too long. He was signaling that he noticed and she wanted to barf. He was old enough to be her father. Out of the corner of her eye she saw Denny wink at her. The game was on.

Oscar waited for his drink and sat down on a couch across a coffee table from her. "You mind if I sit here?"

She really did mind, but this man was the key to more information and she had to work him. She had never played the flirting lady role in her life. "Not at all. I was kinda bored anyway."

"Well, I like getting out and meeting people. My job keeps me at home in solitary confinement you might say."

"Well, its L.A., let me guess, you're a screenwriter."

Ericka turned up the smile. Oscar took a sip of his drink. He had a smug look that he was probably not aware was broadcasting what he was thinking. *'I can't believe my luck.'*

"I've had my work adapted for the screen, but, no, I'm a novelist." Ericka snapped her fingers and pointed acting like she was trying to figure out who he was.

"You're uh...Wait don't tell me...okay, tell me."

"Ozzy Hill. I wrote—"

"*Rocking the Cradle.* I love that movie! You're awesome! I'm Ericka, by the way."

Ericka had read about how much Oscar hated the big screen adaptation of his novel, where the ending and all the major characters were changed. She was surprised that he was able to maintain his smile.

"It's an early work, but my new novel..."

"You're still writing?" Ericka smiled and played dumb this time she knew what she was saying. A new Ozzy Hill novel came out like clockwork as winter settled in November. His publishers flooded the Thanksgiving weekend airport bookstores and like magic he hit the top of the *New York Times* bestseller list every year. His light breezy mysteries were designed for airline reading.

"Oh, I love writing. I have a new book almost every year," Oscar smiled.

Ericka could see him as the same man in the face, but he didn't feel punk in any way, shape or form now. She would never have guessed who he was, that was for sure.

"How do you find time to write, and, uh, stay in shape like that?"

That was over the top, and she knew it. He wasn't fat, but not skinny like he had been when he was younger. Behind them Denny dropped his head on the table with a smack. He looked back to see what made the sound but quickly turned back to Ericka.

"Would you like to have dinner with me tonight, Ericka? I'm a fantastic cook, better cook than an author."

Ericka didn't want to wait to get information, but she knew he would be gone. She felt uneasy about it, but it was time for plan B. The plan she refused to consider when Denny suggested it. She leaned forward and he did too.

Their faces were inches apart over the table. She was grossed-out by his teeth, which were yellow at the bases. He was seriously in need of a good floss. She tried to act turned on even though his breath reeked like tombstones.

"Why have dinner when we could have dessert right now?"

She felt him watching her as she got up. He saw the punk patches on her hoodie and she wondered if he got nostalgic for the old days. What better way for him to re-live his glory days than lay a young punk chick? He watched her walk to the bathroom. She turned as she opened the unisex bathroom and beckoned him.

He got up so fast he didn't notice Denny stand up right behind him. Despite whatever fantasies Oscar had of Ericka when he opened the door, he didn't find them. She wasn't waiting twirling her underwear. She didn't throw her bra at him.

She stood at the sink with her hands crossed. Denny stepped in his way and pushed him into the bathroom. Ericka reached across and locked the bathroom door. Oscar looked worried for a moment and then checked Denny out. He apparently liked what he saw of Denny too.

"Well, hello," he said as he unbuttoned his pants and smiled at Denny. "My very lucky day."

Denny rolled his eyes. "Keep 'em on, Romeo."

"Hey, buddy." Oscar tried to push past him but Denny held him in place. "Hey, man, she invited me, but I wasn't gonna do anything."

Ericka sat on the counter, and Denny blocked the door. "We don't want to hurt you. We just have a few questions."

Oscar stared at her and his mind reeled off possibilities. He was worth a lot of money. He probably assumed this was extortion. Ericka wondered how many things he had to have that look of fear on his face. He wasn't worried about something happening in this bathroom, not really. He was afraid to be exposed to the rest of the world for something.

"It's about the van. I talked to you yesterday on the phone," Denny said as he leaned back against the door.

Oscar stared in astonishment for a moment; he bit his lower lip and then laughed. "The worst fucking summer of my life. You know I never played bass again. Not once."

Denny looked at Ericka. She slid off the counter. "What is going on with the van?"

Oscar put the toilet seat down and sat on it. "How the hell should I know? That band was more than twenty years ago."

"Yet yesterday you told us to destroy it. Why?"

"How much do you know about The Fuckers? The real history of the band?"

"Quite a bit," Denny said and pulled the old tour journal out of his backpack. Oscar's eyes got wide and his jaw dropped when he saw it.

"No fucking way." Oscar leaned forward to get a better look. "We looked everywhere for that."

"It was in the ceiling between the fabric and the roof over the loft," said Ericka. Oscar tried to grab it. Denny pulled it away. Oscar shook slightly.

"Where is it?" he asked calmly, then exploded. "Where is the goddamn van?"

"We don't know exactly," Denny said.

Denny told him the story. Ericka mostly listened, but added details when she felt she needed to. Oscar was getting more nervous with each minute. He explained as far as Houston, when she noticed he was looking away.

"Hey, just what the fuck happened after Houston?" Ericka interrupted.

"I can't tell you." Oscar looked away.

Denny turned his face toward them. "The van is here in the city. Dickie said that Frank was coming to get him. We think he is coming to get you. Relive a lost chance to be at the Black Flag show he missed."

"That's insane," said Oscar, with fear in his voice.

Ericka stood in front of him. "Look we don't want to cause trouble for you, we just want our friend back."

Oscar looked at them. "Frank's coming for me. He's coming to get me, and now he has your friend to do it. If I tell you what happened, you'll help me stop it?"

Ericka and Denny nodded at each other.

"You got it. We promise." Ericka put out her hand for him. Oscar shook it.

"It started when I shot Frank..."

CHAPTER 31

The bathroom wasn't well lit, and it was probably in Ericka's mind, but as he talked the room felt colder and darker. Something came over Oscar as he thought back to that time. She knew enough about it from reading the journals to know most of that summer was a drug-fueled haze.

"Frank was never right in the head. He got picked on pretty bad before he had that growth spurt and got huge. He never got over that and what happened to his mother."

"His mother?" Ericka and Denny shared a look. Denny shrugged.

"When he was little she was kinda trashy, but he loved her. She was fucking this biker guy and things got ugly. He saw it happen, I think."

Denny shook his head. "Saw what happen?" Denny shook his head.

"He beat her to death. So you see Frank had lost his mind, but I get it. I understand why it happened. Punk was salvation to him, it was everything. So this war he waged, one thing was for sure, he wasn't going to quit. Each time he killed it was for the grand mission. We had to do it. I had to do it. I killed him. Shot him as he sat in the driver's seat."

"You shot him in the van?" Denny asked.

"He was sitting in the driver's seat?" Ericka whispered.

Oscar nodded. "I'll never forget prying his dead hands off the steering wheel."

Ericka looked at her hands and thought about the hours she'd spent holding the same steering wheel.

"We tried to go on and finish the next two shows to get the money to go home. It wasn't the same. He was gone, but, then again, in a way he was still there."

Denny looked at Ericka. She stared into Oscar's eyes. In

the dim light of the bathroom, she could see hurt inside him. Terrible pent-up feelings he had worked to keep buried for decades were leaking out. Tears began to flow.

Oscar found himself whispering as he continued. "We cleaned up, we hid his body, but he was still there. You could feel him in the van. Watching, he was watching us. Judging us. The van was strange too. It would stop and start on its own. The radio would come on. It was weak at first but every day until we got home it got stronger."

"What got stronger?" Ericka said.

Oscar looked at her and shook his head. His earlier confidence was gone completely. "His spirit. It never left the van, and it's gotten stronger. When the tour was over we all wanted to forget about The Fuckers. We were afraid the van would someday get tracked. Dickie was supposed to destroy it. I don't know why he didn't."

"When he killed himself," Denny gulped slightly, "It was right after we got the van. He said he was finally free, something about Frank coming to get him."

"Dickie is dead?" Oscar fought back tears.

"What I don't understand is why he needed Nate? If he could control Dickie enough to make him keep the van why use Nate?" Ericka leaned back against the counter. "Nate's favorite thing in the world is hardcore. He lives for it. It's more than in his blood, it's who he is, his spirit. He'd do anything to protect it. Frank must've sensed that, exploited it."

"Sounds like Frank. He was obsessed."

Ericka shook her head and paced. "No, they're nothing alike. Nate Underhill is a caring sweet and compassionate person. Frank Huff was a thug."

Oscar stood up. He took a deep breath and tried to feel the confidence he had twenty minutes ago, but it was gone. "Only one thing is going to save your friend, and it's the only thing that will save me."

"And what's that?" Denny looked at him skeptical.

"Find and destroy the van. It's the only way to release Frank's spirit."

CHAPTER 32

Nate drove the van through Hollywood unnoticed. He watched the scene roll past him and judged everything he saw. He lowered the windows and blasted a mix of early eighties L.A. punk bands. The mix was heavy on the Germs. Frank bobbed his head to the music and looked out the window.

He had never made it to California when he was alive. He didn't have old L.A. to compare it to. He saw lots of different kinds of people while they were driving. The twenty-first century hipsters were a far cry from the gritty punks L.A. was known for in his day.

"He lives here in L.A., you know?"

"Who?" Frank asked.

"Oscar. He's a writer and he lives here."

"I know where he is," Frank said just above a whisper.

They pulled up to a stop light and waited for the red. They were stopped in front of a TV and appliance store. In the window a row of large flat screen TVs showed Good Charlotte rocking out in a highly produced, glamorous video. Frank squinted, watching it. One of the band members wore a brand new looking Ramones shirt that looked fresh from the rack at Hot Topic.

"What the hell is that?"

Nate looked over his shoulder. "I know, it's disgusting. The shit that passes for punk rock in this day and age. It is terrible. Bubblegum crap they play on the radio."

"What the fuck? We couldn't even get played on the radio. I mean, not just us, nobody could."

They drove on as summer dusk began to darken the sky over the city. Nate kept driving, no destination in mind.

"It's disgusting that shit is even considered punk rock."

Nate liked having kindred spirit to talk to. He always thought Ericka understood. "It's like a virus. They have stores in malls now that sell so-called punk merch, and like every high school has one of those bands cloned. You know what else? Jocks even like punk now."

"That sucks, man," Frank agreed. "That's how they crushed us. We did it to ourselves with the help of those fucking posers. Bought us right out."

"Fucking posers is right."

"So you know what that means right?"

Nate shook his head.

"Are there any of those bands who live in L.A.?"

"Yeah, lots of them."

"Who is the worst?"

Nate laughed. "The bass player and lead singer of the Tilts have a Beverley Hills mansion. His wife is some model or something. They have a TV show."

"They are the enemy. They mock and exploit everything we work our asses off to create. It's our culture that's under attack, and the worst part is they're getting rich doing it." Frank smiled at his young companion. "We seek and destroy enemies of the state. We'll teach those rock star fuckheads a little lesson in what it means to be punk rock."

***

Ericka thought after living in the van for weeks that a motel room was luxury. Oscar's mansion in Beverly Hills was ridiculous. It was packed tightly next to other massive homes, but the amount of space he had inside the house was obscene. She stepped out onto the porch, which was bigger than all of Fort Flop back in Bloomington. It was strange these fancy mansions packed so tightly.

The lights of L.A. appeared and flickered like reflections of the stars popping out with the dusk. The sun dipped out over the ocean, ending another day without Nate. Every bit of her heart and inch of her skin longed for him. She wondered if it would have been better to not have had those days together. They were less than week ago, but felt like another lifetime.

Ericka turned when a screen door opened. Oscar went to a small bar he kept stocked in a cabinet just inside and poured them all a shot of bourbon. He was the only one to drink as he and Denny thumbed through the journal.

Oscar shook his head, his mind blown at seeing this written artifact just sitting right there in front of them after all these years.

"Well, you read it so you know there is not much I remember."

"How could you let Frank do all that shit?" asked Denny.

"Did you not figure out how fucked up I was? It was a different time. I was a different person, so don't think for a second I have an answer." Oscar took a deep gulp, finishing his drink. "I got into punk because I hated my life. I was queer in Indiana in nineteen eighty-fucking-one. I wanted to die or not think about living. No in-between. Besides, I did the right thing eventually."

"How many died first?"

Ericka turned whistled loud enough for it to echo in the brush canyon below the house. "So where the hell was the L.A. show?"

"Yeah, that was bizarre. Frank had read a story in a *Maximum Rock and Roll* scene report about these kids who were doing shows in a giant sewer pipe under the city golf course. Kinda famous. I mean punk famous. Really, there was a working outlet just outside the pipe and the music could be heard off the golf course faintly, but no one imagined where it was coming from."

"So, playing with Black Flag was a ruse? Just a lie to get Gary to do the tour," said Ericka.

Oscar smiled. "Well you've done your research. Two L.A. shows." Oscar held up two fingers. "No, the Flag show happened, but that was the next night, in Huntington Beach, another big old warehouse. Frank will take your boy there for sure. That was our big show. It was everything to us at the time."

Ericka came to the coffee table where she left her notebook. She wrote something down and showed it to Denny. He nodded.

"Well..." Oscar looked around nervous. "What's your plan?"

"We have two options." Ericka smiled. "We can wait here for Frank to go after you."

"I'd like another option."

"Let's check out the sewer show space." Ericka stood up. Since she didn't like waiting, that was her choice.

Oscar put his elbows on his expensive glass table held his hands up with his fists.

"Fucking great," he muttered under his breath.

***

"Her tits were hanging out of her shirt. They do that to get tips from suckers like you," his young wife complained. John Tills' wife owed her career to her cleavage. As much as he wanted to tell her it was no different, he kept his mouth shut. She was the one that wanted to be seen here.

They were doing that. A part of him still couldn't believe she was as shallow as she was, but each day she became more and more of a cartoon. She should understand why he had to tip so heavy, but she only thought about herself.

"Places like this remember who tips well or who doesn't. We won't get a table again...look, I didn't tip well because of her rack, okay?"

Most of their days and nights were in front of the camera. The reality show team followed the couple everywhere. As soon as he was romantically linked to Nicole Mills, the vacant, blonde, soda pop empire heiress, the cameras rolled. He had met her when his band was opening the small stage on the Warped tour, but she didn't give him the time of day.

He was just a smelly, nerdy, punk kid from Riverside County then. After his sugary sweet, poppy punk ballad, "In the days Without You," hit number one, things changed for the Riverside band, The Tilts. And then there she was.

The band had to accept that sudden stardom came at a price they were not expecting. The song and the album became a hit after Disney bought the rights to play it over the final scene of one of their TV stars' first movies. That made them a *Tiger Beat* sensation, and the sales went through the roof.

The teenyboppers loved the ballad, and the next song made them feel like rebellious kids. The ten-million-dollar-a-season reality show deal was a bummer for his band, but it bought him a house in the Hills and the chance to make sex videos (to leak on purpose) of him with Nicole.

They kicked off the second season with episodes about their wedding and honeymoon. The producers suggested they announce a pregnancy in the finale, but they hadn't even discussed the idea of kids. Chelsea Handler did an entire monologue about their marriage, but the only part that bothered Nicole and John was when she said John would always be poor white trash.

Now they were dining at Le Pigeon, a restaurant that catered only to snobby assholes. The world needed to know he could afford it. John had grown up dirt poor in Riverside, and the other members of his band came from wealthy families in Orange County. In his heart he knew that is why they didn't feel the need for the spotlight or the money like he did.

Nicole hardly ate all night, just picked over her salad. She had gotten bored with all the attention of the show and wanted to break up with John. The producers had planned their kid's role on the show while her agent was planning their break-up in the season finale.

The rumors got back to him, and it was underlining all of their off-camera interactions. TMZ was reporting that her spa weekend in Santa Barbara was timed for the visit of her favorite NBA player who she'd had a thing with before John.

"Something wrong with dinner?" John tapped his fork on the table. "You picked the place."

"No, *sweetheart,* it's fine." Nicole looked around. "Why no crew tonight?"

It was the first unscripted thing she had said to him in

almost a week.

"Well, Mitch thought the papanazis could handle the message more subtly. Plus, I leave for tour in two weeks." John put down the fork. "I thought we could get some alone time. I think we need to talk."

"Talk?" She said the word like it was painful to her to even consider the idea. "You want to talk?"

"Yeah, talk like real human beings, not celebrities."

"Excuse me, but the reality show was your idea."

She always said that. Maybe she even believed it. She first pitched him the idea in bed as he lit a post-coital cigarette for her. He hadn't even taken off the condom.

"Yeah, well, I know about Santa Barbara, bitch."

Nicole raised an eyebrow. She was ready for this. "It will be good for ratings. We'll have a big fight and everyone will be speculating on who I left you for. Will the show return? That kinda stuff."

"What if I left you first?"

"Right, is that why you were looking at the waitresses' tits, shopping? You and I both know I am the finest ass you'll ever get your hands on."

John stood up and threw his napkin down.

"The dumbest, maybe." John dropped two hundred-dollar bills on the table and headed for the door.

As he opened the front door, he saw the Paparazzi waiting for him, snapping enough pictures to make him wish he had sunglasses on. John turned around for the back entrance. A waiter was ready and opened the door to the back alley. LePigeon had enough celebrity business that they had this door for this very reason. Out of the corner of his eyes he saw Nicole roll her eyes at him and slink over to the bar.

John pulled out his Camels and fumbled in his pocket for his lighter as he walked into the alley. He had parked his car in valet, but needed to walk around the building. He lit the cigarette and walked down the smelly alley. He had to decide if he was taking Nicole home or ending it right here. He avoided ruining his Italian shoes in a few puddles before running into someone. It was like walking into a wall.

"Sorry, man. I didn't see..."

He looked up at the young man. He was wearing a ratty looking sweatshirt with the logo for a band that read 'His Hero is Gone' and a dirty old Black Flag hat with a bent bill. He could barely make out his face. The guy didn't move or react. John laughed and took a drag off his camel.

"Excuse you," John Said.

"Hey, man, you're John Tills." The young man spoke in a husky voice that sounded unnaturally deep for his size. To John he was just some punk kid. He knew the guy would recognize him. The good thing was punks at least didn't ask for autographs. John walked around and heard the guy turn to watch him. "Fucking sell-out," the young man said with thick venom in his voice.

This stopped John in his tracks, he almost turned around but decided to keep walking and talk with his back to the young punk. "That's right. Every seat in the house, every night. What's your fucking problem?"

John smiled. He loved saying that to self-righteous punk kids. He couldn't enjoy the victory for long. Something wound around his throat and squeezed. John tried to scream and pull at it but it was tight. He couldn't get his fingers under it, but he could feel the gauge.

Guitars had funny strings. He had broken and strung thousands in his professional life, although now he had road crew do it. The lower, thicker strings were burning across his skin and tearing it as his attacker pulled them tight. John tried to scream for help but no air made it into his throat. He couldn't say a thing.

***

Nate had thought it was a waste of money when Denny suggested they bring so many extra guitar and bass strings on tour. As he twisted a handful of them around John Tills' throat and dragged him backwards to the ground, he was glad they had them now. Frank watched him nodding and spinning his fingers, encouraging him to speed up. Nate wasn't prepared for the rage he felt when he said that bullshit about every seat in the house.

"You think that's funny, don't you?"

John couldn't breathe. He waved his arms like he was in the pit at a show. Nate tightened the grip. Words were not happening. His forehead and face turned purple. The only thing his mouth could make was drool.

"You're a fucking insult to everything I stand for,"

Nate felt him dying. He let up the grip on the strings just enough for him to take in a breath. Desperate, he sucked in air before he could think about screaming. Before he did, Nate twisted and tightened the strings again. John blacked out for a second. Nate felt John's body going limp but heard the unmistakable sound of a van door unlocking and then sliding open.

Frank held the door. *"Let's go."* He pointed .

Nate pushed John's nearly-lifeless body into the back. He fought to scream, but couldn't catch his breath. Nate jumped in the back door of the van and sat on top of John. "Shhhh." The door slammed behind him. He looked up and instantly Frank was in the driver's seat. The engine came to life with a big, burbling roar.

"Go! Go!" Nate yelled. Frank nodded as he put the van in drive and it began to roll. John took in breaths that snapped him fully awake. He tried to squirm out from under Nate but his energy was almost gone. He looked up and saw the loft.

Nate could tell he recognized the look of an old school touring van. Nate wrapped a power cord around his hands and tied it as tight as he could.

John screamed, but Nate screamed back louder in his face. The *Circle Jerks* blared suddenly from the speakers. Nate reached for duct tape and worked on his ankles. John began to whimper. He could see L.A. passing outside the window. He wondered for a second if anyone could see Frank behind the wheel. He didn't have time to care.

"What the fuck? I've got money, whatever you want!"

Nate ripped a piece of Duct tape off and considered it for John's mouth.

"Whatever I want?" Nate laughed. The song ended and the *Misfits* song "Horror Business" came on. Frank sang along as loud as he was singing at a show.

"Money, chicks, whatever you want!" John screamed over the music, over Frank like he couldn't hear it. The music faded as Nate spoke.

"You see, that's your fucking problem. Your priorities are totally fucking whack. I don't want your money. I want you to shut the fuck up and leave punk rock out of your bullshit. Okay?"

As if on cue the music turned back up. Frank sang along. John screamed as Nate lowered the duct tape toward his mouth.

"I'll quit the fucking band!"

Nate looked at him for a moment and considered this. It was a lie. He would say anything right now.

"Goddamn it, I'll play something else. Disco, or country, just let me go."

Nate took a slimy Sado-Nation shirt he had worn for three days at the beginning of the tour and jammed it into his mouth. The smell alone under his nose was enough to make John sick.

He screamed his muffled scream. He tried to spit it out when Nate put two small pieces of duct tape on each side to hold it down. The music turned down.

"The damage is done already, I'm afraid."

John whimpered, tears streaming from his face.

"We could just kill you," Nate said as he jumped into the driver's seat. Frank appeared in the passenger seat. "Believe me, that would satisfy me a great deal."

Nate seamlessly sat down and took over the driving and took a right turn. He adjusted the mirror so he could see the crying whimpering corporate punk rocker in the back seat.

"We thought you needed to learn a little history about real punk rock."

John screamed watching through tear-filled eyes as the van drove across L.A.

CHAPTER 33

The golf course was between Torrance and South Central L.A. When it was first built in the late fifties, the area was nicer. It wasn't the most popular golf course for the rich and famous, so in L.A. golf course terms, it was ghetto. As they pulled the Prius up to the golf course, Oscar hung his head low. Denny drove and Ericka sat in the back clutching the tour journal.

"Oh, fuck," Oscar muttered. "You know if we find them, Frank will do what it takes. If it's me or your Nate friend. We need to be ready to do what needs to be done."

Ericka looked at the man who killed Frank in the first place. "I think I can reach Nate."

"Honey, you're cute, but Frank doesn't care."

Denny pulled up the parking brake. "Watch your mouth, Oscar."

Oscar rolled his eyes and stepped out. He looked around the parking lot and nodded. "Yeah, this is the one all right. The bands back in '82 couldn't park here or they would draw suspicion. The bands parked closer on the other side by the apartments to pack one set of gear across the field. All three bands shared gear for the sewer shows. After the gear was loaded we parked the van at that Burger King."

Ericka and Denny shared a look. Oscar squinted. "What?"

Ericka put the journal under the front seat and shut the passenger door. "The van was spotted there yesterday."

"We see that fucking van, we blow it up or something," Oscar whined.

"I'm a drummer, not a Unabomber," Denny said as he looked out over the dark golf course. "We're looking for Nate. You're more than welcome to blow up the van all by your lonesome."

Ericka was already tired of Oscar, who was afraid to be alone. He wouldn't leave them. Every time he threatened to leave, she was more convinced of how afraid he was.

"I should. You know we should torch that fucking van. Burn that motherfucker."

Denny and Ericka waited at the edge of the golf course for Oscar. He looked at the Doc Martens on his feet and sighed as he followed them into the darkness on the course. "I don't have the right shoes for this."

Ericka laughed and walked first on to the greens. Oscar looked at her with a 'What, me' face that only made her laugh harder. Denny laughed with her.

"What is so damn funny?" Oscar was pissed.

"You're such a fancy lad now," Ericka said and Denny laughed with her. "For somebody who had a nose ring in 1982..."

"Not to mention fucking rooms full of people for smack," Denny added.

Oscar stopped. "Wait a second." He was fuming. "I was young and stupid like everybody else. Playing around trying to piss off my parents, cops, the schools, it's a bullshit game of who can be the biggest rebel. Don't look down on me. You'll grow up and see it's all crap."

"Maybe to you. I think punk itself grew up. For me punk was never about pissing my parents off." Ericka kept walking as she talked. "It was about living honestly, doing the right thing even if society doesn't see it the same way. It was always about doing good because the system is just about exploiting our labor and—"

"Give me a break." Oscar was huffing a bit to keep up. "I was wearing spikes and slam dancing before your parents' first date, so don't lecture me, sweetie. I've literally been fucked by punk rock more times than you have friends on MySpace."

"Everything depends on the people involved." Denny was a few steps in front but turned to address Oscar. "There is good and bad in everything."

"You see that?" Ericka stopped them when she saw a

light on the course. The light disappeared under the ridge.

"It's right by the sewer drain." Oscar had a nervous shake in his words.

"Could be nothing," Ericka said, walking.

"Could be something," Oscar said, waiting to go third.

***

Nate grunted as he dragged John Tills across the field. He struggled at first, but exhaustion and a realization that fighting wasn't helping had set into the famous rocker. They were almost to the sewer drain. It was like giant hole cut through a ridge. A light on the far side lit it up. Seeing the drain caused a round of muffled screams.

His wrists bled from struggling against the cord and tape, but it did him no good. Nate had to stop twice to catch his breath. Every few minutes John would scream vainly, but the screams in view of the pipe were more painful to listen to. Nate got down on to one knee and punched him in the gut.

John couldn't stop the whimpering, but got the point and stopped with the screaming. After a few more minutes of dragging, Nate laid him down by a small creek. Nate thought the sound of the water soothed John. He closed his eyes, probably hoping this would end soon.

"Here we are," Nate whispered just inches from his ears.

Nate kept a mini-Maglite on his belt during tour. Sometimes when setting up equipment in dark clubs it was an essential tool. He lifted the light up and shined it on the sewer drain. The inside of the drain was tagged with the faded logos of old L.A. punk bands from the 80s. Some, like Bad Religion, had gone on to success. A few other names and logos were ones Nate didn't recognize.

Nate tapped on John's shoulder and pointed in the direction of his light. He shined on the spray painted ST logo of the band Suicidal Tendencies. "This place was a legend," Nate told the bound rock star. "For some reason when the city built this drain, they installed a power box."

Nate shone a light on a small concrete slab that was inside the drain. It looked like it was built to be a stage. "Can't explain that, but it has a stage."

Nate put away his flashlight and pulled John into the stream. He dragged him across the rocks and the cold water shocked his system. Now he couldn't control it. He screamed into the shirt in his mouth harder than he had before.

He knew this was the end of the line. In the distance over the trees and the greens of the golf course, Nate could see the orange light from the city and then the strangest thing.

Lightning flashed in the sky. *Lightning in L.A.?*

The silence broke and Nate's ears were overwhelmed by three chords of raunchy guitar. Up on the concrete slab a band played. Leather jackets and spikes on their bodies and Mohawks and stubble on their heads.

A circle pit stomped in the stream around him. The guitars were as thick and sludgy, the bass sounded distorted and fuzzy, and the drums like trash cans. The cracked cymbals and out of tune guitars were enough to drive Nate to mosh, but this crowd ate it up like redneck seniors at the Country Crock Buffet.

"Fuck, yeah! Can you feel it, John? Real punk rock! Fucking vital, man."

Fists flew, boots stomped, and the dirty sewer water sprayed in the air. John looked up at Nate, watching him mosh around the pipe to music he didn't hear. The storm of the pit exploded around Nate.

He forgot that John laid on the ground and stomped around in the pit. He spun around, slamming into spikes and sweaty shirtless bodies. Silver flashed in his eyes as a head full of spiked hair swung back and hit Nate in the face.

He shook his head and when he opened his eyes, the band and the punks were gone. John laid on the concrete stage looking up at Nate. Frank stood beside the crying man. Nate pulled out the blade he'd picked up in the city. Rambo would have been jealous of it. He stepped closer.

"He is the reason, Nate. Sell-outs like him are why punk is so diluted now."

Nate spun the blade around and cut John's hands free. John could only beg with tear-filled eyes. The maniacal smile on Nate's face scared him enough. Even though John's hands were free he was afraid to search his own skin for wounds. His whole body was soaked, as his hand reached up his shirt he felt liquid some cold, some of it lukewarm. His fingers reached his throat and he felt the skin opened up.

John didn't scream. He didn't have the energy, just closed his eyes for the last time. Nate brought the knife down.

As John's body slumped, Nate stood straight. A light shone across the tunnel on him, reflecting off the parts of the blade not dripping with blood. Nate looked up, but couldn't make out the newcomer.

"Nate!"

It was worse than "Put your hands up" or "Drop that weapon." The voice cut through the fog inside his mind. It was Ericka. For just a moment Nate remembered who he was and what he had just done.

CHAPTER 34

Ericka couldn't believe her eyes. Nate stood over a bloodied, torn up body holding a dripping knife. Denny came up behind her and gasped. Oscar swore and stepped completely out of view. Ericka shook slightly but held the light on Nate.

A look of total fear came over Nate for just a moment. Then malevolent hatred returned to his face. He shook the blade, clearing the blood from its shiny surface. "Get that fucking light off me."

"Nate," Ericka fought back tears. "What have you done?"

Nate laughed and stepped out of the light. Ericka followed him with the light. "Nate?"

He laughed and held up his hand trying to block the light. "Nate's not here at the moment. Would you like to leave a message?"

Ericka's heart broke. Denny walked up behind her.

"What are we gonna do?" Denny whispered to her. Oscar hid behind a bush, praying. Nate took a step closer into the light, holding the blade up to reflect it. Ericka and Denny squinted.

"Nate, I know you're in there somewhere," Ericka said.

Nate laughed back at her, stepping quickly back into the shadows and closer, holding the knife up. Denny and Ericka stepped back.

"We should have brought a weapon," Denny whispered.

"Stop or I'll shoot," Ericka lied, hoping he was blinded still by the light.

Nate stopped for a moment. He tilted his head, but the glare was still flashing on his retinas. He couldn't tell.

"You know it's not too late to finish the tour. I've been thinking about our sound. We need a little harsher edge. Of course, most times that is just a matter of attitude."

"Nate, it's all bullshit. Frank Huff was a violent thug who didn't know shit about Hardcore," Ericka's voice got shakier as Nate stepped closer.

"Shut your mouth, bitch." Nate spun the knife and held it in stabbing position and got closer.

Ericka took a step back, clearing the path to the van. His Nate's eyes darted to the left, to the clear path, for just a second.

Nate lunged and lifted the knife to bring it down on Ericka. Denny dove, tackling Nate. Ericka dropped her Maglite and in the glare and darkness lost Denny.

She heard the struggle but couldn't see it. She stepped closer and saw the knife on the ground. She picked it up and threw it deep into the drain. Denny had his head buried into Nate's gut. Nate was slamming his elbow into Denny's back.

Ericka looked into his eyes and saw Frank. He laughed and threw the hacking and coughing Denny off of him.

Ericka tried to block his path, but Nate pushed her into the stream and ran. Ericka felt the stones in the stream slam against her tailbone and watched Nate take off in the field. She saw Denny struggling to get up but took off after Nate.

She was slow and sopping wet, but she took off on to the green. She could see Oscar popping up to look, but kept going. Nate had turned at a tree and crossed over a ridge.

Ericka got to the top of the hill and he was gone. The van was pulling away

"Fuck!"

CHAPTER 35

Oscar helped Denny limp out of the sewer drain. Denny was already pulling out his phone.

"What are you doing?"

Denny looked back at John Tills' body still draining and mixing blood into the sewer.

"Calling the cops. There's a body."

"What kinda punk are you?" Oscar asked in disbelief. "We can't trust them to understand what the hell is going on!"

"He's right," Ericka said "Although he's just protecting his own ass. We'll call from a pay phone when we're clear."

Denny looked at Ericka who seemed different, as if something had snapped inside of her. He was afraid her will to go on or try to save Nate was gone.

"What's next boss?" Denny asked.

Ericka took deep heaving breaths. "Destroy the van in Huntington beach."

"Fucking A!" Oscar said.

Denny looked at him and shook his head. "You gonna help this time?"

"I did," Oscar stared at them in disbelief. "I was waiting in case he came out that way, I mean ambush. Come on!"

***

Nate walked in the California sun and smiled each time he passed a newspaper rack.

Emo-rocker found murdered. Rock 'n' roll murder in Hollywood. Sex, Drugs and Murder for John Tills...

Nate stopped in several spots to watch the reactions, shock, and dismay. The grieving wife had already issued a statement to the media expressing her grief and plans to contest his will. She was already a person of interest. *Entertainment Tonight* was covering the story. "Punk Rock in the 21ˢᵗ Century." Nate stopped at a newspaper box in front of a Hot Topic-like punk fashion store and took out a sharpie. He looked around to make sure no one was watching.

He wrote quickly but neatly.

Punk's not dead, but John Tills is.

"That's true." Frank laughed and grinned at Nate. His ghost stood next to him in the California sun and it didn't even make him blink. A couple walked down the street, passing through him.

"Try to keep a low profile, huh?"

"We have one more thing to check out in L.A.," said Frank.

"The Huntington Beach show."

"Well, yeah, and kill Oscar, then we can move on. Start a new band."

An old school punk with liberty spiked mohawk and his green-haired girlfriend in a full-on, spiked dog collar walked toward Nate.

"I like it here," Nate said and the punks looked at him strangely.

"Stay focused. There are enemies everywhere."

Frank disappeared, but Nate knew he wasn't alone.

***

It hadn't changed in the two decades since it was home to barely legal punk gigs. More cracked pavement, more growth of weeds and spider webs. It had been a camp for the homeless in the late 80s and the location for post-apocalyptic action films, but now a large chain link fence blocked it off.

The Prius rode silently up on its electric motor to the gate. Denny turned to look at Oscar in the back seat. He nodded. Ericka closed the journal knowing they had found the place.

Oscar got out with a hammer and a spray bottle. Ericka

didn't understand what chemical it was but he sprayed it on the lock. He beat on the old rusty lock several times before it cracked apart. He pushed the gate aside and waved the car forward.

"Better hide it when you park. We don't want him to know we're here."

Denny nodded but Ericka knew he was worried that Nate was already inside, hiding. Denny's back was still sore from the pounding. This time Oscar had a handgun, which Ericka didn't want him to bring, and Denny was carrying a baseball bat. A little more prepared. In the truck they had two cans of gasoline for blowing up the van.

Ericka opened the trunk and pulled out a blue tarp for covering up the car. Oscar walked up behind her and helped her place it over the car.

"Why did you guys always play old warehouses?"

"I think the better question is why you young bucks don't? Look, man, nobody wanted us, clubs wouldn't book us, not even the rock and roll crowd understood what we were doing."

"I gotta admit that Fuckers 7-inch is pretty fucking raw," Denny said getting out with his bat in hand. "In a good way."

Oscar hadn't felt much respect from Denny. He smiled. "I haven't listened to it in twenty years. You know how it is... bad memories."

"I'm pretty sure I'll never listen to it again." Ericka looked around.

Oscar pointed to a warehouse door. He kicked it open. "You see, there was nothing like Flag or Bad Brains before them. You kids don't understand what a fucking revolution it was."

Oscar walked into the old warehouse. Ericka held her nose for a moment when she hit the stale air of the former meat-packing plant. The meat hooks still hung after thirty years from the ceiling. Denny whistled looking around the scene. The dust was ankle deep. The building itself was as dead as a tomb.

"Where was the stage?" Ericka panned around not sure

where it would be.

Oscar had gone chalk white looking at another ghost of the past. "I'm sorry, it's just so weird being here." Oscar tipped his head. "Can you hear it?"

"Hear what?"

Oscar pointed at the back part of the room. "Right there in that spot. All the greats. Flag, the Kennedys, The Germs, fucking X. They played right here. That raw power and energy exploded like a super nova in this spot. That is the thing that can't die. It is too powerful to ever die."

"It empowered Frank," Ericka whispered.

Denny wasn't impressed. "Okay, as fun as this will be let's find somewhere to hide."

Oscar and Ericka looked at each other considering Denny's suggestion.

"I'm voting for the car," Denny said through a grin.

***

The sun was going down over the Pacific Ocean as Nate drove down the Pacific Coast Highway towards Huntington Beach. It was impossible for him to avoid the level of anticipation he felt. He rocked a party shuffle of Black Flag CDs during the drive. Nate had the window rolled down and the stereo blasting as loud as the speakers could handle.

He didn't have directions, but he had a feeling Frank knew where he was going. The turn signals came on and he followed. Before right turns, the van slowed on its own. The closer they got, the more the van moved before he could even think of the motions. They passed several meat-packing plants that were now dead and had long ago moved their operations farther away.

The van made a hard turn towards the gate of one of the plants. The gate was open and invited them in as the last rays of sunlight turned the sky purple. Nate wanted to pause and look around first, but the van itself inched in through the gate. He put his foot on the brake when he saw the busted lock, but it pushed back.

The van inched forward into the complex. The sky filled with lightning flashes, and this time Nate just closed his eyes and let the transition take him. For a moment he saw the complex as it had been in 1982, cars and tour vans lined up along the building and huge groups of punks standing in front of the building, drinking, smoking, and talking.

Nate floated free in the van watching as the young Oscar drove the van slowly towards the building. A guy holding a beer with a large flashlight in his back pocket walked up to the van. "Fuckers?"

"That's us," Oscar said as the guy looked in the van.

"Sorry to hear about your singer. You still want to play?"

"We're still hoping he shows up, actually," Oscar lied with a ridiculously obvious fake smile.

Nate poked his ethereal finger at Oscar who of course couldn't feel or hear a thing. *"Fucking liar."* He spoke to only himself.

Oscar turned suddenly. Nate felt like he was looking at him but it was impossible.

"You guys hear something?"

"Hear what?" Dickie asked.

"A voice?"

"You're panicking, Oscar. Frank's dead," Gary said but he didn't sound convinced.

***

The guy directing them tapped on the hood of the van and pointed to parking space reserved by the loading dock for them. As they pulled into the space, Gary started rubbing his hands together.

"Flag, dude. This is awesome." He laughed a bit as he stepped out of the van.

Oscar sat at the wheel motionless after he turned off the van. Dickie sat quietly in the passenger seat.

"I just want to get home," Oscar said just over a whisper.

"He's still here." Dickie put his hand on the dashboard. "Say what you want, Gary, but I can feel him watching us."

"Something," Oscar said as he leaned back in the driver's seat. Gary appeared all smiles in the window. "Come on, we're first..."

Nate watched as they unloaded their gear.

***

Ericka had fallen asleep in the passenger seat of the rental car. Denny had the driver's side seat back, and Oscar was crashed in the back seat. They still had the tarp covering the car. She opened the door slowly, needing to pee. She intended to find someplace to unobtrusively take a piss. Her bladder was so full, she was afraid to sneeze.

She walked back into the nearest corner dropping her pants before squatting to pee. The water flowed and the sensation of relief was immediate. Ericka looked up and followed a moon beam t just twenty feet away. The van was parked and pointing at her. She couldn't stop peeing, but felt the need to hide.

It was too late. Nate probably already saw her. The element of surprise was gone. The seconds like hours passed as she finally finished with her pee. She pulled up her pants. Her breath was fast, but the moments passed and she assumed Nate wasn't in the van. It still felt like she was being watched.

Maybe he was behind her? Ericka turned quickly. He wasn't there. A minute passed and she carefully stepped out into the glow of the moonlight that glowed down on the van. With each step, she got a better look and saw that the van was empty. Behind I the door to the warehouse was open. She wanted to look inside, but couldn't get the nerve to walk in front of it.

Ericka kept her eyes on the van as she walked past it. At the door to the warehouse, she simply poked her head into the dark room. A small beam of light shone in from the window over the door. Nate stood still in the room beyond the light, but close enough that she could see him.

***

What remained of The Fuckers opened their set with "Dear Congressman." The amped crowd didn't hesitate to slam into each other. Oscar began rocking and almost forgot on the fourth time they played the riff through that he needed to get up to the microphone. By the second verse Oscar could barely breathe and his voice was cracking. There was a reason he didn't sing for a band.

Gary went nuts playing his parts cleaner and more accurately than he had since the first week of tour. In the middle of the punk storm, one kid stood still, unaffected by the crowd. He didn't move, oblivious to the skanking and moshing madness around him. Nate watched him from the center of the crowd, and he had the feeling that in that moment Oscar saw him. Oscar sang the chorus "Dear Congressman." Nate sang along pointing at him just in time to sing "Fuck you!"

It was wrong. Everything about it was wrong. Oscar had no right to sing Frank's words, no right to take over the band he started. They practiced in his grandparent's garage. Frank had booked every show they ever played, had found the van, had done all the hard work while they just showed up and played.

Now they stood on stage playing those song like they even gave a shit about it. After all he did for the band, they killed him and left him to rot in the desert. Nate laughed and let the rage build. He put his thumb up making his hand look like a pistol.

The song transitioned to the next verse and Nate dropped his thumb like he was firing his imaginary gun. Oscar suddenly felt a slight pain in his heart and screwed up the lyrics. He stepped back playing the music but forgot about the lyrics. When he looked up again, Nate was gone.

***

Ericka turned around and ran back to the car. She grabbed the tarp and ducked under it. Denny almost jumped out of his skin when she lightly tapped on the window. Oscar jumped up and pulled his hand gun out. Ericka jumped back and smacked the window.

"Put that away," she whispered. "He's here!"

Denny got out of the car and looked at the van. Oscar got out and smiled when he saw it was sitting by itself. Denny pulled the tarp off and opened the trunk. He looked at the two gas cans and took a deep breath.

"It's showtime."

Ericka took off running towards the warehouse. Oscar took two steps after her.

"Where are you going?" Oscar flirted on the edge of yelling, but kept his voice at a whisper. Denny didn't watch her, just grabbed the two gas cans out of the van.

"He loves her, and she wants to be there for him."

CHAPTER 36

Ericka hadn't prayed since she was little. Her family wasn't a religious one. The only time she had ever been in churches were for weddings and funerals. When she got into punk rock she thought of it as salvation and she never had a moment in life when she felt so desperate that she prayed to god or anything.

Every fiber of her of her being was rattled by that desperation. Now she prayed. She didn't know what she would find when she went through that door into the warehouse. She hit it running, fell through it into the dark room. Only a beam of moon light cut the darkness. Nate looked frozen, his head tipped back, his eyes closed.

"Nate!" She called out. He didn't move even as his name echoed back to him. This time she screamed "NATE!"

***

The sound of the scream snapped Nate back into the present. Ericka stepped into the building. She stopped inside the door. He turned and looked at her. Their eyes locked, for a split second.

Reality was still murky, his retinas still flashing with the fading light of the show in the past. His ears ringed from the assault of The Fuckers playing. It wasn't in his mind. He was there.

"Nate, please!"

A breeze came through the shattered windows. The moonlight was all they had. She stepped into it. She was beautiful, but Nate couldn't allow himself to be fooled by that. He didn't move as she walked through the clouds of dust she kicked up.

The breeze coming off the ocean pitched up and made a howling sound through the broken windows. The meat hooks hanging high off the ceiling clanged together gently like wind chimes.

Nate's anger towards Oscar, the posers, to the scene, all of it, melted away. Ericka smiled at him. He could just go home. He smiled ready to run toward her. His legs didn't move. It was like they were sinking into wet cement.

"You know I hate to admit this." His heart sank when he heard his own voice. "Nate protected you the last two times I wanted to kill you."

Ericka closed her eyes. The tears overcame her and rolled down her face. "Let him go."

"I can't do that, sweetheart."

Ericka looked at his face. She thought of the good times, the person he was, and saw something different now. The evil had taken total control, and she knew now. She tried to center herself and stopped about ten feet from Nate. It was his body standing there but she only felt Frank's presence in the room. He looked her up and down, and grinned.

"Oh, don't be so upset. You and I had fun too. I'll cherish our time together."

Ericka felt sick to her stomach, angry and exposed.

"Nate is a good person," Ericka said firmly. "How could you do this to him?"

"Oh, that's sweet, that's why you're here, huh? For love? See, I think I get and understand Nate better than you ever did. His love is on that stage, in those records, the zines. The real scene is what he loved all along."

"I love Nate dearly, and I'm going to get him back."

Nate's eyes looked over her shoulder back towards the door. As the broken warehouse door swung in the wind, there were loud sounds coming from outside.

Nate's eyes got wide. "You didn't come alone. It won't work. I'm gonna kill all three of you."

***

Denny ran to the warehouse and watched through one of the broken windows. He couldn't hear everything, caught some of it.

Oscar yelled at Denny. "Come on! We don't have time! Your boy is long gone!"

Denny nodded and ran back to the trunk of the Prius. Oscar put his hand out, expecting Denny to hand him the gas can. Oscar had waited this long. There was no way in hell he was letting someone else have the glory.

He ran to the van and poured gas on the front windshield. Denny took the gas cap off and stuffed a shirt in it. He shook with nervous excitement as he walked the length of the van pouring the gas. Denny opened the back doors to the van. Oscar came up behind him.

"What are you doing?" Oscar whispered.

Denny reached in and grabbed his bass drum. "My drums, and Scott's guitar. It's a Fender. It means a lot to him."

"Fuck the gear, man. I'll buy you new shit, let's go!"

"It will just take a minute.

The open doors blocked their view of the brake lights as they glowed into life. Denny grabbed a snare drum.

"We don't have time for this shit," Oscar pleaded as he grabbed his shoulder. The engine suddenly roared to life. They both looked up. Oscar knew there was no one in the driver's seat. He also knew it didn't matter. The brake lights went dark after the gear shift snapped into reverse.

Denny threw the snare drum as Oscar pulled him away. The van was already moving backwards. Oscar tried to jump out of the way, but the door clipped him. Oscar fell backwards, trying to move on the ground away from the van. He looked up at the open back doors and realized the gear wasn't secured.

The van stopped suddenly as the brakes caught. The band's remaining gear became examples of physics. They flew out the back and crashed on to the ground. Oscar felt the guitar cabinet land on his leg. He screamed as his kneecap broke into pieces. Denny managed to roll out of the way. "Goddamn thing is protecting itself!"

The van pulled back into the parking lot and turned around. The headlights snapped on blinding Oscar for a moment. Despite the pain he tried to move. Denny jumped into action and moved the guitar cabinet off his legs.

Oscar rolled over and faced the burning headlights of the van. Denny tried to help him up, but he just screamed in pain and pushed him away."Light that motherfucker up!" Oscar screamed. "Go!"

Denny seemed frozen in the headlights among the ruins of his band's gear. Oscar tried to stand again. The waves of pain shooting up his leg were too much. He fell back to the pavement.

"You gotta do it, kid. Wake the fuck up!"

The engine in the van roared as if someone was gunning the gas, like a bull dragging its leg before charging. Oscar pulled his Bic lighter from his pocket and put it in Denny's hands. Oscar put up his arm to block the blinding light.

"Oh, god, Frank, fuck you! Goddammit fuck you!"

Denny stared at the blank driver's seat. They both knew Oscar couldn't get up, and that was what the van was waiting for. A direct kill shot. It was daring him to stand. "Goddamn it, Denny. I need help," Oscar screamed.

Denny whispered. "I lift you up and we're dead." Denny picked up his snare and threw it with a bang at the van. The van suddenly turned and smashed into the rental car, pushing it back against the wall. It pulled back again, facing them with the headlights.

Denny breathed heavy. "Fuck you, whatever you are."

***

Ericka heard the screaming and yelling. She turned back to the door, not sure if she should go to them or stay with...

When she looked back for Nate he was gone.

"Nate!" Ericka hated to do this. "Frank? Where the fuck are you?"

Her voice echoed in the empty warehouse. Ericka pulled her Maglite out and pointed it at the sounds of shuffling feet. She only saw his shape disappear further into the building.

More yelling outside. Oscar in pain. Denny cursing. Ericka considered running after Nate, but knew she should help her friends. Ericka ran out the door following the sounds of screams.

"No!" She screamed when she saw the headlights of the van shining on Denny and Oscar. She stopped in the door way, shrieking back into the empty warehouse. "Frank! Stop this shit!"

Her voice echoed, but there was no reply.

The van engine roared, and the wheels spun creating a small dust storm before the van took off toward her friends. Denny tried to lift Oscar by his shoulder. Ericka couldn't watch, involuntarily closed her eyes. She heard a thud and two screams.

"Fuck you, Frank, goddamn it!" Oscar's voice was cracking from the strain. Both Denny and Oscar were dropped to the ground. Denny reached for a lighter out of his reach. She knew they must've poured the gas on the van already.

Ericka was protected from the van's movement by the door frame. It had to run into the building to get her. But the lighter was out of Denny's grasp. He appeared too hurt to get it.

Denny and Ericka made eye contact. Both of them looked at the lighter and back to the van. He knew what she was thinking.

Denny shook his head. "It's a fucking trap! Don't do it!" The van revved, sounding hungry. Ericka looked at Denny, and he shook his head again.

"Somebody light that fucking van!" Oscar screamed.

Denny tried to stand, but his leg had been crushed when the van hit him. He crumbled back on the ground, screaming in pain. He pushed through the pain and inched across the ground toward the lighter. It was perfectly between him and Ericka. The headlights shined on the lighter daring them.

"Fuck it!" Denny looked up at Ericka. "You save him."

"NO! Denny, don't!"

Denny screamed and pushed through to the pain to grab and ignite the lighter. The van almost peeled out. Oscar was in the path and sat up in time to give it the finger. Ericka turned away before the thud and the sound of bones being crushed. With her eyes tightly shut she heard Oscar groan in pain, still alive.

Ericka slowly opened her eyes to see Denny under the van. It backed up to reveal his blood-soaked and crushed body.

"No!" Ericka ran up to his body, but when she got there she was too freaked out to even touch him. She fell back and stared into the blinding headlights and wept. He didn't even make it to the lighter. He died for nothing.

She nudged Denny's body with her Chuck Taylor's but he didn't move or respond. He was lifeless. Oscar groaned in so much pain beside her. Denny and Oscar's blood pooled and mixed with the gasoline under them. The rank smell of death mixed with hydrocarbons.

Ericka looked for the lighter. It was gone. She was ready to let it rip and burn along with the van. The tears came in wave after wave. The band was dead, Denny was dead, and Nate was gone.

She was so close to having every dream she ever wanted. She felt the rage boil in her. In New Orleans, lying in bed with Nate finally, still sweaty from playing shows and making love. Love and punk rock. It was everything she ever wanted. Not fame or fortune, just him and the music.

She was ready to end it now. She felt around in the blood and oil trying to find the lighter. It was gone. In anger she screamed at the top of her lungs.

The van revved, drowning out her screams. It inched forward and shifted before inching back. Ericka turned and stared into the light. Oscar screamed and then whimpered as the van grew quieter. He wasn't dead, but Ericka knew he was dying near the van.

"Goddamn it! Frank, stop!" Ericka said as she slopped

through the filth to his side.

"He won't stop! He's gonna fucking kill us," Oscar screamed over her.

"You have the lighter, Oscar?"

Ericka reached him and saw the holster on his belt loop. His 9MM Glock was illegal in the city. He said he got it for research and for stalker fans. He looked at her and saw she was emotionally ready to use it.

"No, it's gone, but take the pistol."

"I can't!"

Oscar shook his head. Ericka cringed and took the pistol from his holster. Behind her the van revved again.

"You know how to use that?" Oscar asked, his voice cracking in pain. "First round is in the chamber."

Ericka never imagined she would fire a gun. It was heavy. She was afraid that the trigger was more sensitive than she expected. She pointed it at the van. The gun blasted like thunder. She wasn't expecting the power.

She dropped the gun after the bullet sailed through the windshield. The gun bounced on the pavement. Ericka was scared it would fire and kill her. Oscar reached for the gun. They both did. It was just inches from her fingertips when Ericka felt a hand on her shoulder that grabbed her shirt and pulled her back into the warehouse.

Ericka kicked the handle of the gun so it spun toward Oscar's hand. He couldn't get up but he could grab it.

"Not dead yet!" Oscar said as he picked up the gun. He pointed the gun at the pool of gas on the ground. He looked like he didn't know if it would work, but he wanted to ignite the whole thing.

Ericka watched in slow-motion as Nate stepped through he door way holding a short board with two rusty nails. Ericka put her hands up, but it was too late. He was swinging the board. Oscar lifted the gun as the board streaked at his face. The sounds were awful.

The rusty nails hit Oscar's neck. He couldn't scream as the nails tore through his Adam's apple and sent pieces of it into the parking lot. The pistol twisted down in his hand and fired at his already crushed leg, splattering pieces of it on the pavement. Nothing ignited.

Nate moved the board right and left before he could pull it and the nails out of Oscar's neck. Ericka screamed as Nate walked in front of her holding the board. Blood dripped from the nails. Somehow Oscar clung to a shred of life. His body spasmed in death throes. His eyes grew wide.

Ericka wondered if he saw Nate or Frank when he looked up.

"I didn't plan that, but damned if that isn't poetic. Don't you think, Oscar?"

Nate kicked the gun further away.

"Have any final words, Oscar?" Nate laughed and looked at Ericka. "I suppose not." Nate swung the board into the top of Oscar's head. Oscar's eyes froze as the nails buried into his skull. Nate tried to pull the board free but the nails were stuck. "Oops, it's stuck."

Ericka looked at the Prius and hoped that Denny left the key inside and the doors unlocked. She jumped past Nate who had to let go of the board to try and grab her. She slipped past his fingers and fell.

When she hit the ground she was surprised to feel the Glock beside her. Ericka lifted it in the air and leaned against Oscar's body as she pointed the gun at Nate. He turned with his arms outstretched.

"Shoot me and you kill Nate."

Ericka shook with the gun, but held it with both hands pointed at him. "Just let him go and we'll walk away. You can keep the van."

"I waited a long fucking time for this body, this spirit. I am afraid I'll have to hold on to Nate."

Ericka shook her head.

"We have a lot of work to do, Nate and I. You had your chance, bitch. So did Denny, so don't cry me a fucking river now. Oscar was it. Dickie killed himself after you bought the van. Gary's been dead for twenty years. We did it. We finished the tour. We won the battle, but the war is not over. Let Nate go."

"No, you're done."

Nate grinned. "You know Nate believes in you. The reason he loves you is because he thinks you understand punk rock. That you live it. This is the crossroads, baby. Nate gave himself to me so I can save the scene. No more pop-punk poser assholes. No metal crossover shit. No more merch in the malls. I am going to strip it down and restore the scene. It starts tonight."

The van revved up and rolled off of Denny's body, and turned again so the headlights shined on Ericka. She fought tears as she stared clearly at Denny's corpse. She looked up at the van and realized she was straight in its path.

Ericka looked back at Nate who was smiling and taking careful steps closer to her. She moved the gun so it was dead center on Nate.

"Shoot and you only kill Nate. It will slow me down, but I'll find another. After I run your ass over and live forever."

Ericka looked down and saw the lighter sitting on the ground, just past the reach of Denny's crushed wrist. There it finally was. She thought about trying to shoot Nate where it wouldn't kill him and diving for the lighter. She wasn't exactly a sharpshooter.

Nate carefully watched her, trying to figure what she was thinking.

"We could use a bass player," Nate said, smiling, and for a second it reminded her of who he was. "How about it?"

"No way."

"Too bad."

The van roared, Ericka looked at it in time to see the headlights overtake her. With Nate's last moment of control he closed his eyes and blocked out her screams.

EPILOGUE

August 4, 2008

"You ever played in L.A. before?"

"Nah." Scott hated this subject. He focused on pulling his amp out of the van. One of the guys working the venue had offered to help him. He played in one of the local bands that played their Orange County show the night before. "My old band toured, but we never made it to California."

"Oh, yeah," he said as he propped open the back door of the club letting the sound of the opening band blast out into the alley. It was a raw old school sound. It wasn't the first retro punk band he heard on tour. A song ended and the crowd barely had time to clap before the band launched into the next song.

"You were in People's Uprising right?" the tech yelled over the music.

"Yeah." Scott didn't hide his frustration.

"Sorry, I didn't mean to bring up..."

"Just forget about it,"

Scott hated this conversation, but ever since the tour started, and people realized he was in People's Uprising, they wanted to ask. They wanted to know. Being the only survivor came with questions and guilt he was unable to outrun. He never thought he could be convinced to tour again, but after Mel dumped him he was desperate to get something going in his life.

He moved out of Bloomington to Louisville and joined a pretty popular hardcore band, Force of Movement, on second guitar. Six months after he joined they hit the road in a van pulling a U-haul. While his new bandmates respected that he didn't want to talk about People's Uprising, everywhere he

261

went people awkwardly danced around the subject.

His People's Uprising bandmates were never seen again and the legends and rumors about the haunted tour van spread like wildfire. The same van The Fuckers toured in and their singer never came back alive.

Scott hated talking about it. He had known Denny since they were kids so he missed him most of all, but it was his first band that gelled so he missed them all.

He rolled his amp into the side stage area. The show was in a venue in Koreatown, near downtown L.A. It looked old-school, with a skate ramp inside and tagged band logos on the wall. The shows on this tour were almost all well attended and promoted every night. It was a far cry from his last tour experience.

Their vocalist, Parker, had gone to talk to the promoter about what time they went on, but the local opener was already playing. Parker came out of the crowd and yelled in his ear.

"It's a local band and then we're up next. Go ahead and start loading."

Scott and Jimmy moved the cabinet into the air conditioned club, but the heat was still overwhelming. Better than outside, Scott told himself. Scott saw there was a space beside the stage where they were supposed to put their stuff on deck. They moved that way, his back to the stage.

The band playing had a dirty old-school sound that belonged in the early Eighties. Dirty guitars, old broken drums. When they put the cabinet down Scott turned around to watch the band from back stage.

The drums looked cheap, a pillow sticking out of the broken bass head. He laughed, not realizing anyone still did that. He stepped closer and got a better look.

The singer was leering off the edge of the stage screaming his guts out. His voice was harsh but familiar. He stomped on the stage with spiked combat boots, and his spiked hair shook but stayed solid due to a full can of hair spray. He was wearing a denim jacket with the band's name "The Slimy Bastards" written on it. The picture on the back patch was of a familiar looking Chevy van, and the name of their first EP "The Tour from Hell."

"Talk about old school," Parker said, laughing.

"What do you know about this band?"

Parker laughed. "From Portland, I think. Assholes. Real punk fucking rock man. Crusties love 'em."

Scott laughed with him and was just turning to leave when the singer turned slightly and he saw his face. He knew the face, but didn't want to believe it. He watched, knew some of the movements. It was like hearing an old friend's voice on the phone. He was different, and this was hard to reconcile.

The song ended. The vocalist thanked the audience and dropped the mic. Scott had to talk to him. Dancing between moving amps and patch cords, Scott reached him.

"Nate?" Scott grabbed his shoulder.

The vocalist looked back at him. The face was the same, the eyes were different. There was a moment of recognition. Something inside told Scott to let it go. To forget he ever saw him. Then he was gone.

AFTERWORD

Thanks for reading *Punk Rock Ghost Story.* I am proud of this book. From the first time I outlined the novel in 2007, until its release in 2016, it was a project I never stopped working on. The first draft of this novel was written in July 2007, over a period of thirty-three days. Last year I threw out that first draft and started from scratch. It is the same story, better told in every way.

I wanted to explore the difference between punk rock in the early days, and the contemporary scene. With the advent of certain mall stores, certain television music shows and the internet, the acceptance of or co-opting of punk into the mainstream has been crazy—something that no one would have predicted in the 80s. I thought the ghost story genre would be a fun way to explore this.

I had the idea that if I created a book based on a fictional punk band, it would be fun to convince people that it was real, a kind of *Blair Witch* style promo campaign. This novel was written before *Amazing Punk Stories*, and *Boot Boys of the Wolf Reich*. My publisher and I chose to release my other punk horror books first, so I would have years to plant the seeds of The F*ckers' mythology.

Clearly The F*ckers were never a real band. I spent years telling people that they were. This was part of the project and the experiment that was and is *Punk Rock Ghost Story*. I can't thank enough the people who played along and helped me to create the hoax. My conspirators and I did several things to create authenticity. We recorded and pressed an actual record—The F*ckers' only release - and made a documentary that is on youtube. Search *Punk Rock Ghost Story* or "The F*ckers documentary" if you have not yet seen it. I also collected a few video-recorded interviews from people in the punk scene in Indiana.

In this section, I have included photos and credits for the things we did to make The F*ckers a real band:

The F*ckers 7-inch

Music recorded in England, produced and engineered by Rat.

Guitar/bass/ drums—Rat
Vocals: David Agranoff
Back-up vocals: Anthony Trevino/ Garret Sisti
Frank F*ckers' on-stage banter: Anthony Trevino
Vocals recorded and engineered by Garrett Sisti

Picture of full cover:

Cover artwork: John Schipper
John nailed it with the cover art!

Record pressed by:

My Studio
5 bis Bd Léon Bureau
44200 Nantes
tel : 06 74 25 20 40

In 2007 when the novel was conceived, I knew I wanted
to do a record and possibly a People's Uprising record. I
thought it would be essential to creating the belief that the
band existed. I thought I would have to put a band together.
In 2013 my old friend Rat, from England, (the grandfather of
Vegan Straight Edge) offered to record soundtrack songs for
my skinhead novel *Boot Boys of the Wolf Reich.*

Rat wrote the music, and I wrote the lyrics for two OI!
style anthems. He played everything and recorded it in his
home studio. I asked him if he could write some old-school
American style hardcore, and I would do the vocals this time.
I sent him links to The Zero Boys, who would have been the
local heroes of The F*ckers, and Circle Jerks' *Group Sex,*
and asked if he could make it sound like that.

The initial recording was far too polished. Rat dirtied up
the guitars a bit, and he even did a "live" version with shittier
sounding guitars, feedback, and more. Once I had the music,
I took songs titles which were already written in the novel,
and turned them into real songs. "Us vs Them," "God Hates
Sports," "Conformity Factory," and "Carter Sucks" were all
mentioned in the novel. I listened to each instrumental song
dozens of times trying to find the perfect fit.

The fifth song, "Fifteen-Year-Old Punk Kid," was written
by a joke grindcore band that I was in during the summer of
2000, called Moshed Into Oblivion. That band played 1.5
shows, and that was my favorite MIO song. In 2007 I started
mentioning to people that this song was a cover of a classic
Indiana punk band.

In March, my friend Garret Sisti (podcaster, filmmaker
and sound engineer), let me into the studio where he works
his day job, and in four hours, we recorded all of the vocals.

For the "live" version of *"God Hates Sports,"* I cracked my voice on purpose, and we recorded Anthony doing on-stage banter. We looped the chorus, but when we noticed, we added some feedback.

I wanted fliers for a Zero Boys show, so I asked my friend Ryan Love, who has amazing photo shop skills, to doctor a flier. This was for a show in Cincinnati, summer of 1982.

One time I commented on a facebook post that I was working on a novel about "The F*ckers, a legendary Indiana punk band". John Schipper, who was already working on the cover art, posted this picture. Cracked me up. Well done, buddy.

The F*ckers' 7-inch was hanging on the wall at the famous Taang record store in San Diego. The store is a record collector's heaven. After someone buys a rare record, Taang leaves the price tag on the wall. This remained at Taang.

I once posted this photo to my facebook with "At TAANG Record Store. They leave the price tags up after they sell classic records. Damn you just missed a chance. But you will be able to read about them soon. I would NEVER sell my copy."

Interviews for the documentary

To add to the legendary status, I thought it would be fun to make a simple documentary about the band, as if they were real. Everything was recorded on smart phones, and my buddy and screenwriting partner, Larry, edited it all together into something cool. Larry has a video blog about being a disabled video gamer, so he is becoming a great editor - all self taught.

For some of the interviews, I asked a few well-known people from the Indiana scene to talk for a few minutes about the band like it was real. One fun note is Bru-dawg, *the* real life Bru-dawg, who inspired the character in my novel *The Vegan Revolution...With Zombies*. He is the biggest record nerd I know, and he really added to the discussion of the band. I also liked the connection it created to *Vegan Rev...*

Written by David Agranoff and Larry Hall
Edited by Larry Hall
Directed by David Agranoff

Austin Lucus
Ian "Bru-Dawg" Duncanson
Rose O'Keefe
Jeff Burk
James Chambers
Matthew Whittaker
Curtis - Taang Records
John Zeps
Rob Tavares (As Dickie Abrams)
Kat Himmel (As Lizzie Plague)

JOHN ZEPS
GUITAR-TRANSGRESSION/BURN IT DOWN

MATTHEW WHITTAKER
BASS-THE BELGIAN WAFFL

CURTIS OF TAANG! RECORDS
HILLCREST, CA

DICKIE
DRUMS-THE FUCKERS

JAMES CHAMBERS
AUTHOR OF
THREE CHORDS OF CHAOS

Special thanks to Garret O'Sha for filming interviews in Indiana, and Anthony Trevino for filming several interviews.

Acknowledgments:

My wife Cari, James Chambers, Edward Morris, and Anthony Trevino, who all edited this book at various stages. My publishers, Rose O'Keefe and Jeff Burk. Larry Hall, who put tons of work into the documentary. Rat, Kat, John Schipper, Garrett O'Sha, John Zeps, Clark Giles, Austin Lucas, Mary and Bru-dawg, Brian Keene, Matt Whittaker, Garret Sisti, Ryan Scott Love, Curtis and Taang records, John Skipp, Laura Lee Bahr, Ross Lockhart. All of the San Diego writers: Ryan C. Thomas, Cody Goodfellow, Bryan Killian, Miguel, Essig. Everyone who kept the secret. Everyone who shared the songs, the documentary, or the link online. No one was paid; everyone did this for the sheer punk fun of it all.

I sincerely hope that I have not forgotten anyone.